Tales From The Western Queen

A Novel By

Ken Gordon
and
Laurie Day

The Western Queen © 2024 by Ken Gordon and Laurie Day. All Rights Reserved.

All rights reserved. No part of this book may be reproduced in any form or by any electronic or mechanical means including information storage and retrieval systems, without permission in writing from the author. The only exception is by a reviewer, who may quote short excerpts in a review.

Cover designed by Cover Designer

ISBN: 9798878858991

This book is a work of fiction. Names, characters, places, and incidents either are products of the author's imagination or are used fictitiously. Any resemblance to actual persons, living or dead, events, or locales is entirely coincidental.

First Printing: April 2024

Table of Contents

About The Authors 6
Acknowledgements 7
The Prologue 9
The Ship's Tale 17
The First Captain's Tale 31
The Nurse's Tale 61
The Steward's Tale 87
The Engineer's Tale 113
The Boatswain's Tale 131
The Marconi Man's Tale 143
Captain Olaf's Tale 167
The Epilogue 183

They that go down to the sea in ships and occupy their business in great waters…

From Psalm 107

About The Authors

This is Ken and Laurie's second book together. Their first, *The Wave Makers*, charted the rise and fall of Bulford Trading over seventy or more years, mirroring the decline of the British Shipping Industry during the 20th Century. Their latest work focusses on just a few of the characters, both good and bad, that graced the decks of the cargo-liner, *MV Western Queen.*

It isn't surprising that both books have the sea as their backdrop. Ken was at sea for a lifetime, rising from navigation apprentice to Master. He sailed most of the Earth's oceans and visited ports on all continents. When his sea-going career ended he worked as a Harbour Master in a small fishing port in the West Country, then completed a four-year term lecturing at Warsash Nautical School before joining The Maritime Coastguard Agency as examiner of Masters and Mates. He ended by auditing Nautical Colleges from Plymouth to Stornoway. Always possessed of a deep, inquiring mind he completed his Doctorate, Doctor of Education (EdD) (Lifelong Learning) when he was sixty-five. Having survived cancer, he now is dealing with the long-term effects of Parkinson's Disease.

Laurie by contrast, is a landlubber. A career in the food industry – he claims that at one point he made all the *Bisto* in the world – saw him finish as a senior Human Resources specialist. When the opportunity came to assist Ken on *The Wave Makers,* he jumped at it. He had always dabbled with words and had written a few short stories himself, but here was a chance to write on a grander scale. "Ken has the vision, I have the words; Ken is the architect, I am the painter and decorator."

Ken is already back at his draughtsman's board, so watch this space.

Acknowledgements

We owe special thanks to Monica Fulford for the many hours spent in the careful reading of our manuscripts and for her patient and sensitive explanation of our errors. Any that remain are ours alone.

Our thanks are also due to Richard West and Terry Johns. Your insightful comments helped us tremendously in making Tales From The Western Queen a much better read.

A ship in harbour is safe, but that is not what ships are built for

John A Shedd

The Prologue

I am known to anyone who cares to enquire as the *MV Western Queen*. It's painted on my stern, which also bears the legend *Panama*, and on my bows. At the time of writing, it is 1967; I was built in 1935, so, for a ship, I'm getting on a bit, and it shows. I've been called, amongst the more printable epithets, a 'rust bucket', 'a heap of junk', 'a floating disaster' and 'an accident waiting to happen'. But I've sailed roughly 70,000 miles every year that I've been in the water, carried cargo, crew and passengers more than two million miles in that time and been to most of the ports of the world that you could mention and quite a few that you probably couldn't. I've had a dozen Captains, survived a war, and battled through some of the worst weather to be found on the planet. So, a 'rust bucket' I may be, but I'm a tough old 'rust bucket', make no mistake about that.

As they say, 'start at the beginning', so I suppose I should. My story really started back when the Industrial Revolution was getting underway. You see, I'm the last in a long line of ships that have been owned and run by members of the Grace family. By all accounts they were landowners up in Yorkshire, near Whitby. They also channelled some of the money, which was made by good honest means, into financing the slave trade, but that's another story for a different time.

My keel was laid in William Doxford's yard in Sunderland in 1933 and I was ready for my maiden voyage in the spring of 1935. My sister ship was started six months later in the same yard. Alas she is no longer with us, having hit a mine in the Atlantic in the Second World War. The economy was beginning to look up when I was launched, and I was soon carrying a lot of passengers and cargo; the company was earning a good return on its investment and felt vindicated in its decision to build us. So, things were hunky dory, a phrase that I picked up on my trips to America. Unfortunately, a certain Mr Hitler was growing in confidence and power in Germany and only four short years later I was requisitioned by the Admiralty and refitted as a depot ship, eventually making my way up to the fleet in Scapa Flow. There were all sorts of comings and goings;

boys from the fleet came to me for a bit of R&R, to let their hair down. I have to say the Officers were just as bad but had better accents don't ya know. We carried all sorts of spares and provisions, and people were on and off all the time; it was really busy. I liked it like that. What I didn't like I can tell you, were the attacks that took place. I hadn't long arrived when a German submarine got into our so-called impregnable anchorage and sank the *Royal Oak*. I know she was an old ship, a bit like I am now, but she went down with the loss of over 800 men and boys. Terrible it was and it came as a great shock to the nation. As if that wasn't enough, I had a narrow escape a few days later when a bomb from a Ju88 dive bomber exploded mightily close to me, sending a massive fountain of water up into the air and making my plates quiver like fury, albeit, thankfully, I was unscathed. Sadly, it was during that raid that we lost the old *Iron Duke*. In early 1940 the powers that be decided that Scapa Flow couldn't be properly defended from air attacks and so the fleet moved out, me included. I was lucky and escaped the attentions of the U-boats that were waiting for our departure.

From Scapa, I went to Harland and Wolff in Belfast, to be fitted out as an armed merchant cruiser. Now, if you haven't heard about one of these, then you need to know that to all intents and purposes, when viewed from the sea by a submarine, or a warship, I looked just like any other merchantman, except that in reality, I carried six six-inch guns and had four three-inch guns in support. They were well hidden behind screens which could be removed in a matter of minutes if need be. I also had a selection of differently shaped screens that could be fitted when in harbour, so that my appearance could be altered from one trip to the next. If a submarine spotted a merchantman like me, they would sometimes surface, fire a warning shot across it's bows, inviting it to stop. Then, they might board to see what cargo was being carried, what signal books were in use and any other pieces of information that might be had to help their war effort. Finally, they would either put a skeleton crew onboard and sail it off to a German port if they liked the cargo or sink it with surface fire.

I accompanied a few convoys in this guise without any problems, but we did take part in one exciting battle that ended up with a U-boat being sunk. U-boat commanders didn't like to use their expensive torpedoes, of which they had a limited supply, unless they had to. So, if they felt it safe to do so, they would surface as I said, and sink a ship using their deck gun, which was powerful and could fire a lot of rounds quickly. Well, we had been on an Atlantic convoy, my tenth as it happened, and were returning to Liverpool when we came upon a U-boat sitting on the surface, probably re-charging its batteries or some such thing. Luckily, we had seen it quite early on and had our guns cleared and ready for action at about the same time they did. Our Navy gunners were good, they had practised a lot I have to say. Used to give me quite a headache, all that banging and vibrating. Well, we got in the first hits, taking out their gun and damaging the conning tower. It tried to make off on the surface, but we followed and sank it. The whole chase lasted about an hour. My crew were jubilant, but it had a big effect on our Captain. You'll hear more about that later.

I sailed quite a few thousand more miles in that guise before being taken off in 1943 to a yard at South Shields to be fitted out as a hospital ship. It took four months, working day and night, but by the end of that time I'd been transformed. Gone were the guns and protective shields; gone was my drab paintwork. Now I was painted all in white with a great green line going all around me. There were two big red crosses on each side which could be seen from miles away. The changes they made to me internally were significant to say the least. A complete emergency lighting system was installed, and an electric lift was put in to help carry the stretchers. New freshwater tanks made sure we didn't run out at a vital moment. There were two operating rooms, an X-Ray machine and virtually all the apparatus of a land-based hospital. My Merchant Navy crew sailed me as usual and I had a whole team of doctors and nurses and naval orderlies to do the heavy lifting and shifting, which included the patients.

The conventions of war meant that we were supposed to be able to sail the seas unmolested, in no danger of attack. 'Inviolate' I think the word is. That wasn't quite how it was in reality. My first tour of duty came in June of that year when we sailed into the Mediterranean and supported the Sicily and North African campaigns. We sailed backwards and forwards, carrying our poor wounded boys back to safe ports. We were supposed to carry the wounded from any country, but I can only remember that happening on a few occasions when we had some Germans on board.

After that we sailed back up to Southampton and got ready for D-Day. Boy that was some experience. We had a team of twenty doctors, forty nurses and a load of navy men to act as porters and service the ship. Initially we were moored offshore, with the wounded being brought out to us on landing craft, lifeboats and the like. We could handle a hundred stretcher patients at a time and double that number of walking wounded. When the time was right we would depart for Southampton, and later to Cherbourg and Dieppe, and drop them off taking care to avoid the mines that were still in abundance in the waters we travelled. As I've told you, my sister ship wasn't so lucky and went down with all on board. Then, after my hospital markings were removed, I was used as a troopship for a while, trips to the likes of Canada, United States, India and South Africa, before returning to Mason Grace Shipping in 1947.

I was refitted back in Sunderland before resurrecting my role as a cargo liner and life became quite routine, as I travelled backwards and forwards across the Atlantic. My route didn't vary much, typically Southampton to New York, but occasionally we ventured further south, and I paid my first visits to South America during this spell. There were to be many more of those let me tell you, but in the early fifties, life was fairly humdrum. And then I was sold to a new owner in 1955.

I don't know why; perhaps the Company took seriously the warnings about the potential impact on passenger numbers that cross-Atlantic flights were going to have and wanted to get out early; perhaps the Grace family felt that I wasn't earning them enough money, or perhaps the costs of a refit to bring my 20-year-old structure up to modern standards was too much. Or maybe it was simply a sign of the deepening malaise that the British shipping industry was starting to feel. The dreaded flag of convenience was really starting to make itself felt. You may know that ship owners were, and are, required to register their ships with an 'authority' and typically a British ship owner would register 'under' the British flag, a United States ship under the 'Stars and Stripes' and so forth. That was the way it was done. Back in the 'twenties there had been a well-publicised contravention of this when two ships, *The Reliance* and *The Resolute* registered under the Panamanian flag so they could sell booze on board and get round the Prohibition Laws, but there hadn't been a lot of further examples up until now.

Ships are covered by the laws and regulations of the country under whose flag they are registered. Some countries' laws and regulations are a lot less demanding than others. If, as an owner you wanted to lower your tax bill, pay lower wages to your sailors, run with fewer crew and avoid those annual inspections for seaworthiness which were costly, then, under certain flags, you could. And much more besides. If you didn't want people to know what you owned, you could set up shell company to hide your identity far more easily in certain domains. All of which amounted to, if not a license to print money, which in many cases it really was, then at the very least, it was a way to save on your operating costs.

The Grace family, still true to their Quaker background and principles did not wish to seek to diminish the safety standards for their vessels, nor exploit their crew members and so they chose not to go down that route. Euro Shipping, to whom I was sold had no such scruples and I was soon registered under the Panamanian flag.

I didn't have to go in for a dry dock inspection when I was re-registered, which saved an awful lot of money; the crew numbers were reduced; and where I had heard mainly English being spoken by my crew, a whole new array of languages were soon flowing over my decks. Over the years that followed I was barely inspected at all, and when I was, things that in my previous ownership would have been repaired and returned to their full operating standards without question, were done in a quick, cheap fashion, or not done at all.

I was sold again last year. My appearance has steadily declined; no longer am I freshly painted, the wood of my handrails is no longer smartly varnished, and my brass is dull; rust bubbles through my dingy old paint in many places, and you don't even have to look hard to find it. The grand days of a full First-Class Saloon are long gone; on most journeys now, like my current one, I carry no passengers, only cargo. And in train with that, the number of crew needed to sail me on my journeys from the ports in the Far East to South America, has fallen. I used to carry 80 crew of all shapes and sizes and skills when we had our full complement of passengers; now there are only 45.

I'm currently bound for Montevideo with a cargo of scrap iron and then I'm to return to Yangon with a cargo of wool. I've heard whispers that I might be heading to the scrapyard in the next two or three years, but I'll meet that eventuality when I come to it. From what has passed in these pages so far, you can see that I've had quite an eventful career. But being at sea is not only about the places you visit and the hazards you overcome but it is also very much about the people who live on you and within you. Thousands have come up my gangplank over the years. Without them I would have gone nowhere of course. A mix of the good, the bad and the ugly as they say; it is to a few of these characters and their stories, that I would now like to turn your attention.

A journey of a thousand miles must begin with a single step

Laozi

We do not exist in isolation; we are the outcome of history.

The Ship's Tale

Nathaniel had been born to William and Sarah Grace at their estate in Dunsley, near to Whitby, in 1742. It was a difficult birth and at one point it was touch and go as to whether the mother, the son or either would survive their shared ordeal. But survive they did, and although Sarah would never be able to have another child, the care that she and her husband lavished on their only son resulted in his growing into a strong, healthy, and cheerful boy. He was thoughtful, outgoing, and gregarious with a kind and generous nature. When not studying, reading books or painting, he was often to be seen out with the workers on his father's lands, helping and hindering their progress, as they harvested the grain and fruit crops, planted the next season's potatoes, or worked in their woodland, coppicing and laying in logs for the fires up at the Hall.

Growing into his teens, he heard the estate workers speak often of the Society of Friends, and being an inquisitive lad, asked if he could go with them to one of their meetings, which he duly did. Thus started a lifelong association. He liked their philosophy of non-violence, of simple living and of providing support to those who in some way had been marginalised by society. Those views went much against those of his father, who like most people in his position, a member of the landed gentry, a pillar of the local community, was convinced that his way of doing things was the right way, the only way, and the way that should continue to be followed for centuries to come. Anyone who thought differently was seen by him as an idiot, or a troublemaker, or both; someone who needed to be watched carefully and, if it came to it, be put in their place by whatever means was appropriate.

Amongst the topics that Nathaniel heard discussed at the meeting he attended, was the slave trade. Being his father's son, he had always accepted that it was the normal way of things. To his astonishment, here were people who opposed it and wished to see it ended. The more he listened, and the more he thought about it, the more he came to agree with them, growing over time to see it as an abhorrent business. This placed him in a difficult position. After much thought, he decided if he did not say something about his family's involvement in this inhumane enterprise, he would not be able to look at himself in a positive light again. He could not live with that he thought. Eventually he plucked up courage to raise the matter with his father; it would not be an easy conversation he knew, since his father made a lot of money from it, but it had to be done. So it was that one Monday morning he stood outside his father's study, heart pounding, stomach churning, and knocked upon the door; hearing a voice bid him enter, he went in, closed the door, and waited to be invited to sit.

"Well Nathaniel my boy, what may I do for you? I don't often see you in here. Not done anything that you shouldn't I hope?" and he gave his son a conspiratorial smile.

Before Nathaniel could reply his father continued, "Sit down, sit down. I'm glad you've come to see me. I was going to ask you to do so as I wanted to talk to you about your future. Before you say anything, I know you have been interesting yourself in the running of the estate, but it is high time for you to take up a proper responsibility, one befitting your station. You're sixteen and a bright boy. You can't go running with the estate boys forever, much as that might be fun. No, it's time for you to take on a proper role. To that end, you should know that I have been talking with William Devonport in Liverpool and I'm pleased to say he is prepared to take you into his office, so you may begin to learn the trade."

By this, he meant the slave trade; Devonport owned a large company engaged in its activities, running ships on the three legs; goods to Africa; slaves to the West Indies; and raw sugar cane back to England.

Nathaniel was both shocked and appalled by this news. He wished to have nothing to do with slavery; why, wasn't this the very subject that he had come to discuss with his father after all; to persuade him to stop his involvement with it. He had no wish to leave his beloved Yorkshire to go to some awful office on a dusty Liverpool street. He wanted to stay here on the estate where he had grown up, doing.... he knew not what he suddenly realised, but not slavery, no, not slavery. A further thought crossed his mind; there was a girl on the estate that bordered theirs, a daughter of Sir John and Matilda Whetherdyke. He met her when the two families came together on formal occasions and at church, and whilst they had talked but little, his heart definitely beat faster when he saw her. He thought, or at least hoped, that his feelings might be reciprocated. So, he stood before his father, his mind in turmoil, an awkward silence growing between them.

"What, cat got your tongue boy?"

"Er, no father," he stumbled out. "It has come as a surprise I must confess, and I need to think about it," he said, seeking to buy time.

"Well, there's nothing for you to think about Nathaniel. I've agreed it with William, and you start there at the beginning of next month. That will give you time to sort out whatever it is you must sort out here, and then you may be on your way. Right Nathaniel, you may go, I have matters to attend to." And with that, he was dismissed from his father's presence.

Sitting alone in his room Nathaniel tried to handle the turmoil raging within. If he did as his father had dictated, then he was doomed to spending time in a business he had come to loathe. If he went against his father, then what would happen he wondered? He wouldn't be allowed to stay on the estate, of that he was certain. His father might disown him. Where would he go? Where could he go? He felt bemused. What could he possibly do?

When he had gone to the Friends' meetings, he had often talked with a man called George Fell. Fell had told him of their founder's trips around England a century before, of that man's philosophy of piety, faith, and love, and of the growing battle with the legislature over slavery. Nathaniel felt George was someone he could turn to, someone who would listen to him, someone who might just possibly have some answers as to the way forwards. Sure enough, after listening to Nathaniel's story, George said, "let me ask you a couple of questions then Nathaniel," and he continued, "Number one; how strongly opposed to this career are you?"

"Totally," said Nathaniel.

"So, number two, what do you think your father will do when he hears of your decision to reject his direction?"

"He'll explode, and even when he has calmed down sufficiently, well, then he will still probably disown me I suppose. I don't think I will be able to stay at home. I will have to move out."

"Number three: is there any way that you might be able to persuade him to delay your appointment? Is there something you can think of that he would find acceptable as an alternative to what he is proposing? What are the elements of the business that you will have to learn? Can you suggest anything to him which would make you even more acceptable to Devonport if you became skilled in one of them before you joined him? At least that would give you some more thinking time and who knows, by then you might be able to talk him out of his plans for you entirely."

They talked on for a while, and when they parted, George had said, "Trust in Jesus. Talk with Him and together you will find a way, of that, I am sure."

Two days later Nathaniel knocked once more on the door to his father's study and went in. Once more he stood in front of his father's desk.

"Father I ...."

Without inviting him to sit, William Grace cut across his son.

"I have some bad news for you Nathaniel. I am afraid that I will not now be sending you to that scoundrel Devonport. He has fallen far short on the profit I was expecting from him; some nonsense about the plantation owners out in the West Indies putting up their prices for the sugar cane. I wrote to him, 'that's not my problem Devonport,' I said, but he wrote back and said we all had to take some of the shock, it was part of our arrangement, and well, it has all gone rather downhill from there I'm afraid. I'm thinking of finding someone more reliable than that bounder. And then we'll see about you once more."

Nathaniel tried not to show the relief he felt at this news; perhaps his talk with Jesus had done the trick after all.

"What a shame Father. But perhaps it provides us with an opportunity. There is something I have been thinking about for some while now, which I would like you to consider. I feel it could make this family quite a lot of money, for only a small investment."

"Oh yes, what is that?" William said, apparently absent-mindedly, his thoughts seemingly already having moved on to other matters. However, he had heard 'money' and 'investment,' so he did listen to what came next.

"Well father, I have heard talk coming from Whitby that there is a growing and not inconsiderable amount of money to be made in shipping coal down to London. They are building lots of colliers there; it's a growing trade with a big future. I think it is something we should investigate."

He was going to add, because he had rehearsed it before going into the study, something along the lines of 'besides, there are already signs of a growing discontent with the slave trade; it may not always provide the income we have enjoyed up to now, as your experience with Devonport might well foretell'. But he decided against that. Devonport was out of the picture for now, no point in bringing him up again. Even though he was comparatively young, he had observed his father well enough to know that with him, it was better to sell the advantages than rake up disadvantages.

Instead, he said,

"I know it is not something that we have been involved in before, but you also know I can learn quickly. I am, after all, my father's son." He smiled at his father at that point and saw the face relax a little. "If you were to allow me one year, a small sum of money and a few of the estate workers, I really do think that we would do well in it. Would you at least let me try? But if it doesn't deliver as I think it will, then at least I will have some knowledge of shipping and trade to take to the employer you find for me. Will you please let me try?"

Two months later, Nathaniel left the port of Sunderland in a small barge with fifty tons of coal, headed for London. It did not turn out as he had hoped; with only a couple of the crew having been to sea before, the rest having come from the estate, it was not long before they were in difficulty, and in only moderate seas it must be said; after two days the barge was lost on the shore near Hornsea. Everyone had managed to get ashore alive; it was an inconspicuous start.

Nathaniel's father was livid. Fifty tons of coal; cost £50. Barge; cost £45. A total loss of nearly £100.

"I thought that you said this was the way for us to make money, not throw it away," he shouted angrily at Nathaniel.

"I know father. And I am truly sorry. But please, do hear me out. As you are aware, in the last two months I have got to know a lot of people in Whitby's seafaring circles. I have spent time with them, talking about what is happening in their business. People are building big, solid boats as fast as they can, for coal, for the Navy and for the timber trade. It really is a bustling, growing industry. People are making good, reliable money from it and I still think we can make a decent profit from it if we were to persist."

Again, he saw the look on his father's face. He hurried on,

"I have learned a hard lesson Father; we nearly lost good men and boys and I will never let that happen again. If you are gracious enough to allow me to carry on, I wish to become an apprentice. I know now I must learn everything there is to know about ships and sailing them before we set out on our own venture." His father made to speak but Nathaniel carried on. "I know a company that will take me; I will not be paid much but it will not cost you a penny. I'll be sailing out of Whitby, and I'll be learning all the time. Please allow me this last try Father. I will not disappoint, I promise you."

Nathaniel was older than many of his fellow apprentices, who typically joined at the age of fourteen, but he applied himself well and set to learning the ways of the sea and of ships, in the proper manner. There was so much to learn. Initially as a deck hand, he was involved with the rigging and sail setting, the use of the capstan, the loading and unloading of the ship, its cleaning and repair and how to care for its fabric. It was a tough life with no let-up from hard, physical labour. His captain, having noted Nathaniel's application and obvious intelligence, started to teach him navigation, sail-setting and watchkeeping. After eighteen months he found himself at the Mate's side, learning all the while about his new world. As more months passed, he became ever more proficient; stowage, provisioning, riding out bad weather were all added to his armoury. Unlike many Whitby colliers, his ship was chiefly engaged on trade to the Baltic, bringing back timber, tar, hemp and other naval supplies. He loved it; he loved the camaraderie, he loved the chance to visit foreign ports and see countries he had never thought he would ever see; and he loved overcoming the challenges that were constantly thrown their way by their friend and enemy, the sea.

They were moored up in Copenhagen and had taken on a large cargo for the Navy. Captain Mason, who was eager to be off with the tide, stood at the gangplank of *The Faith*, scanning the passing throng, becoming more and more agitated as the Mate, who had earlier gone into the town, failed to return to the ship. His impatience grew as time passed and it was obvious to all those watching him, that he had, at last, come to a conclusion. He gave orders for the ship to clear the port, and when it had, he took Nathaniel to one side.

"Well Nathaniel, if you feel you're ready for it, I think your time has come. I've been impressed with the way you have conducted yourself and now we seem to be missing a mate, I'm thinking that you might step into those shoes. What do you say?"

On each visit back home to his parents, Nathaniel had kept them spellbound with tales of the countries and ports he'd visited, their different ways, their different foods, their wines and beers, their beautiful buildings. He minimised the dangers and maximised the beauty of the sea for he did not wish to cause concern for his mother. And they were pleased for him. He had grown into a fit, strong, good looking young man with a great air of confidence and self-reliance. Even his father, who had only grudgingly given permission those three years back, was pleased with what he saw. And on each visit back, Nathaniel would urge his mother to arrange social events that would give him further opportunities to meet Miss Wetherdyke, Annabelle, as he had come now to call her. A romance was in full bloom, and whilst there was some reticence initially in her family, 'walking out with a sailor for goodness sake,' he managed to charm Sir John and his wife into accepting him; he was, after all, the son of a prominent and wealthy landowner.

And then a tragedy befell their ship and his captain. They were coming up from Calais, just off the Hook of Holland and on their way back home to Whitby, when a sudden squall came up through the English Channel and overhauled them. Before they knew it, they were engulfed in a massive rainstorm; the sky became black, lightning flashed, and violent gusts of wind seemed to be trying to rip anything and everything off their decks. Johnny, one of their young deckhands, was hurrying across the deck to take in sail, when he was picked up and tossed over the side by a giant wave. They still had too much canvass up; frantic efforts were being made to take it in when a vicious gust, stronger than anything that had gone before, caused a spar to break. It came crashing down onto the deck, knocking Captain Mason off his feet and over the side. Just like Johnny, there one moment, gone the next; Nathaniel couldn't believe what he had just seen; chaos was everywhere. He knew that if the ship and any of them were to survive, the responsibility was now his and his alone. His years of training came to the fore, he became clear about what had to be done. By the use of hand signals and arm waving, grabbing and pulling and pushing his sailors, for words could not be heard above the noise of the wind, he began to get the crew to start the process of taking back control of their boat. Rigging was cut, sails taken in, and the broken spar was lashed to the side. The helmsman, who knew his business well, gradually turned her to face into the seas and little by little they got their ship back. And then, as suddenly as it had come upon them, the storm passed, the sun came out and *The Faith* sat, almost serenely on a quieting sea, as though nothing had happened. That was often the way with the sea, thought Nathaniel, beauty and the beast. They slowly limped their way back to port.

A few days after the memorial service for Captain Mason, Nathaniel received a request from his widow for him to visit her. After being admitted to the neat, comfortable house in a fashionable street in Whitby, the offer of tea accepted and provided by the maid, Mrs Mason said,

"Thank you for coming to see me, Nathaniel, and thank you for helping to save our ship. Captain Mason always spoke highly of you. I think he thought of you as the son he had never had." A tear slipped down her cheek which she wiped away with a fine lace handkerchief. She then sat upright in her chair, composed herself and said,

"Well enough of that. Please forgive me. I've asked you to meet with me today to discuss the future of *The Faith*. I think you know she will need extensive repairs, and she will be out of the water for a while. Since I have no family who would wish to carry on with her, and I cannot do so, I am afraid I am going to have to sell her. I wanted you to hear that from me Nathaniel. I know Andrew would have wanted that. Perhaps a new owner, if there is to be one, will offer you a position; you will be highly recommended, of that I can assure you. But for now, I am afraid there is no work for you or the rest of crew. I'd be grateful if you would tell them all this and pay them whatever is owed to them, if you'd be so kind."

"Of course I will Mrs Mason," said Nathaniel. "Captain Mason was a very fine man. He taught me all I know about sailing. It is only because of him we were able to bring the ship home, he had built a very good crew. I owe him my life, as do the others."

He paused, allowing them both to savour their thoughts of the man.

"Mrs Mason, If I may venture a suggestion?"

"Of course you may."

"*The Faith* is still a fine vessel and, having looked her over, I'm sure she will be able to sail for many more years once the repairs are carried out. It has occurred to me that if we might come to some arrangement as to the price you are seeking for her, then I might be able to take her over and sail her, as her captain. Or, perhaps, we could have some form of partnership arrangement, where I run her, and the business, and we share the proceeds. How would you feel about that? I must confess to you I have already had talks with my father, and he has said if a suitable position could be agreed between us, then he would be prepared to fund the repairs and meet your needs in regard to the price of purchase, full or joint."

And that was how Nathaniel Grace came to be a ship owner at the age of twenty-one. A three-quarters stake initially, which, after three years became full ownership. He prospered, carrying coal from the northern ports to London. Within seven years he had two vessels and by the time he was forty he had ten, sailing to all parts of the country where coal was needed, as the Industrial Revolution picked up pace. He no longer sailed of course; he was a businessman, office bound, and the only course he charted was that of the growth and prosperity of *Mason Grace Shipping.* He worked hard for the rest of his life to make his business grow. He married Annabelle Wetherdyke when he was twenty-two and they had four children, two boys and two girls. He died in his bed when he was seventy-four.

§§§

Contrary to the currently received wisdom that a family business typically fails in three generations, Nathaniel's descendants looked after *Mason Grace Shipping* well. It survived all the things that the world could throw at it; family disputes and arguments; famines; wars, of which there were many, chiefly with our continental neighbours; economic depression; technological change in the design and building of ships. It ended up owning the largest fleet of colliers in the country by 1932.

The Great Depression was in full swing. Coal production had been falling gently since its peak in 1913 and this current depression had knocked it further; the last three years had seen a reduction in output of thirty million tons or more and that was bad for business.

The latest Grace to inhabit the Chairman's seat was Frederick, or to give him his full title, Sir Frederick Mason Grace. On this day, he and his senior directors were sitting in the Board Room. They had been aware for some time that change was necessary if they were not to see a steady, slow decline in their fortunes.

Sir Frederick looked in turn into the faces of Miles Mitchelmore, his Finance Director, Sean Griffin, the Company's Chief Engineer and Iain McDougall, his Operations Director.

"Well gentlemen, it's probably not the first time this has been said in this board room but on this occasion I think I am truly correct in saying that this is the most important meeting this company has ever held in its long and successful history. As Miles has told us repeatedly," here he paused and looked across at his accountant with a smile on his face, "as he has told us repeatedly, our revenue is falling by about two percent each year and whilst Ian and Sean have been working hard between them to keep our costs under control, our profits have taken somewhat of a hit. It is obvious that we cannot simply sit back and wait for things to improve; if we do, then I think we will continue to see a decline in our fortunes. Whilst there are no signs of improvement in the state of the economy yet, it will come, we all know it will, and when it does, we must be ready to take full advantage of it. So today gentlemen, I repeat, we are probably going to be taking some of the biggest decisions this company has seen since Nathaniel Grace persuaded his father to buy *The Faith*. We all know what the proposal is. We all know the numbers, but I'd like us to go through it all, just one last time before we make that final judgement. Perhaps Miles you'd like to start us off with an outline our financial position one last time."

In his forties, Miles Mitchelmore was tall, balding and of pale complexion. He looked round the room at his fellow directors through a pair of thick glasses. Clearing his throat, he picked up his papers and spoke, his accent giving a hint to his Cornish ancestry. "Thank you, Frederick," they dispensed with the 'Sir' when they were alone together. "By the way, it's 2.7 percent at the last count." They all laughed. He continued, "you have the figures there before you. We have checked and double checked, and I can tell you with certainty that we have an investment fund available to us of £1.8m of our own funds and the potential for a government grant of a further £1.2m. Luckily, the Government is very concerned that the Germans, the Italians and the French don't steal a march on us; as you know, they've been laying down new keels at a rate of knots if you'll pardon my pun. We have the funds available gentlemen, so it's a question of how much we spend, on what, and when. I think we have some answers, don't we Iain?"

He looked round the table for a moment. They all nodded.

"Well Iain, shall we turn to the proposal? Would you talk us through it please?"

"Yes Frederick, of course. To confirm, we have been looking at various sectors of the shipping market very carefully over the last year or so. As a result, we believe we should build two ships in the next four years and those ships should be passenger and cargo combinations. It's a new departure for us, we haven't carried passengers before, but those of us who have studied it believe it to be a profitable market that we can exploit. We know there is a call for passenger berths as the recent laying down of that Cunard keel in Clydebank demonstrates, and as Miles has said, our continental neighbours are going in this direction and at some pace too. So why not just a passenger ship, or ships, you might ask. Well, we have thought about it long and hard, and we think the provision of some cargo carrying capacity will, how shall I put it, 'hedge our bets' a little. We have pretty much finalised a design, which Oswald will tell you about in a moment, but we're thinking of something carrying 200 passengers split between first and tourist class and a cargo capacity of 8000 tons."

"That is large," said Frederick. "You really think we can carry it off, that we shouldn't go just a tad smaller?"

"Yes, I do Frederick. I know, it's a lot larger than most cargo liners, but I think that would give us the edge over our competitors; we could be quite an attractive proposition to the larger shipping companies who might well wish to charter us because of our bigger passenger potential. A charter with a big company like Cunard White Star would be very profitable. And, as we know, ships are generally getting larger these days."

They continued to discuss the implications of such a dual-purpose vessel for some time; crew numbers, possible cargos, most profitable routes, likely profitability and a myriad of other details and facts. Ian finished by saying,

"I think this proposal marks a significant development in our company's history and a very profitable one. Miles has checked our figures and thinks them sound. I would urge we get underway as quickly as possible."

They broke for lunch.

When they reconvened, it was Sean's turn. In his fifty years on the planet, Sean had started under canvass, worked on steamships of various sizes and shapes, spent time learning the design business in Swan Hunter's yard at Wallsend and built diesel engines in Sunderland. He knew his stuff. If he said they would use marine diesels the Board listened; if he talked of the latest Marconi technology, they took his statements at face value; if he said that the loading derricks had to be placed just-so, they agreed. They agreed because they knew how very thorough he was, that he had carried out extensive research, and had costed everything down to the last rivet. Over the previous six months, in company with Ian, he had visited the various yards that could build these ships, discussing lead times of steel plate, engines, cordage, cabin fittings, galley equipment and all the other ten thousand and one things that were required to bring a ship to life. They had discussed the availability of slip times, what design team resources would be allocated to their build, provisional build costs, and completion dates. And now Sean took them through it once more.

At the end of a long day, Sir Frederick said,

"Gentlemen. This project was mooted nearly two years ago. You and your teams have all done a first-class job, to my way of thinking, to bring it to this point so quickly. What you have achieved in that time is a wonderful example of British skill and ingenuity at its best. If we agree today, I think we will truly be setting Mason Grace shipping on an exciting and profitable new course. Let's take the vote."

One by one, they assented to the proposal to build two cargo liners, both twin screw diesels, capable of 18 knots at twelve tons a day fuel consumption, of carrying 8000 tonnes of high value cargos and 200 passengers housed in 150 cabins. It would take most of their available funds, but the forecast returns were high.

The subject of the ships' names was raised.

"As you might expect gentlemen, I have been giving that some thought. I would propose that our first ship be named *Western Queen* and her sister ship *Western* Princess. And it was so agreed.

Sir Frederick called for champagne and invited his colleagues to toast to the success of their two new vessels.

They rose as one, raised their glasses and said,

"To the success of our two new ladies, the *MV Western Queen* and the *MV Western Princess*."

Success or failure is caused more by mental attitude than by mental capacity

Walter Scott

I once overheard a conversation between two gentlemen who were taking their brandy and cigars in my First-Class Saloon. They were obviously men of some standing, you know the sort; educated, well-off, important in their own worlds, the sort that others looked to for guidance and approval. The elder of the two said, "Don't laugh Bertie, but between you and me I can't wait for this to end, to be free of it all, to be free of the pressure." Bertie had given him a look of great surprise. "What do you mean Graham old chap? What pressure? You're as steady as a rock. You're talking poppycock. You can't possibly be thinking of giving it all up."

"I've never said this to anyone before Bertie, but I dread the day when someone is going to find out that this is all a front, that I am all front, an imposter; that I shouldn't be where I am, doing what I'm doing."

Bertie had spent the rest of the evening reassuring his chum that his fears were groundless, and it reminded me about the pressures attached to playing a role that doesn't quite fit. Pressures that I have witnessed.

The First Captain's Tale

At the age of three, Percival Jackman was pecked by a large white goose. His father kept a flock of them on his estate in Norfolk for use at Christmas for himself and his friends, and for their eggs, to which he was rather partial. The goose intended no harm; it had simply seen a small, tottering invader and was warning it off. For Percival, it was a seminal moment. He was a quiet, mild-mannered boy, taking after his mother in his ways rather than his burly confident father. The bird's attack had both shocked and frightened him and he had started to cry and call out for his mother. Most small boys and girls, would have got up, wiped their eyes and carried on with their lives, possibly even running back at the offending bird to scare it away. But Percival was not most boys. Sitting on his mother's lap he promised his small self that he would find a way, and the goose would suffer, but going near it again was not an option. It set the tone for his approach to difficult situations for the rest of his life.

Percival had been born to Mavis and Algernon in 1906 and was their only child, unusual for that generation but there it was. Algernon perhaps had more desire to run his estate and his farm machinery business than producing a large brood. But he did love the boy, and when time permitted, he would play games with him, explain the rotation of the seasons and name the animals and birds that they saw when out walking. When it was time for bed, he would regale him with Tennyson's stories of King Arthur and the Knights of the Round Table and other tales of adventure and daring do. He was told the history of Nelson, who had grown up in Burnham Thorpe, a Norfolk village not far from his own. The young Percy so much wanted to be like him.

Percival was not by nature an outgoing boy; he had few friends and little opportunity to make more since he was schooled at home. He did love their estate; it gave him plenty of opportunity to explore, containing as it did, a small wood, a folly and a lake. The folly was an attempt by a previous owner to create a prehistoric cave and was formed from massive boulders that had been imported from somewhere in Spain, so his father told him. He would climb up onto its roof and imagine himself on the quarter-deck of *The Victory*, giving orders to seamen to go 'hard a 'larboard', or commanding them to 'run out the guns' and 'fire on the up-roll'. He spent hours like that, spyglass to his eye, wooden sword at his waistband. When fishing in the lake, for the roach and tench and carp that abounded, his thoughts were often of the sea and of how he would command a ship someday.

The Great War started when he was eight, and little by little Percival became aware of something big going on outside his own small world. He was a bright boy and his tutor had taught him to read both quickly and well. He would pick up his father's paper and study the headlines. He learned of the Battle of Jutland and of how it had secured British dominance at sea. He heard of Arras and Ypres and Verdun and of their awful losses and of the mud and trenches. If truth be told, what he read frightened him, all those deaths, all those losses. But they had died as heroes, the paper had told him so and in some perverse fashion the triumphs and the tragedies fuelled a desire in him to become part of something when he grew up; something that would make his parents proud of him.

He read copiously; books by Stevenson, Ballantine, Captain Marryat, Defoe, Fennimore Cooper, consumed one after the other. He wanted to be on *The Hispaniola*, dealing with Israel Hand, or sailing the Mediterranean Sea, as a midshipman fighting Napoleon's navy. He saw himself on *HMS* Victory alongside Admiral Lord Nelson as together they won the Battle of Trafalgar. That the sea was a dangerous place in its own right, and the fact that Nelson had been killed at sea, again raised some tremors in his breast, but he put those thoughts to the back of his mind once more and assured himself that, when the time came, he would be alright.

His parents noted his growing infatuation with the Navy with some concern but eventually agreed when he was thirteen, with reluctance, to send him for officer training to a naval college. It was a requirement that he attend as a boarder, coming home for two weekends a month from the college which was in Lowestoft.

Percival arrived at the college at the beginning of September 1919. His parents accompanied him on the journey and noticed a growing nervousness in his demeanour as they got closer to the town. He would be all right, they thought; he had always performed well for his tutor. He was a bright boy. He would fit in and make friends, and all would go well. These thoughts they hugged to themselves as they watched him drag his trunk down a long corridor to his dormitory behind a college servant, after they had tearfully hugged him goodbye.

As he wiped away the last of his tears, he entered his new, spartan quarters. He spotted what he thought to be his bed in one corner of the room, but before he could move to it, a large boy, dressed in the uniform of a cadet of the college, thick of figure, low of brow, with pudgy features and a nasty sneering look moved to block his path.

"Oh my goodness. Look what the cat's dragged in here boys. Are you snivelling, lad? Is that a tear I see hanging off the end of your nose?"

Percy made an involuntary movement to wipe the offending article away, then stopped, knowing there was nothing there.

"Did your mummy give you a big hug and tell you to be a good little boy, did she, and that you'd be fine, did she? Is that what she said to you? Your dear mummy."

Indeed, she had, but Percival didn't think it wise to admit it to this oaf. He tried once more to move over to the vacant bed of the four in the room, but the large boy moved to block his path once more.

"Well boy, what have you got to say for yourself? I take it you can talk, can't you? You do have a name, do you? Let's see. What might it be? What do you think boys?" He turned and looked at his companions who both were smirking, happy that they weren't the focus of the brute's attentions at that moment.

"Is it Little Lord Fauntleroy by any chance? You look a bit like one of them to me. Or perhaps it's a Jeremiah. He looks a bit of a moaning Jeremiah, don't he boys? Or is it Mary? Yeh, I think it's Mary." He laughed uproariously, his colleagues following suit. This was fun they thought.

Percival hesitated a moment and then said

"I'm Percival Jackman. Can I get to my bed please? I need to get ready; I was told that I must be in the Great Hall in ten minutes, in my uniform."

"Oh, it does speak," the boy mocked. "Well Percy, I still think Mary is a better name for you; those two are Rodgers and Brown and I'm Ellis, but you will call me Sir. Understood?"

When Percival didn't reply, Ellis shouted in his face, "Is that understood little Percykins?" and when Percy nodded his agreement the malevolent Ellis again shouted at him, "speak boy" and Percival returned a hesitant "yes… Sir".

From that moment on he was Ellis' plaything. He was made to clean his shoes, make his bed, press his clothes and attend to many of the other domestic chores that their communal living brought upon them. And there was no real relief when they attended their lessons. Practical training was given on an old, wooden, decommissioned ship of the line, even though the age of sail in the Navy had passed. Their tutors were old, time-served Petty Officers who simply loved making the 'Young Gen'lemen' suffer; out in all weathers, climbing rigging, beaten with knotted rope ends, their 'starters' they called them, if they failed to respond quickly enough. It was a brutal introduction to life in the Navy. Percival found out very quickly that he did not like heights. When he looked down from a spar as they were reefing in sails his head would go dizzy, he would begin to feel a little faint, and his breakfast would rush up to his mouth, trying to force its way to freedom. Nor was he much better at any of the other physical things they were forced to do. To his great annoyance, Ellis proved himself to be sure and nimble and dextrous at each successive task they were given, rapidly gaining the approval of his teachers. He took every opportunity to mock Percival's physical ineptitude, branding him a coward and a weakling and 'not fit to be in this man's navy'. The tutors did nothing to intervene.

Luckily, Percival found he was far more assured in classroom lessons. He showed a gift for maths and the basic science that they covered; he could solve navigational problems quickly and accurately. He loved the history of the sea they were taught, the exploits of Drake and Raleigh and Captain Cook. He privately rejoiced that he had found something at which he could best Ellis, something which could make Ellis look completely foolish as he stumbled through some trigonometry problem that Percival solved in a matter of minutes.

This spurred Ellis on to even further heights in his humiliation of his roommate; his classmates could see what was happening and whilst some of them felt sympathy for Percival, they were after all, only thirteen and the pack mentality ruled. You fitted in with the strongest or you suffered; they all knew that. Once more Percival became a lonely figure. He would lie in his bed at night, quietly crying, replaying that day's taunts and jibes, and racking his brain for some way to rid himself of the pestilent boy. And then an idea came to him. His idea was not a pleasant one, anything but, but Ellis deserved it he thought; like that goose of so many years before, no one thing, no one person, would attack him and get away with it.

In his wanderings of the college grounds and buildings, something he did whenever he could, simply to get away from his persecutor, he had noticed that there were quite a few traps laid for the rats that were their constant companions; those traps contained a poison. Percival started to collect small amounts of it, which he stored in his trunk. He was sure that if he somehow got Ellis to eat it, bit by bit, it would make him sick. And when Ellis was sick, well, he wouldn't be able to carry on his bullying ways, would he?

He began his campaign; every day, when he fetched Ellis his porridge, it was one of the demeaning tasks that he was forced to do for the boy, he would sprinkle some of the powder onto the cereal and mix it in; if people had been watching they would think it was just salt, or sugar he thought. His tests had shown it to dissolve easily with no trace of colour or smell, and as he subsequently found out, no taste; Ellis showed no signs that anything was amiss as he gulped down his cereal. He did this for a week. Much to Percy's dismay there was no obvious outcome, and Percival started to doubt his plan would work. The bullying continued. He increased the daily dose.

And then, on the seventh day, Percival noted that Ellis was twitching a little; they were both in the classroom at a geography lesson, when he heard Ellis let out a curse. He had been laboriously writing the name of a country on the map that he had been drawing, when his hand gave an involuntary shake, and his pen dripped ink onto the work below. For a few moments he couldn't seem to stop this from happening, and then, as suddenly as it had started, it stopped. As the days passed, other things began to happen; he suffered an occasional, momentary loss of vision; he would lose awareness of what was going on around him; or forget what it was that he had come to tell that dratted Jackman to do. It was working out the way Percival had hoped it would.

Ellis went to the Matron, but she shrugged him off with a spoonful of castor oil and advice that he go a little easier at night on the thing that young boys did when in bed. It all came to a shuddering end three weeks after Percival had put his plan into motion; they were back on the rigging one morning when Ellis fell from a spar and broke his back on the deck below. Those around him at the time said that he simply seemed to pass out, and that was that. Percival was free.

Mr and Mrs Jackman had been noticing a gradual change in their boy's manner on each of the weekends he had come home to them from the college. Their cheerful, loving little boy, for that is what he had been even though he was thirteen, had disappeared from view, to be replaced by a quiet, morose young man with little interest in anything around him. He talked little of his college and the things he had been learning, nor of his friends. When they came to collect him at the end of the school term, they asked to see the Chief of Staff.

They were shown into his study and saw a tall man, dressed in full Admiral's uniform. He had white hair and a pleasant smile. After they had exchanged the usual pleasantries and had sat down, Mr Jackman started their conversation.

"Thank you for sparing the time to see my wife and me Admiral Halton. We know you are a very busy man, so thank you. We wanted to speak with you about our son Percival. We are concerned about him you see."

The admiral nodded, assumed a serious expression, and said,

"Mr and Mrs Jackman, I assure you it is no bother, and if you had not asked to see me, I was going to ask you to come in for a talk in any case. I've been receiving reports of Percival's first term with us d'you see and I'm afraid we are wondering if he really is right for the Royal Navy." He looked steadily at them, first to one, then to the other.

"Academically he is very bright, a good head on him, quite gifted really; but in matters practical I am afraid that the reports paint a picture of a young man lacking in confidence and skills. He has few friends – 'a loner' - his teachers say. And since that episode with Ellis, well, he seems to have shrunk even more into his shell. I'm not sure he is right for us, or us for him I'm sorry to say."

Mr Jackman said,

"I am shocked Admiral. We have seen a change in him as I indicated, but we were not aware things were as bad as you have described." He paused for a moment and then continued,

"And we have heard nothing of any 'incident' as you term it. What was that?"

The Admiral described the manner in which the boy had fallen. "Been sound as a bell up till then, as good at the practical stuff as your son is at the academic. But that's the end of his naval career I'm afraid. He will be a cripple for the rest of his life."

They talked for a few more minutes then left, having agreed that Percival would be withdrawn from the college. As a final act the Admiral had added that if Percival was truly fixed on a life at sea, then he was sure that he would eventually make a success of it. The Merchant Navy, as George V had recently termed it, might offer a better way ahead he had offered as his passing thought.

Over the next few weeks, they saw the boy they knew return. He said little about his time in Lowestoft, but their boy was back, and he still wanted to follow a life at sea. They talked with him several times about it, raising as gently as they could, the matters of practical ability the Admiral had recounted to them. But he was adamant. He was to be a sailor and he would join the merchant navy as an apprentice. The 'practical stuff' as they put it did not feature heavily in the life of an officer; nor did the modern navy have very much to do with climbing masts and taking in sails.

§§§

Twelve years later he had his British Master Foreign Going certificate. It meant he was qualified to command any merchant ship, of any size, anywhere in the world. He was proud; his parents were proud. He had served variously as a deck apprentice, a third mate and now, at the age of 26, he was first mate. He had spent 10 years at sea, covered enough miles to have sailed round the globe several times, on ships ranging in size from 1,000 tons to 6000 tons. He had proven himself to be a first-class navigator; he understood how to use the Marconi man to good effect; he could organise both stores and people; he could give clear orders when granted space and time to think things through. He did things 'by the book'. And yet, given all there was to admire in him, his men simply did not like him. That once happy little boy had turned into a deeply introspective man with none of the bonhomie of most of his peers. His relationships were typically formal, cordial but cool.

The one exception to that general rule was the engineer on the cargo liner they were sailing, backwards and forwards to America; Southampton to New York and back. Percival was the First Mate and Jimmy Royston was the Chief Engineer. Jimmy was a quiet, taciturn man from Long Beach. In his mid-forties, he was of average height, built like a whippet, with brilliant blue eyes set in a pale face that was lined and moustachioed. He had a habit of not quite looking at you when he talked with you, which was quite off-putting for most with whom he came into contact. Jimmy and Percival would often find themselves alone together in their mess, their colleagues suddenly finding the need to be elsewhere when either one of them came in to eat. And through this enforced togetherness they began to forge a bond of brotherhood, so much so, that when they docked in New York one Friday night, Percival found himself accompanying Jimmy to his home.

It was a pretty house with a little porch and a neat front yard; lights were shinning out through the windows as they arrived.

"Honey, I'm home," Jimmy called out as they went in, to be answered by, "OK Babe, be with you in just a second." A few moments later a pretty, red-headed woman came through a door, wiping her hands on a tea towel, and threw her arms around Jimmy, giving him a big hug and a kiss on the lips. Then, catching site of their guest, she pulled back and said, "Oh gosh, oh my, oh, you must be Percy. Jimmy said he was bringing you, oh my, what must you be thinking?" She was blushing impressively, which went well with her dark red hair.

"Mrs Royston, please, it's a pleasure to meet you at last. Jimmy's told me so much about you, I feel as though I've known you for years. Please don't be embarrassed on my account. I can see why he's always so eager to get home." Percy smiled, she smiled, and Jimmy smiled. The evening progressed from there.

It became a regular thing for Percival to accompany Jimmy home when they were in New York. Jimmy had talked a lot about his daughter, but Percival, or 'Percy' as he was in the Royston house, had never met her. She was at an upstate college, taking a degree in the Humanities; she was going to become a teacher. He had seen the photographs around the house of an attractive young woman, nice figure, auburn hair, and lovely green eyes but this did nothing to prepare him for the first time he met her. His breath was quite taken away and his stomach seemed to do a somersault when they were introduced. He thought she was the most beautiful girl he'd ever seen. He stammered out a greeting, feeling so foolish; it was obvious to anyone looking at him that he had been smitten. It would have been no surprise to anyone had Cupid appeared, his bow string still twanging and removed his arrow from Percy's heart. For her part Chrissie did not seem to be distressed by his reaction.

It took a while; they met infrequently at first but then Chrissie started arranging her visits home to coincide with the ship's return and within eighteen months, just after Chrissie qualified as a teacher, they were married. It was a blissful period. They rented a small flat not far away from her parents and fitted in as much sightseeing and lovemaking as they could in the three or four days the ship had for its turnaround. Percy had never been so happy. That was about to change. Percival's undiluted life of pleasure could not continue forever. He had been first mate for two years when his Company called him into their Southampton office 'to discuss an opportunity'. He was offered the chance of his own captaincy on one of their smaller ships, a few passengers but mainly cargo, on a regular route between Boston and Puerto Cortes in Honduras; consumer goods out and knitted goods or bananas, or palm oil back. It would mean less time together for the newlyweds, but Percival had to think of his career. Advancement would benefit them both, wouldn't it? More money, a better flat, money for a baby. It didn't take him too long to accept the offer.

With the Captaincy came added responsibility and he quickly felt the pressure; he was the one everyone looked to for a final decision, when and if one was needed. Most of the time, of course, it was plain sailing so to speak, but occasionally a little something out of the ordinary arose and that was where the captain was expected to step in. He knew he was not good when forced into an immediate decision, when he didn't have time to think things through and issue calm thoughtful orders. And so, he was either over fussy in the planning of his voyages and in the detailed orders he gave, expecting rigid compliance, allowing no questioning or modification from his team; or he simply froze in difficult situations. His subordinates talked amongst themselves about him going 'walkabout', both physically and mentally at those little times of crisis, not that there were that many. But they noticed, and amongst his senior crew he became known as 'the Aborigine'.

They were on the approach to Puerto Cortes at the end of one trip when their lookout hailed the bridge and advised them of a ship approaching fast, on a course that would result in a collision unless they took some avoiding action; the other ship, which was a large tanker, seemed blissfully unaware of their presence and it was obviously down to Percival to take that action. He ran out onto one wing of the bridge and then raced across to the other; the helmsman looked to him for guidance; the mate stood ready by the engine room telegraph to relay the captain's orders, but nothing came. For what seemed like an eternity, as the two vessels converged, Percival stared wild eyed out of the bridge window; then seemingly coming to his senses, he issued the order to the helmsman, "starboard 10." Nothing wrong in that; it would take them out of the tanker's path; but he had forgotten the sandbank that lay to their right, clearly marked by a line of buoys; his decision would take them on to it within minutes. The mate came quickly to his side and said,

"Captain, may I respectfully suggest that we hold our original course and bring her to dead-slow ahead, Sir? The sandbank sir, do you see?" and he pointed the buoys out on the starboard side.

Percival gave him a withering look and said,

"Mr Mate. When I need your advice, I will ask you for it. Until then you will remain silent. I was about to issue that order" and he quickly said, "dead-slow ahead, Mr Mate and helmsman wheel amidships." Two long, agonising minutes later, Percival issued a further order to the helmsman to bring the ship a further seven degrees to port.

They narrowly avoided the collision, and the sandbank, and moored safely at their berth in the harbour. Percival later registered his displeasure with the captain of the tanker but received no apology, which further soured his mood. Relationships on the bridge on their return leg home were to say the least, strained.

§§§

About two months after the Puerto Cortes incident, Percival received a letter from his father. He opened it and read it quickly. Then he read it again and then again.

My Dear Percival,

I hope this finds you and Chrissy well. I write with news of something I think you might find quite exciting. I was in my club in London the other day when I happened to meet Freddie Grace, Sir Frederick Grace as he is now. I was at school with him, and we've kept in touch over the years. Well anyway, we had lunch together and he told me something rather interesting. Apparently, his company, Mason Grace Shipping, has taken the decision to build a new ship, two in fact. They're starting to build up in Sunderland in about three months. One thing led to another and, long story short, I've managed to get you an interview with his people if you want it. They're looking for a Captain, somebody keen and with fresh ideas, to oversee the build project and then sail her after that. Freddie knew about you of course, but I brought him up to date with your career and he was interested. So, if you would like to be considered, he's willing to give you the opportunity to chat to his Operations Director.

And here's the even better news. This man, Iain McDougall is his name, is coming over to New York in two weeks' time. He could meet you there if you're not away sailing down to Honduras.

Let me know what you think. Send me a telegram and we can get things set up if you want it.

Your Mother sends her love,

Your Loving Father

"If I want it" he shouted out and went rushing off to find Chrissie to tell her his news.

He was due to be away when Iain McDougall was in New York, but a 'bout of illness' and then the use of some leave he was due, took care of that. Dressed in his best naval uniform with his gold braid shining brightly, Percival approached the grand entrance of the recently opened Waldorf Astoria on Park Avenue at 11.55am. A white gloved, uniformed doorman saluted and pulled the door open to allow him to enter. He was staggered by the beauty and opulence that greeted him. The Deco design was amazing as was the Waldorf Clock in the lobby, covered with beautiful, bronze relief figures. He thought to himself if this is what working for Mason Grace Shipping gave you then, yes please, I really want this job. He approached the reception desk, and a pretty girl greeted him.

"I'm here to meet with Mr Iain McDougall. If you would kindly let him know that Captain Percival Jackman is here to see him.

Two hours later they shook hands and Percival went home on the Long Island Railroad. He went back over every moment of their meeting. He thought it had gone well, from first meeting to their parting pleasantries. He had been given the opportunity to talk through his career, which he had done in a calm, clear and simple way. He had been questioned about his apprenticeship; his experience of shipyards, of which he had a fair amount having been on ships undergoing refits; what did he see as his greatest assets? His patience, his attention to detail, his experience of captaincy, his seamanship, his detachment and his steadiness under pressure. He was asked for examples of these things, especially of the latter and he simply reversed his actions and described the actions of those who had saved his bacon. Of his weaknesses he could summon a few, like not taking no for an answer; it sometimes caused friction didn't it, but it was necessary on occasions. He did admit to having no actual experience of a build from the start, but he had read a couple of books in his local library in the intervening period between his father's letter and the interview and had the terminology and the process learnt off by heart. So, all in all, a good start he thought. Iain had asked him to ring him at 4.00pm the next day at the hotel and he had been provided with the number to call.

He couldn't sleep that night; he went backwards and forwards over the answers he had given, groaning when he thought of a better response. He and Chrissie had talked about what it would mean should he be successful. A move for her to England obviously, living in the Northeast during the couple of years it would take for the build and sea trials; she would be able to come home and see her parents at regular intervals, especially if he was paid what he thought captains of large ships were paid. And he would be home a lot more often during the build period than he was now. She could go and stay with his parents from time to time, they would love to see her and look after her, he assured her. They had only met the once before, when they got married in New York, a quick trip over, but she thought they seemed nice, and they had liked her. On and on they talked, deep into the night.

At four o'clock the next day he could hardly dial the number his hands were shaking so much. He waited an eternity for Iain to be found, hoping he had enough coins to see the call through. Eventually he heard Iain's voice.

"Hello Percival, sorry for the delay. Percival, I'd like you to come in and see me again, tomorrow morning at 10.00 if that's possible. I'd like to talk a little further with you about the position."

Iain went over some of the ground they had covered in their first meeting, and seemingly satisfied by what he heard, said,

"As you know Percival, these cargo liners are a new venture for us. We think the first ship should be ready in about thirty months from the time her keel is laid. If you were to be her captain you would, of course, be heavily involved in her being built. We'd like you to meet our Chief Engineer, Sean Griffin, and talk through a few things with him; you'd be working closely with him if you are appointed. Unfortunately, he can't get over to New York anytime soon, so we'd like you to come to London. You could also meet Sir Frederick. I'm sailing back to England day after tomorrow. I know it's a lot to take in, but do you think you could accompany me?"

Percival hesitated only momentarily. He said,

"I'm just thinking about my current Company Mr. McDougall. If I go to London with you, well….."

"Yes, I understand. We thought you might raise that. Whilst I have not been authorised to offer you the position as yet, it is for Sir Frederick to take the final decision, I can tell you we will offer you a role in Mason Grace Shipping on at least as favourable terms as you enjoy currently.

And I would ask you to remember, we are going to build that second ship too you know."

Two days later he found himself accompanying Iain back to England on the world-famous *RMS Mauretania*. It was, of course, far bigger than the ship that he might Captain, if his meeting with Sean Griffin went well, but who knew what lay in the future.

And again, all did go well when he met the Chief Engineer. He was shown the plans for the vessel and asked for his thoughts, not knowing that they were an earlier version of its design. Did he foresee any issues from a seafaring standpoint? What might he change? What might he add? Percival offered a few thoughts, a couple of which drew a look of approval from Sean. He was impressed by the young man's intelligence and particularly by his methodical and analytical approach to answering his questions and his attention to detail. He seemed to have a sound grasp of the build process and had been able identify potential process bottlenecks

From a personal point of view, Sean thought that whilst the man before him wasn't the most outgoing chap he'd ever met, they had conversed easily enough as the day progressed. He could work with him, and he could teach him a few things about the ship and the building process that would stand Percival in good stead in the future. He seemed keen to learn. Building a ship was a lengthy process and you needed a relationship that would endure the ups and downs of that process. He felt that he could have one with this man.

When Percival met with Sir Frederick, he was offered command of the vessel with the Yard Number 823.

§§§

Percival arrived for his first morning at William Doxford and Sons Ltd and was stunned by the magnificent gate at its western entrance; three arches, exquisite wrought ironwork, a mixture of tall windows and great curving windows, high chimneys and sloping roofs of slate. It was a sight to behold, something you would expect to see guarding the approach to a great country house. Inside the gates, it was just as impressive, with long office buildings, three massive berths that would allow a build of up to twelve thousand tons in each, and a giant radial crane. It even had its own railway.

Checking in at the porter's lodge he was directed to the office of the yard manager, Billy Blenkinsop; Sean was already there and carried out the introductions. Thus started the most hectic thirty months of Percival's life. He and Sean shared a desk in the office of the design team, a great oblong room, well-lit by windows on either side, and housing ten long, wide tables down its centre. Percival came to know it well, came to know its people well as they spent hour after hour in discussion about the exact design of this hatch, the actual height of that derrick, the form the wood panelling should take for the first-class dining room and cabins and so much more. When he could, he would get out of the office and simply walk around the yard, visiting the chippy's workshop, the welder's shed and the marine engine and boiler works; he was totally fascinated by it and in his element.

A small ceremony was held to mark the laying down of the keel. Sir Frederick and the rest of the Board attended. Sir Frederick said a few words about the importance of this moment for Mason Grace Shipping, shook hands with the yard's management team and waved at the workers. A quick lunch in the yard manager's office, a few words of encouragement to Sean and Percival about delivering the best possible vessel in the shortest time possible, and he was gone, back to London.

Eighteen months later, they were all back together again for the launch. Sir Frederick's wife, Helene, was to carry out the naming ceremony. There was a brass band, there were drinks for the launch party, the shipyard workers were gathered, with their wives, to raise a cheer and throw their caps into the air as the ship, now named *Western Queen* by Lady Helene, slid smoothly down the slipway. She came to a halt in the River Wear with a rattling of chains and great clouds of rust as they took her weight and stopped her progress.

Fitting out took six months. Percival busied himself, roaming the ship several hours a day, plans in hand, checking progress and the quality of the work. He gained a reputation amongst the workmen of being very pernickety, pointing out every little thing that he thought to be at odds with the design, or badly executed, no matter how big or how small. And they did not like his manner; aloof, arrogant, in short, a pain in the backside. The ship did not yet belong to Mason Grace Shipping; the handover would only occur once all the fitting out work had been finished and the sea trials completed successfully. But that didn't stop Percival. He didn't speak with the shipyard workers directly at all, and only occasionally with their foremen, but typically he would walk into the yard manager's office every afternoon with a carefully written list of items that required attention. He would carry out an inspection on the following day to ensure matters had been attended to, and woe betide the yard manager if there had been little sign of rectification; this would result in a further visit from Percival, who, in cold, clipped tones, would recount the yard's shortcomings.

Percival and Billy Blenkinsop did not get on. Their relationship had gone into decline long before the daily lists started to appear. The build had been progressing well. Percival was on the deck where his cabin would be and was walking its space when it occurred to him that it was going to be rather small, not something befitting the status of a Captain. He had called the foreman over and had said,

"This cabin is too small."

He stared at the man in front of him; short, wiry, leather belt cinched round his waist, striped collarless shirt with rolled up sleeves, a dark waistcoat, a flat paddy hat and a flamboyant pair of moustaches. He waited for a response. None came immediately, although the look on the man's face might have told Percival just exactly what he was thinking.

"I said, this cabin is too small. What are you going to do about it?"

The foreman said that he would go and talk to his boss and left an impatient Percival pacing the deck.

After what seemed to be an age to him, but was only ten minutes, Billy Blenkinsop appeared, plans in hand. In brusque tones he said,

"Right Captain. I'd like you to look at these plans," and he opened them out on a trestle table. "There's this deck, there are the cabins, there's the captain's cabin, your cabin, and there's the dimensions. You and Mr Griffin have been over these countless times with me and have approved them. Look, there's your boss' signature." He pointed to the corner of the drawing where Sean's signature was clear for all to see.

"And now you're telling me it's not big enough?" his voice rising throughout, a tone of high exasperation and incredulity evident. "Well, it's too late to make changes now; the steel's been cut. If we were to change it, then it would delay your build and add to the cost, and besides, if we were to make it bigger, we would have to reduce the scale of the chief engineer's cabin and he's not going to be exactly delighted, is he; it's small enough as it is. So, just what exactly do you wish me to do?"

Percival thought for a few moments. He did want a bigger cabin, one where his office space could be separate from his sleeping quarters. But was it worth annoying Sean over it? He had after all signed off on the plans. Was it worth being seen to add to the cost? Was it worth a possible delay on the build? But then again, he WAS the captain, wasn't he? Surely that should count for something; the cabin should befit his status, shouldn't it? And what if the chief engineer had a smaller space? That wasn't of concern to him. But it might be to Sean, he was an engineer after all.

The silence grew longer and longer. The yard manager was looking at him, the foreman and his men were also standing watching in silence. What was he to do? Finally, he said,

"Well Mr Blenkinsop," with significant emphasis on the 'Mr', "I would have thought a properly run yard would have been able to accommodate a simple change like this without all this fuss. I shall bear your conduct in mind."

And with that, he turned on his heel and walked out of the deck space. As he went, he could hear the yard workers talking behind him and it wasn't very complimentary.

The fitting out ended, as did Percival's lists, much to everyone's satisfaction. Sean had had a word with him about letting the men get on with their work as they knew their business, which both angered him and frightened him. Obviously that useless Blenkinsop had been talking to him, how dare he? But Sean was his boss, could damage his career if he chose to, so he now let the lists slide, raising only matters that he saw as serious contraventions of the design brief, and there were few of these.

And still Percival couldn't get his hands on the ship. That had to wait until the sea trials were over and successfully completed. Whilst he and his crew were present, the conduct of the trial was in the hands of a Trial Master and his crew, all independent of Mason Grace Shipping. In the week that had been allowed, the ship's performance was tested to its limits. The contracted speed had been for eighteen knots, and this was tested over four runs between posts set up on the coastline at a known distance apart; the ship averaged eighteen and a half. Then she was run for twenty-four hours at maximum speed. There were checks on all her systems, on her ability to transfer fuel from one tank to another, on her pumps, on the derricks, and all the other pieces of equipment that would need to work together to keep her above the waves, pointing in the right direction and carrying crew, passengers and cargo to their promised destinations. The *Western Queen* passed in all regards with only a small list of minor defects. The week had provided Percival and his crew an excellent opportunity to learn their new ship. They had accompanied the trial crew on everything they did, asking questions, getting answers, and even covering the 'what if….' scenarios that were raised.

Percival had not had much say in the selection of his crew. That had fallen to Iain and Sean, who had chosen for the senior roles from the current employees of Mason Grace Shipping, people they knew and trusted. They, in turn, had been left to recruit their teams. On the journey from Sunderland to Southampton, the first voyage of the *MV Western Queen* under Percival's command, he was keen to see how they would perform. He had them carry out a series of exercises so he could see how they worked as well as helping them to become further acquainted with their ship. Emergency stops; ship evacuation procedures; docking against imaginary quaysides; going astern; full steam ahead; and so forth and so on. Percival began to get the feel of his ship, started to identify the capabilities of the crew, and began to build a working relationship with the First Mate, Barney Oxlade, a small, tanned man with brown hair who hailed from Whitby and had been captain of an 800-ton collier prior to moving to the *Western Queen*. He had been at sea for ten years and was on his way up the chain of command should he perform well in this bigger role. Like Percival, he was a stickler for process, for planning, for drills and practices. In addition, he had what Percival lacked, a rapport with his men. Iain and Sean had felt this might be a necessary quality to have near their captain, especially in the early days of their new venture.

§§§

On Thursday 28th November 1935, the *Western Queen* sailed from Southampton on her maiden voyage. It had been much publicised by Mason Grace Shipping and the passenger list for their journey to New York was almost full. The night before their departure, the Board took all the senior officers out for dinner at a local hotel. When they had eaten, Sir Frederick rose, and the room fell silent

"Gentlemen, I hope you will forgive me for interrupting this fine dinner, to offer you a few thoughts before your maiden voyage tomorrow. I shall be brief, since I know there is still much to be done before you cast off." He paused to allow the ripple of polite laughter to spread throughout their room.

"Tomorrow marks a great day in our history, in the history of Mason Grace Shipping, and a major addition to the services that we are able to offer to our public. I know you have all done your bit to bring this project to fruition since it was approved in 1932. The fruit of all your labour is sitting at the quayside not more than 500 yards from here, for all to see, a truly beautiful vessel. But now the real work starts. Tomorrow Captain, you and your crew will take our first 150 passengers on their voyage to Miami. I am sure when they leave the *Western Queen* in twelve days' time, all they will be able to talk about are the levels of service, comfort and care they have experienced. It rests in your hands Gentlemen, and I am sure you will deliver for us all. Allow me to propose a toast."

They all stood and raised their glasses,

Sir Frederick said, "To the *Western Queen.*"

"The *Western Queen*" they replied.

As they had all hoped, the first voyage was a great success. The ship performed well, the crew did likewise, providing their passengers with the quality of life they had expected for the money they had paid. Percival enjoyed the trip and proved an interesting and informative host to those who graced his table; they were no threat. Barney Oxlade was left to his business and performed well; he found his Captain to be both business-like and respectful.

And so began a long spell of voyages backwards and forwards over the Atlantic. When in New York, Percival would often visit the Roystons, bringing letters and presents from Chrissie who was still back in England. The one present Mrs Royston was hoping for had yet to materialise and she would often drop phrases such as 'the patter of tiny feet' into her conversations with Percy. Getting no real response, she would carry on, hiding her disappointment and promising herself that 'it would happen in all good time, the Lord would see to that'.

Both of Mason Grace Shipping's new vessels were performing well and the company was making a good return on their investment. Plans were being considered for the addition of a further two vessels, their route would take them down to Cape Town. There was, however, a growing problem that concerned not just Mason Grace Shipping but the whole of Europe, war. Its possibility had been known for some time and whilst there had been a great deal of planning for the 'what ifs', when it came, it came with a ferocity and a closeness to home that shocked all onboard the *Western* Queen, which was sailing home in mid-Atlantic. The news of the sinking of the *SS Athenia,* a ship carrying nearly 1500 souls, on 3rd September 1939, just 250 miles off the coast of Ireland was devastating. The Germans weren't allowed to attack civilian ships, nor was anybody else for that matter, and here they had gone and done just that dreadful thing only hours after war had been declared by Britain. All on board the *'Queen'* were shocked. When the Marconi man had come to him with the signal requesting all vessels near the stricken ship to come to its assistance, Percival's first thought was 'thank God we are nowhere near it' followed by a flicker of guilt for even having thought such a thing. He told the wireless operator not to pass the details of the signal's contents on to anyone and then started to consider the arguments for and against making this knowledge public. He called his senior team to a meeting; he told them of the contents of the signal; by the looks on some of their faces he concluded that the Marconi man had let slip the information, whether before or after he had told his captain he wasn't sure, but he vowed to find out.

"Right gentlemen, it is my view that we don't pass this on to our passengers. They were jumpy enough when they boarded three days ago, heaven knows what this will do to them if they find out and I don't think we want our Purser and his team having to deal with a bunch of rioting passengers do we?"

Having said that he looked across to Trevian Grey, a paunchy man in his mid-fifties whose team had most interaction with the passengers, working as they did in the cabins and the dining rooms of the ship.

"No Captain, indeed we do not, but I fear, sir, that the news may already have reached them." His gaze fell to the tabletop as he let out the last few words.

"Is this true Mr Mate?" Percival's voice had acquired a cold edge.

"Yes Captain, I'm afraid it is. Our Marconi man was not as discreet as he should have been when he received the signal. I expect the news will be moving steadily all around the ship by now."

"Mr Mate, please instruct the Bosun to bring the loose-lipped fool to my cabin in ten minutes. Purser, please prepare a meeting in the main dining room in thirty minutes for our first-class passengers and invite them to attend to 'hear something of importance' I think you may say."

"Yes Captain," the Purser said. "Will you be addressing them, Captain?"

This took Percival by surprise.

He started to say "What? No. Of course …." Then he caught sight of the faces round the table looking at him, the beginnings of surprise starting to show.

"Why I…Well perhaps…..Of course. Purser, I'll be there in thirty minutes, after I have dealt with our Mr Cuthbert."

§§§

When the ship finally docked in Southampton, many relieved people, passengers and crew alike, had uttered a collective prayer of thanksgiving for their safe arrival. Percival thought that he had handled the matter quite well but was angry with himself for showing that little hesitancy in front of his team. He should have made it clear that he was personally going to address the passengers. It had been his intention all along, hadn't it? Yes. Of course it had and how dare they doubt him. He had confronted Mr Cuthbert, the unfortunate Marconi man, before his meeting with the passengers. Cuthbert had admitted that perhaps he had let the news slip out before seeing the captain. As a result, he then felt the lash of a very sharp, very cold tongue. He was advised that his actions were in direct contravention of the Telegraphy Act, which required a wireless officer to pass information received to the captain of a vessel and to no one else. His contract would be terminated as soon as they arrived in port. Furthermore, his company would be receiving a detailed report of his shortcomings. Percival had finished by advising him that he should consider himself lucky if he was ever able to find work again as a radio operator. The smirk on Mr Cuthbert's face told Percival that he couldn't care less what the captain thought of him.

"There is a war on you know. Someone with my skills is going to be in even more demand now, you, you jumped up little sailor."

And with that, the odious man had left his cabin. Percival's anger overcame him and those nearby heard him shouting and cursing and throwing things at the walls.

§§§

The *Western Queen* did not make its next scheduled Atlantic crossing after it had docked that September day. An emissary from the Admiralty had visited Sir Frederick Grace at his London office and had asked him, being the true patriot they knew him to be, if he would have any objection to the King's Royal Navy requisitioning her to act as a depot ship for the fleet up at Scapa Flow; '…be a great help to us Sir Frederick; Mason Grace Shipping would lose no money by it; several favours would be owing at an appropriate time….'. Sir Frederick knew that he had no option but to agree.

After a brief refit at Doxfords, Percival and his crew guided the *Western Queen* to Scapa Flow. The mooring allocated to them was in the Hoy Sound, off the eastern coast of Hoy in the Orkneys, at the top of Scotland. It was full of history; Viking ships had moored there; the German Fleet had scuttled there in 1919; the Royal Navy had used it in World War 1 and were now back. Whilst the Admiralty felt comfortable in using it as a base once again, the First World War defences had fallen into a bad state of repair and, in reality, there was little cover from a determined enemy attack. It was a nervous Percival who looked out onto the placid waters that surrounded his ship after they had taken up their given mooring in early October. The *Western Queen* had brought up much needed supplies from the mainland for the fleet; weapons, ammunition, steel, engineering tools and a good quantity of navy rations and drink. Their main purpose was to provide a base for the crews of the warships and submarines so they might get some rest, some decent food, and some immediate medical care, were that to be needed.

Percival had to call upon all his inner reserves after the sinking of *HMS Royal Oak*. A German submarine managed to sneak into the waters of Scapa Flow from the poorly defended east end and after several attempts went on unchallenged to send three torpedoes into the old ship. It sank within fifteen minutes of the final attack with the loss of over 800 men. Percival had thought they were in a relatively safe place; it was a long way from Germany, it had defences; and then, bingo! One of their own was sunk. How could that be? His presence on the bridge, where he had been a constant figure since they had docked two weeks before, was suddenly noted by his senior officers to have diminished rapidly. Where he had been a fastidious nit-picker, of process and performance – spotless decks, hawsers stowed in the proper fashion, no rust tolerated, polished handrails, polished brasses – he was now a convert to operating through his officers from his cabin. And this became all the worse a few days after the submarine attack when four Ju 88 bombers broke through the British defences and badly damaged *HMS Iron Duke*. A couple of bombs fell close to the *Western Queen*, causing some shrapnel damage but little else. After that he was rarely seen in the open, receiving visiting RN officers in his cabin and ordering the first mate to guide any inspection tours they requested.

The British worked day and night to strengthen the defences around the harbour; bombers continued to harass the Flow so it was a great relief to Percival when the fleet was ordered to leave its base for a short while in March 1940. The *Western Queen* was never to return to those waters. Instead, she sailed to Belfast, to Harland and Wolff, where she was fitted out to perform the role of a convoy escort as an armed merchantman.

§§§

The work to fit the armament, the false bulkheads, fake deckhouses and an extra funnel that could be taken down and put back up, with great difficulty it has to be said, took two months. During that time Percival re-appeared. The crew noted his presence with some interest and saw the attention to detail return. He had lost weight and colour during their stay up in Scapa but these were now beginning to return.

Chrissie had gone back to New York before the war had started and Percival wrote to her on a regular basis, typically trying to keep his letters light and funny, leaving out any mention of attacks, or death or peril. His jottings were of the quiet time they were having, sailing, but not out on risky seas. 'Can't tell you where though Darling, careless talk costs lives don't you know', and all his letters had been of that nature. But seeing the guns being bolted to the decks and the depth charge launchers fitted and then screened off, brought home to him the additional perils he was about to face.

Ten days later the *Western Queen* was sailing across the Atlantic escorting a convoy from Liverpool to New York. There were scares: some possible sightings of submarines; the sound of aircraft in the distance; the loss of a vessel to a mine. But it turned out that their first trip was uneventful, and Percival got to see Chrissie for a couple of nights when they docked., Things however began to get worse as the year rolled on. France fell, and the U-boats found harbours further south on the French Atlantic coast than they had previously enjoyed, giving them greater range and time at sea. Allied losses began to mount and the submarine commanders experienced 'the happy time' as they called it, taking a heavy toll on the Allied convoys, often sinking more than a quarter of a convoy's participants.

As this toll mounted, and news came in almost daily of ships lost to German submarines and surface craft, so Percival's state of mind and health deteriorated again. He sat in his cabin and wrote Chrissie a letter.

My Darling Chrissie,

I hope this letter reaches you and finds you well. I'm fine. Our ship is in dock at present, but we will soon be back out at sea, so I have some little respite now from this dreadful war. I know my previous letters have made light of it, but I have to tell you how much I hate it. I know I must do my duty, and I will, but it is awful, it drains me beyond belief. My Darling, I can say this only to you, no one else can know, but I'm so scared by it. I don't know how it all will end; nobody does. I just long to be with you in our home in New York. I think of you all the time, of how beautiful you are and of how gorgeous you would look if you were pregnant, lovely I know. And how happy that would make our parents. And then I think of how that may never happen, of how I may never see you again and I weep hard hot tears in my cabin. I shouldn't tell you this I know, but it's how I feel. I really don't know how I can see this through to the end, whenever that may be. But when it does come, I shall never return to the sea again. I have truly had enough.

Think of me my Darling, as I think of you, and if my worst fears come to pass, know that you have given me the happiest years of my life, years that I will treasure as I go to meet my maker.

I will write again soon

All my fondest love and kisses.

Your Percy

He put the letter in an envelope, sealed it, wrote the address, and then put it in his pocket to be posted later.

His senior officers had talked amongst themselves about what they should do in the event of his total collapse. Would it be mutiny if they relieved him of his command? They weren't sure, so they agreed amongst themselves to keep a very close eye on Captain Jackman.

Towards the end of 1941, the arrangements for convoy escorts changed. America had entered the war; the Canadians had increased their fleet significantly and escort duties were now shared. At an agreed point, responsibility would pass from the British ships to those of North

America and vice versa. The *Western Queen* was headed back towards Liverpool, escorting a convoy carrying food and munitions. In light seas, Percival was on the bridge watching the sun rising in the east. Barney was near him, keeping a watchful eye as ever, but his view was that his man was holding it together, just.

"I can't wait to get back, Captain," Barney said. "My brother's home on leave and is getting married next week. The wedding is in Liverpool, and I shall be there to see it happen, which is just as well since I'm his Best Man."

Percival took his time to reply. Most of his thoughts had been turned in upon himself, but the mention of a wedding took him back to his own, all those years ago in New York. He smiled and relaxed, thinking about that happy day again.

"Well Mr Mate, I hope it goes well for your brother and his bride, I really do."

He was about to share some further thought when a shout came from a lookout,

"Bridge ahoy, submarine bearing 40 degrees off the starboard bow."

All eyes turned to that point, binoculars were raised in unison, and a collective gasp was released as the dark shape of a U-boat came into focus. It was sitting on the surface, moving slowly, possibly recharging its batteries. It was clear it hadn't spotted them yet, since they were approaching from the west and it was still dark behind them.

"What shall we do captain? Shall we ready the guns? If we could get a little closer, I think our Navy friends could do some damage to that blighter."

Percival seemed frozen to the spot. He looked from the submarine to the expectant face of his First Mate and then back again.

"I... I...I think I'm going to my cabin."

"What?" The word exploded out of Barney's mouth. All eyes on the bridge turned to look at the pair of them. "Sir, Captain, we need you here, Sir. May we close and get the guns ready Sir?"

"Yes Mr Mate. You may carry out my orders."

Another incredulous look passed over Barney's face, and then he snapped into action, issuing orders to bring the *Western Queen* onto a course that would bring her in from behind the submarine, to reduce the possibility of her being spotted until it was too late for their enemy to do anything about it.

"Full speed ahead and aim straight for him."

The hinged bulwarks were released, and the guns became prominent, their crews buzzing around them, readying themselves for their first action in the eighteen months that they had been on board. Everyone had a job to do, but anxious eyes kept looking up from dials and switches and the like to see what progress they were making in bringing their enemy to account. Time seemed to stretch, breaths were held until chests were bursting, and then they all saw action on the deck of the submarine. Crew members were climbing up the conning tower, making efforts to get back inside, wash was coming from the rear of the submarine as its speed began to pick up; they had been spotted. It was obviously going to dive, and slowly it started to submerge, but the *Western Queen* had the advantage and the shells from their six-inch guns started to home in on their target. Bright splashes of colour showed they had made their mark and more and more of them were landing home. It became obvious to all that the conning tower had been damaged sufficiently to put any thought of diving out of the submarine captain's mind, but it was still increasing its speed, seeking to outrun its attacker. More shells landed on their target and a hit on her stern, close to her propellers, seemed to slow her down.

"I not sure we can take her out by guns alone Captain, but we can ram her. That'll settle her hash, Captain, and good riddance."

"Give the order Mr Mate," said Percival. He watched with a sense of dread as the two vessels closed on each other, a dread that changed to a rumbling, tumbling sense of exhilaration as the bow of the *Queen* made contact with the submarine. A wild, shrieking laugh of triumph escaped from his mouth and then it quickly died as Percival saw the face of the submarine's captain; he had been caught by the conning tower's hatch as he had been going below. Perhaps a shell blast had distorted it, but whatever had caused it, the captain was there, his eyes locked on those of Percival. He saw such a look of hate, such a look of loathing and arrogance and fear, that it shook him to his very soul. And then it was over. With a final roar of metal on metal, the *Western Queen* rode on over the submarine's deck, pushing her below the waves.

All on the bridge cheered and yelled their joy at what they had just achieved; an enemy defeated; an enemy who had no doubt sent many fellow seamen to their deaths. Good riddance. All that is, except Percival. He sat in his chair, numbed by what he had just seen, revisiting the look on the fallen captain's face. Such hate. He had just allowed people to be killed, by his ship. He stumbled up and left the bridge and locked his cabin door behind him.

When they did eventually gain access to his cabin, the bosun and the first mate found Percival curled up in a soiled ball on his bunk. Six days later, the port doctor declared him to have had a major breakdown and to be totally unsuitable for sea-going duties for the foreseeable future.

Two months later, a pregnant Chrissie was unpacking Percival's belongings which had accompanied him back home to her. She was hanging up his jacket when she discovered a letter addressed to her. She opened it, began to read its contents, and burst into tears.

The bamboo that bends is stronger than the oak that resists

Japanese Proverb

It takes a certain type of person to stand against the commonly accepted; to speak against the majority; to act independently. They need courage, determination, and stubbornness. Without them, things will not change, and those changes can sometimes be for the better, sometimes not. You can be the judge of that.

The Nurse's Tale

Margaret Elizabeth Burnett, Peggy to her friends, stooped to make a quick assessment of the unfortunate young soldier that had just been brought on board the *Western Queen*. The ship was lying off the coast of Normandy. The sounds of battle, the pops and cracks of rifles, the whump of shells from large guns and the occasional crash of an exploding bomb reached her from across the water. It was only the second day of the offensive and it seemed to her that she had been on duty for most of that time, dealing with an ever-increasing flow of wounded men, many of whom looked little more than boys. Some came on stretchers, others simply walked or limped, in varying degrees of pain. Mud splattered, blood spattered, they were a sorry sight, these men, men who had once no doubt, been looking forward to lives of work and women and family, and normality.

Now, they were dying, or set for a path of recovery which might see them eventually sent back to that intense, living hell that warfare became for short periods; for the rest of the time, it was mainly boredom and training and drudgery. Or, they might be sent home, minus a limb, or their sight, or some other key part of their body or mind, meaning life would never be the same again. No more football, no more dancing or cycling up a countryside lane in the summer sunshine with their loved one. No more peace and contentment. All taken away in seconds; such is life and death in war; destined for crutches, a wheelchair perhaps, having the drool wiped off their chins by their mothers or their wives, spoon fed, nappies changed.

She shrugged her thoughts aside. Whatever lay ahead of them, it was Peggy's job to direct each patient to the right source of treatment; immediate surgery; a wait for a minor process, stitches, a plaster cast; or simply a quiet place to die with a warm hand to hold theirs, as they slipped away. The young man in front of her now, no more than twenty she thought, was gasping in pain and she could see the hastily applied field dressing to the right of his chest oozing blood, running in slow but steady rivulets down his side and onto the fabric of the stretcher, the blood turning to an odd colour on the khaki.

"Take him down to Operation Room Two," she said to the two orderlies that had brought the young man on board. "And tell them that I think this lad is a category one. If they get to him in time, they may well be able to save him. The bullet looks to have passed right through, but I can't tell how much damage it has done."

The young man's eyes sprang open, and they stared right into hers, fear written across his blood-stained face.

"Don't you worry young man, our doctors will sort you out, they're very good and know what they're doing."

She smiled down at him, patted him on the shoulder and moved off to see the next stretcher case, whilst making a mental note to herself to try not to scare her patients with her comments, something she had said to herself many, many times before. The team below needed some guidance, and she didn't have time to whisper, or be coy about it did she.

They came on board thick and fast, brought out to the ship by a variety of boats. Getting the stretcher cases up the side was not easy, but somehow the orderlies managed, straining every sinew to minimise the discomfort felt by their already damaged charges. Peggy must have seen over a hundred patients in her twelve-hour shift, and at six in the evening she went down to her bunk in the nurses' quarters and fell asleep in minutes.

When she rose the next morning, she found they had docked in Southampton overnight and the last of the casualties were being unloaded to be taken off to the local hospitals. The undertakers' vans were also in evidence on the dockside. Peggy went into the mess and had a breakfast of porridge, a big cup of hot, sweet tea and some toast and began to feel ready to face the new day. It was a rhythm that she had become used to over the months she had been serving on the hospital ships. She knew she would have some time before they were back on station, but there was work to be done before they got there. Fresh medical supplies had to be brought on board and then stored in their rightful places, the operating rooms, you could hardly call them theatres, had to be cleaned up and made ready for the new stream of wounded and dying. For the umpteenth time she wondered why men couldn't sort out their differences by means other than war, and for the umpteenth time she decided that it was just men being men; like dogs they had to pee on each other to prove their masculinity, their superiority, and this was the inevitable consequence of their bravado. Women would have dealt with it differently she thought, reached alternative accommodations that wouldn't have seen their sons and brothers and husbands and uncles sacrificed in their thousands on the altar of male pig-headedness.

§§§

She thought back to her father, Alexander Burnett, who had stayed true to his Methodist beliefs and joined the Royal Army Medical Corps when conscription was introduced in 1916. He would always support his country, he was a true patriot, but he would not kill men for it. He would help to save lives, not take them. She had always been proud of him for his moral courage, and it was in part, after a shaky start to her working life, why she had chosen to become a nurse. She could hardly remember him; she had been only three when he had been killed, blown up with another 'conchie' as they had been carrying a wounded soldier out of no-man's land on a stretcher, at the battle of Messines at Ypres. There were a few photographs of course back home; of her parent's wedding, her dad in his stiff suit and polished shoes, her mother in a flowing silky dress and floral headdress, smiling at the camera; her with her dad when she was born, him looking down at her with large moustaches and bushy eyebrows, grinning a silly big smile. She loved that one.

Her mum Jenny had gone to work two years after she was born, in 1916. The nation was crying out for women to take on roles in manufacturing and farming and transport, roles that had previously been the domain of men. Many of her friends and neighbours had opted to work in munitions, which paid comparatively well, but that was not a route that Jenny wanted. Like her husband, she would help out the nation in its time of need, but she would not help one man to kill another. Instead, she opted to go on the buses, becoming a clippie on the routes round her home town of Dunfermline. Peggy's grandmother was enlisted to look after her. She had loved those times spent with her granny, a big, soft woman with white hair; playing with her dollies, cooking gingerbread men, games of hide and seek. She remembered her granny wasn't too good at that, being a large woman in a small house. She couldn't remember the passing of her dad; she had just had a vague feeling that something wasn't quite as it had been.

The war ended, the men came back, and the women lost their jobs. A case of 'thank you very much, now off you go and wash our clothes and cook our dinners and have our babies, and just let us get on with our real jobs'. Jenny did receive a widow's pension and an allowance for Peggy, but it was hardly enough to keep them, and Jenny found work, as a maid, in one of the big houses in the town. It didn't pay a lot and the hours were long, but it enabled them to survive. Peggy had to remain in school until she was fourteen; that was the law. She left as soon as she could and got a job in 'Gregory's the Drapers' which added to their weekly income, allowing the occasional treat of a visit to the cinema, or a cup of tea and a pastry at the local tea shop.

She always had been a pretty girl and as she matured, she grew into a quite beautiful young woman. She was tall, shapely, had a heart shaped face, green eyes and deep auburn hair. She noticed men now looked at her differently than they had before. At first this unsettled her, but she soon became used to it. A year after she had started work, she was sorting out some bolts of cloth in the storeroom at the back of the shop when Mr Gregory came in, carrying some papers. Nothing odd in that, they'd been together in that room on many occasions before. Today though, something was different she thought. There was something about his manner, he seemed a trifle tense.

She heard him say, "you do know you are a very pretty girl Peggy, don't you?" as he stood behind her. She tensed up and turning round to face him, she was surprised to find him almost touching her.

"Now my dear Peggy, come and give your boss a nice kiss," and he put his arms out to draw her into his grasp.

He was old enough to be her father she thought. She was outraged. How dare he? She put up her hands to ward him off.

"Mr Gregory, please don't do that! Your wife wouldn't like to hear about this would she, and you have a daughter of my age. Please stop, and if you try that again I shall go and get the police in here and tell them what you've done."

"Don't be silly girl," he said. "No one would believe you even if you did tell them. An established member of the community, a happily married man, and as you say, a father of two. Nobody is going to take your word against mine."

He made another move towards her, and she slapped him in the face. He pressed on pushing her back against a workbench. It was then that she brought her knee up against him, and he let out a loud gasp of pain and sank to the floor. Peggy pushed passed him, grabbing her coat from the peg by the door and as she left the shop, front door wide open, she could hear him shouting out,

"...and nobody will ever believe you, you stuck up little slut."

Her mother and grandmother were shocked at first, when she told them what had happened. Then they both told her nothing would be gained by making a fuss about it; it had always been the way and as far as they could see, it always would be. Peggy told them that some of her friends, working in other jobs in the town, had often encountered the 'wandering hand brigade' as they called them. She had been lucky that it had taken so long to happen to her she thought. Something should be done about men like Mr Gregory. Perhaps if her dad had been around, then Mr Gregory might have had a comeuppance on a dark night, but that was not to be.

"Best forget it mum. But I do need to get another job. We need the money."

"I don't know what you might do. I could always ask Mrs Arbuthnot if any of her friends are looking for a maid. I haven't heard of anything, but I'll ask."

"No mum, I don't think I want that kind of thing. I don't ever want to work in a shop again either, that I do know. I want to do something useful with my life, something like dad did, something medical, become a nurse perhaps."

"You won't earn much by nursing Peggy" her mum replied. "It's long hours and hard work. And dealing with all the blood and poop and stuff. Are you sure that's what you want? I think I'd run a mile if they asked me to deal with things like that."

"You did it for me, didn't you?" Peggy said. "You didn't run a mile then." They both laughed.

Then she said, "Yes, it is what I want to do. I've been thinking about it for some while, the shop was always boring, well until yesterday anyway."

They both laughed again.

"Clouds and silver linings, eh pet?"

§§§

One month later Peggy was the lowest of the low in their local hospital at Leys Hill Road. Her mother's predictions about poop and vomit and the like had become part of her daily experience. But she loved it. She saw up close how the nurses worked, how they reacted to their patients in all the scenarios that could arise: joy, despair, sadness, acceptance, rage and anger. She saw how they dealt with patients' relatives, how they managed their expectations both good and bad. She saw their humanity and strength. And she longed to join their ranks when she was old enough.

Romance, real romance, not the Mr Gregory sort of stuff, did pay her a visit in the form of one of the young porters who worked at the hospital. Angus was a tall lad of seventeen, curly brown hair atop a tanned, smiley face. One day, he joined her and her friends at a table in the canteen. They were talking 'girl things' when he simply sat down without being asked. The conversation dribbled to an awkward halt. They all looked at him and, looking back, he blushed. But instead of getting up and moving off to another table as a lesser being might have done, he said,

"My mum swears by Lifebuoy. She says it's the best you can get."

He had obviously caught the end of their conversation. They all looked at him in amazement, and then began to giggle.

"That's a wonderful chat up line Angus, where did you get that from eh?" asked one of the girls.

And it just grew from there. Angus became a regular member of their table when his duties allowed. Over the coming weeks it became clear to everyone that Peggy was his favourite. When they were on their own, the other girls constantly asked if Angus had asked her out yet. "Oh

Peggy, I do think your hair is so pretty. Oh Peggy, I do like your coat. Oh Peggy, I think you can walk on water……" they mimicked in as close an approximation of Angus' tones as they could muster. And eventually Angus did pluck up the courage to ask her to accompany him to the cinema to see *All Quiet on the Western Front,* which had just been released and was causing quite a stir.

That was just the beginning. Their romance blossomed. They talked endlessly. They were both lovers of the outdoors; they laughed at the same things; they liked the same things. However, there was one area where they did not think alike, and this became apparent on that first date. The film had led them on to a discussion as he had walked her home, about what a country should do if attacked. Angus said he could understand why the pupils at his former school had called Paul Baume, the hero of the film, a coward when he had gone back there to talk to them about the war. He had told them of the horrors, the dangers, the death and the dying. Angus said, 'A man's duty is to fight for his country, not wail on about how horrid it is." That led Peggy to tell him of her father's approach in World War One. At first Angus was taken aback by this turn of events, fearful that he had damaged his chances with her, but he recovered by saying, "Well at least he went, didn't he. He wasn't a coward, was he." She still kissed him when they said goodnight.

§§§

By the time Peggy was twenty-one she was expecting Angus to ask for her hand; they had been going out together for nearly five years after all. In truth she'd been hoping he was going to ask her a couple of years before that. The day of her birthday came. Her mother had planned a birthday tea after work for her and her friends. As they were leaving the hospital together that evening, Angus said,

"Would you mind having a cup of tea with me before I go home and change. I have a wee present that I'd rather not give you in front of the others." Her heart gave a jump; was this it? Was he going to ask her to marry him at last?

"Oh, right you are then. I have a few minutes before I need to get home," she said in a voice which she hoped didn't betray the inner, expectant turmoil of emotions that she was experiencing.

"Och, I canna wait any longer," Angus blurted out, and right there and right then, he got down in front of her, with passers by giving them strange and enquiring glances, and on one knee, with a box open in his hand which held a small, golden, sparkling ring, he said,

"Miss Peggy Burnett, would you do me the honour of becoming Mrs Angus Liddell?"

Tears welled up in her eyes as she said,

"Oh Angus, I would love to become Mrs Angus Liddell. Yes, yes, yes."

He rose, and they embraced in the street in front of all the pedestrians, who stood and cheered and clapped and wished them well.

§§§

The other momentous change which occurred at that time was that Peggy enrolled into formal training to be a nurse. She had impressed the senior staff at the hospital and when she turned twenty-one, she applied to be a trainee nurse and was accepted. Those at the hospital knew of her engagement to Angus, but since she was yet unmarried, her training was allowed to begin. Knowing this would not be the case were she to marry, she and Angus told everyone that they had agreed to wait the further four years that her qualification would take. They married secretly when she was twenty-two but continued to live apart, snatching time together when they could.

Peggy loved her training and proved to be an excellent pupil. There were, of course, some mishaps along the way. One day, when going to empty a patient's bedpan, she collected it and let out a loud scream!

"It's blue, it's blue," she cried out, and ran off down the ward, heads turning to look at her as she shot out through its swing doors. Doctor Poulton, who happened to be on the ward at the time, scowled after her and asked the Sister just who that stupid girl was. Peggy was unaware that the poor patient was in for an examination of his kidneys and had been injected with a dye to check their function. A stiff dressing down from Sister was followed by the instruction to be more restrained in future, and never to disturb a doctor when he was doing his rounds. Doctors were, after all, next to God in the hierarchy of the medical world.

Peggy saw a lot of things that gave her pleasure during her training and many that angered her. Back in 1867, Florence Nightingale had written a letter, fighting against the common view of the time that nursing was *'being left to those who were too old, too weak, too drunken, too dirty, too stupid or too bad to do anything else'*. Things had moved on from that time, but nurses, especially trainee nurses, were still very low in the medical hierarchy. A trainee nurse could not talk to a doctor directly; instead, she told a nurse, who told a staff nurse, who told the sister, who told the Matron who told the doctor. Surely there was a better way than that? The hours were long and the pay poor, but the joy of being of service, of helping people through difficult times, of seeing people recover and go back to their lives, sustained her, whilst confirming in her an intention to make a difference, when and where she could. She joined one of the recently formed nurses' groups and attended meetings with the public at which they made their case for better work conditions and more respect.

Peggy became a registered nurse in 1939, just as the prospect of war was becoming inevitable. The shortage of nursing staff was apparent to all, especially given the circumstances, and Peggy and Angus felt bold enough to declare their marriage. A rough interview with Matron ensued but wise heads prevailed, and she was given permission to carry on nursing. Then the war really did arrive.

Angus enlisted. "I cannot, in all conscience, just stand by and let those damn Germans do anything they feel like to anyone they feel like doing it to. If we don't rally together and teach them a lesson, then there's no telling what their next step will be. Why, they could be over here, making us do whatever they want, making you do anything they want. I'm not having it." He and Peggy argued about it, but he was adamant. He joined the Royal Scots and was soon in France. Peggy applied to join Queen Alexandra's Imperial Military Nursing Service. She too, soon found herself in France.

§§§

The early months with the British Expeditionary Force were almost like a holiday. There was very little contact with the enemy. Angus was up near the border with Belgium, where they even managed one blissful weekend together, in Lecelles. As the months wore on, the Germans advanced and by May the Royals were just south of Tournai with orders to protect the BEF perimeter. Fighting was fierce and on 26th May, outside Le Paradis, Angus took a bullet to the head and was killed in an instant, along with most of his comrades. Only a handful of the Royal Scots made it back home.

Peggy's workload in the field hospital steadily increased as the Germans came closer. A trickle of cases turned into a stream, and then, in the second half of May, became a torrent. She worked non-stop, snatching a few moments of sleep between the arrival of the wounded who came in lorries, cars, ambulances and even farm carts and wheelbarrows and on foot. The Germans were making serious advances on their position near Dunkirk and then, to everyone's surprise and relief, there was a pause. For some inexplicable reason the German tanks stopped moving forwards, stopped crushing their French and British opponents. Peggy's base caught its breath, restored some order to its chaos and got on with the job of sending the wounded on to the port and back to England.

The respite was short-lived. The heavens opened. Literally. The bombers of the Luftwaffe started to appear; bombs fell; fighter planes flew frighteningly close overhead, firing their machine guns at the Red Cross tents and ambulances and vehicles and people, and the chaos was back with a vengeance. Peggy was running from one tent to another with a syringe of morphine in her hand when a bomb fell nearby and blew her off her feet. She ended up in a crumpled heap, the breath knocked out of her, pressed against something hard. Clumps of earth and grains of sand rained down and she felt as though she had been beaten all over with a stick. She couldn't hear a thing apart from a high-pitched whine in her ears.

She tested the movement of her limbs; all OK. She sat up, with difficulty, and looked around her. The tent that she had been running towards was gone, just a big hole in the earth where it had been, smoke rising from it, bits of debris all around; a singed roll of bandage, the shattered remains of a trolley, someone's arm, its hand bearing a wedding ring. It was an awful sight and she realised, suddenly enveloped in a wave of shock, how close to death she had been. And then she gave a sudden laugh, just couldn't stop. Tears ran down her cheeks and on to the tattered remains of her blood-spattered uniform.

"Oh my God Peggy, are you alright? My God, that was a close one and no mistake. Come on my girl, let's get you up and cleaned off shall we. Let's get you a cup of tea and sort you out."

Sister Winifred helped Peggy to her feet and pointed her back towards the mess tent. Bombs were still falling, but some way further off now, and the pair hardly registered them. She was back on duty three hours later, a wash and a fresh uniform making her look better than she felt. She was still shaking.

The next few days were utter bedlam. The German tanks recommenced their advance and the BEF became tightly squeezed around the port. The evacuation, which had been going on for several days, speeded up even more so, with all sort of craft, ships, boats, yachts and dinghies making their way in and out of the harbour and beaches nearby. Some were blown out of the water before they'd even docked; some were sunk on their way out, back to England, but still they came in their hundreds from all the ports along the south coast, crewed by professionals and amateurs alike. Messerschmitts continued to strafe their positions, chased by a few Spitfires, bombs fell, and shells added to the chaos. The nurses of Peggy's group were given the order to evacuate and head for the docks, after they had destroyed all the medical equipment and supplies that might aid their enemy. This they duly did, and eventually she and her colleagues got away on a small boat and landed back in Dover, a quiet, depleted, and chastened group.

Peggy was granted a few days leave and after a slow and torturous rail journey she opened the door of her mother's house and went in. They fell into each other's arms sobbing as soon as they saw each other and stayed like that for a couple of minutes.

"Aw my pet. Thank God you're OK. I didn't know what had happened to you. I did hear about Dunkirk, and I just didn't know what to think. I was so scared for you. I thought you might be there, but I didn't know. And here you are, all well and right. And, oh, thank God you're alive and well and here."

All of this rushed out of her mouth in a torrent and the tears came again and the smiles and the hugs.

Eventually, when they had both calmed down, Peggy gave her mum a sanitised version of events, leaving out nearly being blown to bits, and the number of deaths and injuries she'd witnessed. Instead, she told of the heroism she'd seen, the sight of all those little boats and their calm heroic captains. And of the thousands that had made it back home safely. Then she said,

"Mum, I haven't heard from Angus. Have you?"

A blank look came over her mother's face

"No pet, I'm afraid I haven't."

Then, brightening up she said

"I'm sure he'll be fine. He's a strong, bright man, he'll be OK, you'll see. He'll have come out on one of those boats and not had a chance to let you know yet."

Five days later, when she arrived back home, she learned that she was a widow. The telegram that she picked off the mat simply said,

I REGRET TO INFORM YOU THAT ACCORDING TO INFORMATION RECEIVED YOUR HUSBAND ANGUS LIDDELL IS BELIEVED TO HAVE LOST HIS LIFE ON 26TH MAY FIGHTING WITH 1ST BATTALION ROYAL SCOTTS GUARDS IN FRANCE STOP I EXPRESS MY PROFOUND SYMPATHY STOP LETTER FOLLOWS SHORTLY STOP UNDER SECRETARY OF STATE STOP

§§§

Returning to her unit in London several days later, Peggy felt a strong desire to give up. She'd nearly been killed; her husband **had** been killed; Britain was losing the war. What was the point of it all, she wondered. Why should she carry on? Her disillusion obviously showed. She was invited to Matron's office. The bespectacled, grey-haired lady, in her full uniform, rose as Peggy entered and showed her to one of a couple of armchairs, taking the other for herself.

"My dear Peggy. I was so sorry to hear about the death of your husband, Angus. It must have been such an awful blow for you, coming on top of all that trouble in Dunkirk. How are you feeling my dear?"

Peggy looked up from her lap to see the look of concern on Matron's face.

"Thank you, Matron. Yes, it's been a dreadful time. We met the once in France you know, but I never thought it would be the last time I'd ever see him."

She paused, a tear trickling down her cheek.

Matron didn't say anything but waited for Peggy to regain her composure and carry on. After a few seconds Peggy said,

"I just wonder what it's all about, Matron, all this fighting and dying. I don't know why we carry on. It's so futile. Good men dying and for what? We had our whole lives ahead of us and now……."

Another silence began which the matron cut short.

"I do sympathise with how you are feeling Peggy. I really do. But you must know you are not alone in all this. We are here to support you. You have your work to do, to look after the poor men and women who are still going to be affected by this whether you like it or not. We can't stop it happening can we, and until someone who can does, well, then it's down to us to look after the casualties of this fight and ensure they get the best treatment possible, the best chance of a happy, fruitful life going forward. I know it's difficult for you to think kindly on my words, but I would ask you to carry on with your work here, to think over what I've said and if you still feel that it isn't for you in a month's time, then we may talk again. But for now, just think of the men like your Angus, and their need for skilled, compassionate care. You are a good nurse. You've shown that. You can offer us and them so much. So please think it over carefully. OK, my dear, thank you for coming to see me, you may return to your ward now."

As the days passed, Peggy did think about the Matron's words and little by little she came to understand that what she had been saying to her had been that if she did stop nursing then the Germans had won, that Angus had died in vain, that her colleagues and friends had died in vain. What sort of person did she want to be? What did she want to be able to look back on in her life when an old woman? Did she want to sit in her armchair when she was eighty and conclude that she'd given in at the first hurdle? Or did she want to stand up on her hind legs and take the fight back to those who had wronged her, and hers, in the only way she could?

Time moved on, the summer had come and now was on its way out as the fighting raged over the Channel, day after day, hour after hour, vapour trails entangled in the clear blue skies, the rattling of the cannons and the screaming of engines providing a dramatic melody to the drama as the exhausted young men of two countries, in their Spitfires and Messerschmitts, fought for supremacy in the air.

Peggy was back nursing with a new determination, her self-doubt and despair having been overcome. She still felt the loss of Angus greatly, it still caused her to weep at the most unexpected moments, but she had a real mission now; each one of the patients she treated was a reminder of her husband, and she brought all the skill and care and sensitivity she could ever have lavished over him, to the care of the poor unfortunates that came her way. Then a new menace arrived. German bombers started to appear over London each night as the skies darkened, dropping tons and tons of bombs down onto the poor people below. Whole streets were obliterated, gone in the time it took to light a candle. Homes, businesses all gone in the blinking of an eye. No power, no water, no mother, no father.

When not on duty Peggy would go with her fellow Londoners down into an underground station, spending many a sleepless night, hearing the blasts from somewhere above, feeling the ground tremble as bomb after bomb fell nearby. When the 'all clear' sounded, they would go back up to the light, to street level, fearful of what they would find. Crushed buildings, piles of rubble, men scrabbling at that rubble, searching for survivors. Bomb craters, smoke, noise, men fighting fires with wriggling hoses, the wounded being carried away to safety. One morning she came across the absurdity of a house left standing, all by itself, its neighbours blown to kingdom come. Its whole front was gone, all the rooms open to view; the settee in the front room, the radio on the sideboard, pictures crooked on the walls.; the double bed, its quilt and pillows still in place, dangling half in, half out, threatening to topple into the street. Such bloody madness, she thought.

Like her fellow Londoners she carried on; you had to, didn't you? The pressure she was under, that they were all under, didn't, however, blind her to the continuing appalling treatment meted out to her and her fellow nurses. Another unforgivable crime in a world that was full of them she thought. She and her colleagues weren't well paid, and their hours were long. Eighty-four hours a week was not unusual, and this was often pushed further. Ok, there was a war on, but war or not, people were people and Peggy felt those in her profession should be treated with dignity and respect by those with whom they came into contact, especially by their senior colleagues; especially when they were all supposed to be working together to achieve a common goal.

The nursing hierarchy was clearly defined. Day-to-day relations between nurses and staff nurses and sisters were generally harmonious. Matrons were a different kettle of fish, but someone had to be the boss and they were typically held in high regard for their knowledge, skill and leadership. Many doctors would tread carefully around the Matrons they encountered but there were a number, mostly senior men, who saw themselves as the lords of their manors and treated the lowlier staff as their serfs.

It had been a long hard shift. The bombing was producing new patients every day, many of whom required surgery. Peggy was working in one of the operating theatres where a thin, middle-aged woman was lying on the table having a large piece of shrapnel removed from her back. She had lost a lot of blood and was lucky to still be alive. The anaesthetist had done his stuff and the team had got to work quickly. The surgeon, Alastair Gollinge, was a man of the old school, a man who expected both competence and unswerving obedience.

"Swab here," he commanded, and a nurse duly obliged. "Scalpel." One was provided immediately, being placed carefully but firmly into the palm of his outstretched hand. As he turned back towards the patient, the scalpel fell from his grasp, hitting the floor and disappearing under the operating table.

"You clumsy buffoon," he shouted at the nurse. "Whoever let you into my theatre? You're no use to man nor beast. Get the devil out of here at once and send in someone who knows what they're doing, not a clown like you. Go on, get out of my sight." Then, addressed to Peggy, "You, come here and take her place. Come on, come on, get on with it, I can't wait all day!"

Peggy who had been watching her friend Alice dash from the theatre in a fit of tears, did as she was told. The operation continued to a successful conclusion and the team went to change.

"Mr Gollinge."

He was washing his hands but turned to view the source of the intrusion. He saw Peggy standing three feet away, her eyes on his, her face set in an angry and determined look.

"Yes nurse, what can I do for you?" and he turned back to the sink to continue his ablutions.

"Well sir, to begin with I think you can do me the courtesy of looking at me when we talk."

At that, he spun round. He took a step towards her, hands dripping water and suds onto the floor, and bent down, bringing his face close to hers.

"I beg your pardon? Just who do you think you're talking to, you impudent girl? Your name at once. I shall be talking with your matron, and you will never set foot in a theatre with me again."

He stood looking at her, waiting for an answer.

"Well girl, tell me your name at once, do you hear me?" He was starting to go very red in the face, and Peggy could see a vein throbbing at his temple.

"My name, sir, is Peggy Liddell. I felt that you should know that I saw exactly what happened in there just now. The scalpel was placed into the palm of your hand correctly, just as it should have been. That it fell was entirely your fault, and not the fault of Alice. That is her name by the way, and she is a very experienced, very professional nurse. Your treatment of her was completely undeserved, rude, inappropriate, and disrespectful, the actions of a bully. Sir."

Gollinge turned purple, took a moment to compose himself and then started to speak in a quiet, cold tone

"Nurse Liddell, you have worked your last shift at this hospital. How dare you speak to me like that. You obviously do not know your place, but I do; it is with the rest of your kind that constantly need to be reminded of their manners and to respect their betters. I shall personally see to it that you never work in this profession again. You are finished in nursing, d'you hear, finished?"

He was shouting at her at this point.

"Never working with you again, sir, will be a blessing. It is time that people like you learned that you cannot continue to treat your nurses as you would treat a soiled dressing, something to be cast aside when it has no further use for you. We are trained, we know our jobs well, we carry out our jobs very well, and at a time like this, the country has a great need for people like Alice and me. You may be good at what you do, no one will dispute that, but the way you treat your colleagues is despicable. As I have said, the act of an arrogant bully."

And with that, with everyone standing watching in quiet astonishment at what they had just witnessed, she turned on her heel and walked out.

And that is how Peggy came to find herself working on a hospital ship. She had been summoned to a meeting with matron at the start of her next shift. After a lengthy dressing down and being told that she would not be able to work at the hospital anymore, Matron had said,

"And I am very disappointed by that Peggy. You are an excellent nurse, with a lot of potential to go further in this profession, but if you cannot curb that mouth of yours, then you will be forced to leave nursing for good. Word will spread and no one will want to take the risk of employing you. Do you understand that?"

Peggy nodded that she understood. Matron relaxed a little.

"Good. Well as I said, I think you are a good nurse with the potential to become an exceptional one, so I'm not going to let you slip away from nursing. I had a chat with a friend of mine in another branch of the service last night and, if you are agreeable, I have managed to secure a position for you on one of our hospital ships. They're always looking for good staff and you could be on board, working, in the time it takes you to get up to Scotland. I'm not going to say that it's an easy life, because that would be a lie. But it is an important role. You would receive our casualties, and sometimes even those of the enemy, and be their first real chance of getting the treatment that could mean the difference between living and dying. The teams are typically quite small, several doctors and not many more nurses. Dare I say it, but I do believe the doctors are perhaps a little bit more enlightened than some of our brethren here, if you understand me, though I can't exactly promise that. So, what do you say?"

As she was leaving the office, Matron said,

"And Peggy, thank you for defending Alice. I'll see to it that she suffers no harm."

A week later, Peggy stepped on board *HMHS Tribune*.

§§§

For the next eighteen months Peggy sailed between Scappa Flow and Aberdeen, transporting wounded sailors from their ships and rescue vessels to hospitals on the mainland. She continued to hate the war and the causes of the war, but she felt blessed she was once again able to make a real difference. That she was a part of the process that took poor, damaged boys and men, sons and husbands, and started them on a road back to recovery carried her through those dark times. Yes, quite a few poor souls did die in her care, but she consoled herself in those moments by thinking their final hours had been better than they might have been.

Hospital ships were supposed to be inviolate. The conventions of war stated that they were to remain unmolested by their enemies. Certainly, enemy troops could board and inspect them to make sure they were engaged in only humanitarian acts and not acting as undercover agents, but no bombing, no strafing; the perils of the sea, including mines, were supposedly the only dangers they faced. In reality, this was not how it worked. Hospital ships, clearly marked, painted white, red crosses in abundance, regularly experienced attacks from the air and sea and, whilst not a frequent occurrence, they were sunk from time to time with the loss of whole medical teams. *HMHS Tribune* was lucky. She was targeted on several occasions, bullets flying above, around and through her structure, but only minor casualties resulted.

This was to change shortly after Operation Husky, the Allied invasion of Sicily, which began on 9th July 1943. The fight lasted for just over five weeks and when it ended the island was in the hands of Allied forces and the Mediterranean was open for business for Allied shipping for the first time since 1941. The *Tribune* had been drafted there to provide its medical services, with several other hospital ships, as part of the Eastern Naval Task Force. The fighting was fierce. Errors were made. Friendly fire downed dozens of paratrooper planes and the Italians fought well and hard to defend their homeland. Vessel after vessel brought out wounded and dying to the ship and the medical staff were on the go for hour after hour. Early one morning as the sky lightened, a Stukka dive-bomber made an approach, the clear markings of a hospital ship making no difference to its pilot. Its bullets raked across the deck and a bomb fell down through an open hold and exploded near the operating theatres, instantly killing three doctors and four nurses.

Peggy had been taking a hasty nap in the nurses' quarters and was jolted into wakefulness by the explosion. At first, she wondered if she was still in a dream, a nightmare perhaps. The room was filled with clogging, cloying smoke; there were sounds of screaming from nearby; debris was lying on top of her; and her ears were ringing. This nightmare was real, she concluded. For a short moment she wondered if this was it, if this was what dying was like, but feeling no pain, she rolled off her cot and got shakily to her feet. She lurched through the smoke towards where she thought the doorway should be, banging her head onto a solid wall; so not there then. She felt the beginnings of panic rising in her chest, but summoning her inner determination, she took a further breath of smoke-filled air, coughed violently, and started to inch her way round the wall, feeling for that elusive opening. Pawing her way along, each passing second caused her panic to grow; eyes streaming, smoke getting deeper into her lungs with every breath. And then, at last, she pushed on fresh air. There was the opening; the light was a bit stronger through it and she lurched her way out into the companionway and towards the stairs.

She crawled up them with great difficulty, the smoke thinning out as she went, her lungs crying out for cleaner air. When she came onto the deck she was met with a scene of devastation; smoke rose into the air from the great, gaping hole that the explosion had caused; the deck plating was buckled, railings had been torn from their mountings and lay in a tangled mess; people were running here and there, searching for friends and colleagues, searching for safety. Peggy could see that the ship was sinking. It had started to list to one side, and it was in that direction people were moving, towards the lifeboats. She stood still, confused as to what to do. Obviously, people would be hurt. She was a nurse. She would need to tend to them. So, she reasoned, she better find out how she could help. She turned to go back up the tilting deck, but as she moved away, a sailor grabbed her hand and stopped her progress saying,

"No, not that way Miss. Come on Miss, you have to get in the boat, we don't have long before she'll be under."

"But what about the wounded? I've got to go and look for them and get them up here too. I've got to go and look after the wounded you silly man." And she made to move off once more.

"No way Miss. In the boat now. If you don't go, I'll carry you there myself. I'll go and look for others, once you're in the lifeboat, but you've got to get in."

More members of the crew appeared, some supporting wounded colleagues, stumbling across the littered decks, falling, heaving themselves upright and staggering on. The one lifeboat available to them, all the rest having been rendered useless by the attack, was filled to overflowing by the time it was cast off from its moorings to sail clear of the sinking ship. Those who could not get in just held onto its sides, or the hands of those already in it. A desperate sight. Ten minutes later *HMHS Tribune* slipped under the water, never to be seen again.

§§§

Their plight had been observed by nearby ships and within an hour they were onboard one of the other hospital ships of the fleet, being checked out for injuries. Peggy had a few cuts and bruises; her lungs were rough and sore from the smoke she had inhaled, but there was nothing major to worry about. What hurt her more, was the loss of most of her nursing colleagues, of the doctors that she had served and come to admire over the long period they had worked together and members of the ship's crew, who to a man had looked after them so well. She cried herself to sleep in her new bunk that night, once more raging at the inanity that was war.

The vessel Peggy now found herself on was *HMHS Western Queen* and after a day or so of recuperation it was agreed that Peggy and her surviving colleagues would continue to serve on it. The Sicilian campaign carried on, providing them with a steady flow of customers, and then, suddenly, it was over. Time for everyone to relax, refresh and prepare.

As she had become used to by now, this 'holiday season' did not last for long. The campaign to invade Italy started in early September and although Napoleon's maxim that 'like a boot, Italy should be entered from the top' was known to those planning the new campaign, the two prongs of the attack focused on the heel, in the area surrounding Taranto, and on the shin at Salerno. The ship became a busy place once again, taking the wounded on board and ferrying them off to the now-safe ports on Sicily. Whilst the new Italian government surrendered quickly in the face of the invasion, the German forces fought tooth and nail and might have even won ground in some areas but for the strategic decision to withdraw and keep Rome in German hands for as long as possible. The campaign continued for months, the *Western Queen* continuing its routine of embarking, treating, and disembarking casualties, whilst avoiding the odd attack.

Things changed in early summer the following year. Fighting in Italy was still going on but there was less need for their services. One day Peggy was in the Mediterranean; several days later she was looking out on the channel coast of England. And then D-Day and the turmoil and blood and death with which she had become so familiar, resumed.

§§§

Two pm; eleven thirty; half-past-six; twelve forty. All just times of the day you might think, but we all have that one moment in our lives that we remember above all others. For Peggy, five-past-two on the afternoon of the 18th of June 1944 would forever be written in letters of gold on her heart. It was at that time a stretcher bearing the wounded figure of one Andrew Woodhouse was lifted on to the deck of the *Western Queen* and placed at her feet. She stepped in to assess him. Obviously a pilot, his flying jacket caked in dried blood, a bandage round his head, fair hair poking out from underneath. He had splints on his left leg and on his right arm. His eyes were closed. As she lifted the blood-stained side of the jacket to find the source of the staining his eyes popped open and he looked right at her, her face no more than a foot from his. He broke into a painful smile,

"I think I must be in heaven." It was an effort for him to speak, but he carried on "you are my lovely angel come to guide me home." And then he passed out. Peggy smiled to herself and carried on with her examination, finding a field dressing on his right shoulder covering a large hole in his flesh. The docket that accompanied him simply noted, "Shot down; parachuted; crashed into a barn and broke limbs; significant loss of blood."

She directed him down to the theatre to have his various needs attended to; a 'category two' in her opinion, not in immediate danger, but needing attention soon. Then she moved on to the next patient.

All afternoon, the airman's pained, smiling face kept coming back to her, and contrary to her usual practise, at the end of her shift she went to see how he had fared. He was out of the operating room and a quick scan of his notes showed that the surgeon had patched up the bullet hole and set proper casts around his leg and arm. There was talk of concussion and a prognosis that the use of his right arm may well be impaired, such a large amount of muscle having been shot away. He was still asleep as she looked at him, thinking that he must be at least thirty; he was also quite handsome she thought, not in a film-starry sort of way, more a sort of competent, capable, intelligent handsomeness, which she found herself liking. As she was about to leave, he stirred and opened his eyes. Looking about him, his gaze eventually came to rest on Peggy.

"Well, if it isn't my Angel." Again, he fell back into unconsciousness.

They were at sea for two more days before returning to Southampton. Peggy found herself visiting Wing Commander Woodhouse at least three times a day and once they had got passed the 'Angel' thing she found him to be as she had surmised, calm, funny and intelligent. He had made light of his wounds and of what had caused them, saying only that he had been a bloody fool not to see the Gerry behind him and it was his own sodding fault. He had learnt about his possible loss of mobility in his shoulder and arm and accepted it, with a resigned good grace.

"At least I'm alive and I've met you, haven't I? So I think I've done very well out of it, even if the Government is short of one rather fine Hurricane."

§§§

Peggy found that she couldn't stop thinking about him. One day a couple of weeks later, when the ship had docked in Southampton, she was handed a letter addressed to her by a man in the Dock office. She didn't recognise the handwriting and opened it with curiosity. It was from Andrew.

'Dear Peggy

6th August 1944

I am writing to you – thank goodness I'm left-handed – from an RAF Hospital somewhere in England. I am on the mend, I'm glad to say. The medics say that I will never return to combat flying, and I can't say I'm truly sorry about that. It does mean that I would have to have a desk job were I to continue in the RAF, but I think that the best option for all concerned would be for me to be invalided out eventually and return to the job I was doing before this damn war overtook us. I was working in a country solicitor's office in Alton in Hampshire. It is to there I shall go, I mean my house in Alton, when I'm released for my convalescence on the 24th inst.

You may think it very forward of me, but I was hoping we might see each other again, when you are free from your duties. I have been thinking about you a great deal of late and I think we have things to talk about. As I say, you may think this very forward of me. I hope you don't; I think you won't, hopefully.

By the way, I live at The Grove, The Westway, Alton, Hampshire. My telephone number there is Alton 213.

I do so hope I shall hear from you, my dear Medical Angel,

With fondest feelings

Andrew

Peggy felt a surge of emotion, of happiness, of delight, of anticipation. Of course she would go to visit him. Nothing, except her duty, could keep her away. Knowing the routine of the *Western Queen*, she would most likely be able to make a trip up to Alton on 28th. The day duly arrived. It was hot and the steam train chugged its way out of Southampton and on to Winchester. Here she changed trains, and after a two-hour journey she stepped out of the 3rd class carriage at Alton Station. Andrew was there to meet her, a broad smile on that handsome face. They shook hands, rather awkwardly and then on second thoughts they gave each other a genteel embrace and left the station. Parked outside was one of the most beautiful cars she had ever seen. It was an Alvis, sports car, finished in red, with big mudguards and massive headlights.

"Your carriage awaits you Miss" he said as held the door open for her to get in.

"Mrs" she corrected him.

His face fell for a moment.

"My husband Angus was killed in France in 1939. He was a lovely man."

"I'm so sorry. I should have asked you earlier. I just assumed, you know, no wedding ring and all that."

His house was a beautiful example of a modest Edwardian country house; set in a small, but beautiful parkland estate, the redbrick house with high chimneys and massive windows glowed golden in the light from the south. Peggy's jaw dropped open.

"My goodness, it's absolutely beautiful" she gasped.

"Yes, it is, isn't it. My dad bought it when it was built. Unfortunately, both he and Ma were killed in the Blitz. It's been my home since I was 12."

Peggy did her sums; yes, that would make him somewhere in his middle thirties as she had thought the first time she had seen him.

That first visit passed very quickly and soon, too soon for them both, she was back on the train to Southampton. Peggy spent her time between the *Western Queen* and Alton for the remainder of the year. The need for hospital ships dwindled as the war marched on to its happy conclusion and in April the *Western Queen* ceased to be HMHS and became the *MV Western Queen* once again, ferrying troops from here to there. Her services no longer required on board, Peggy resigned from nursing and in August 1945 she became Mrs Andrew Woodhouse.

Desperation is like stealing from the Mafia: you stand a good chance of attracting the wrong attention

Douglas Horton

From my observations over the years, I have come to the conclusion that we can plot and plan as much as we like, but we are never fully in charge of our own destiny. Others always have their say and, if you believe in the six degrees of separation theory, that means there are an awful lot of others out there wishing to speak.

The Steward's Tale

Paolo Victor Gambocino, Pauly to his friends, was feeling pleased with himself. His tasks done for the day, the money passed on to safe hands, he was leaning against the drug store wall on the corner of Livingston and Nevins keeping an eye on the comings and goings around him while idly looking at the horse racing section of the paper. He did have a bit of an inside track on such matters; he knew the certainties where 'arrangements' were in place, but he liked to make his own selections on the other races and see how they fared. He was 25, married with two kids. He lived in a decent apartment, not grand but comfortable, and he had money in his pocket. He was doing OK. A made man, he was involved in the grunt work of his family's operations. For his initiation, he had killed his first man at the age of 17, a member of another family. He hadn't enjoyed it, but it was an order and orders were there to be followed. In the main, people generally liked him. He was competent, kept out of trouble, and could be counted on when trouble came calling. For him, the Mafia truly came before his birth family and God. He was, he thought, on his way to becoming a capo and that's when he truly would start to make real money.

Most of his time was taken up with the collection of the *pizzo* from the butchers, the bakers, the candlestick makers of his patch. With an offer of support and protection they couldn't refuse, the little guys handed over their five or ten dollars or whatever the going rate was at the time. Sometimes one of the girls was getting a bit uppity and had to be helped to see the error of her ways; and there was always a bit of activity on the 'powder' side of the business.

As he checked through the various runners and riders for that day and started making his informed choices, he noticed a scruffy urchin of a boy standing on the other corner staring at him intently. He was about 10 years old he thought, thin, shabbily dressed and shod. His little face was unremarkable except for two prominent front teeth which together with his piercing stare gave him the slight appearance of a rat. Pauly turned back to his paper and the next time he looked over to the corner the boy was gone.

The same thing happened over the next four days and even though Pauly was not afraid of very much in his world, except his bosses, he became more and more uncertain about the boy's intentions; was he a spy for another gang, passing information back to them, readying for a hit; was he keeping an eye on him for his bosses? Where else had the boy been following him without his noticing; who the hell was he?

The following day, Pauly didn't stand on his corner; an alley further down the street provided good cover and an excellent point from which to view his little observer. He was there early and waited. Sure enough, he saw the boy come creeping down the street to his normal vantage point and then stand still, obviously searching for his target. Pauly was quickly across the street, grabbed the boys' collar and roughly pulled him into a shop doorway. The lad struggled for a moment and then went still.

"OK kid, what's going down? This better be good or you won't know what's hit you. Capisce?"

The kid looked at him steadily, showing no real sign of fear and said,

"I need a job Mr Pauly. I want to be like you. We need the money, me and my Mom. She's all by herself and working three jobs to keep me and my two sisters alive. I just gotta make money to help her, so you got to give me a job. Anything at all. I can do anything you want; run errands for you; listen in on conversations; tell you what's going down. I need it Mister Pauly. My Mom needs it."

Pauly looked down at the beseeching face. He reminded him a little of how he had been at that age; it was the time of the depression back then, and even though he had a dad, times were bleak, and he had gone to bed hungry on many nights. So, he had some sympathy with the kid, but it was a tough world and there were many other kids in the neighbourhood in a similar position, with dads away at war or killed or just gone from a bad relationship.

"Beat it kid, and don't bother me again," he said and turned and walked away.

The memory of their meeting gnawed away at Pauly. He even told his wife about it, but there was nothing he could do, was there? The kid continued to come every day, just to stand and stare at him. Every day Pauly told him to 'beat it', and he did.

A couple of weeks after their first confrontation, Pauly was on his way to one of his 'customers' for the *pizzo,* when he noticed a commotion on the sidewalk up ahead. The grocer, who was to have been his next point of call, was struggling in the doorway of his shop with a scrawny, wriggling bundle of rags, slapping the head that poked from its top, and shouting at it.

"Don't think you can come into my store and take anything you want and get away with it. I've seen you in here before, you little rat, and I aint gonna stand for it. I'm calling the cops you little, sneaky piece of crap."

He hit him again, a good solid contact that sent the kid staggering across the shop's doorstep and into a counter, where he collapsed.

He was about to repeat the dose when he felt a hand grab his arm and pull him around. As he turned, a punch took him on the jaw and he ended up a wheezing heap on the floor with Pauly standing over him, fists clenched, ready to hit him again. The customers in the shop who had been startled by the goings on, suddenly unfroze and dashed for the exit leaving the three of them alone.

"Hey Pauly, why'd ya do that for God's sake? That kid was robbin' me blind. He deserves everything I give him, the thieving little runt."

"Now listen to me good; if I catch you ever doing that again I'll break your legs. Ya got me? Now give me my money."

He then picked the kid up off the floor, none to gently, and put his face next to his; "and kid, if I ever catch you doing that again, to any of my customers, I'll give you such a beatin' that you won't be able to sit down for a week. Capisce?" The boy nodded, this time a fearful look on his face.

Having been given his dues by the very obsequious grocer, Pauly prodded the boy out of his shop and pointed him down the street. "Come with me," was all he said. A couple of minutes later they were seated in the drug store; the kid had a coca cola in front of him.

"So, what's your name kid?" Pauly asked.

"Michael. My Mom calls me that when she's not happy with me, but normally she calls me Mikey," he said in a scratchy voice.

"Mikey who?"

"Mikey Gordano."

"OK Mikey Gordano, just how do you think you could be of use to me?"

And so it was that Mikey Gordano entered the lowest level of the Mafia family at the tender age of 11.

§§§

Ten years later Mikey 'The Rat' Gordano was a 'made man'. His sponsor, Pauly, was his *capo*. Tall, wiry, with sparse whiskers, he truly suited his moniker; and like a rat, he crept around the edges of his family's territory keeping an eye out for members of the other families, making sure they weren't attempting to muscle in on things that weren't any of their business. He fed his information back to Pauly and, depending on the severity of the noted 'offence', orders would come back for a beating, a kneecapping or an execution, which he and his fellow soldiers carried out; orders were orders after all and, as they said, 'nothing personal'.

Mikey was ambitious. He liked the women and the good times that his money could get him; but he never had enough. The pay of a soldier was okay, but it wasn't that great, and by any reasonable reckoning it would take another ten years or so to become a capo, just look at Pauly; he didn't become a *capo* until he was turned 33. That, for him, just wasn't quick enough. For the hundredth time he asked himself the sixty-four thousand dollar question, how could he get his hands on real money, real quick?

He had racked his brains. He could skim a little off each transaction he was involved in. A dollar here, five there; but, on reflection, he knew that wouldn't work; his bosses knew exactly what money he was due to deliver each week and kept a close eye on it. Any shortfall would be quickly noticed and retribution, of a kind he didn't want to think about, would be swift. No, it couldn't be penny-anti stuff; it had to be something big, something that would give him what he needed in one hit. Then he could disappear, leave this life behind him, and live off the proceeds. But **how**? It took him seven months to work it out, but he got there in the end; an idea that was so dangerous it made him sweat when he thought about it. It would need a lot of preparation, a lot of planning and no little luck. But it was, he thought, a risk worth taking.

And he got his bit of luck. One morning he was standing as usual on "Pauly's Corner" as he always thought of it, when he saw Pauly coming towards him. After their usual greeting was over, the hug, the air kisses, the slaps on the back, Pauly said,

"Well kiddo, things are changing for me, and for you; you heard Reggie Montobano is no longer with us?"

"Yes" replied Mikey, "he died of a heart attack. I went to the funeral."

"Yes, you did, didn't you. Well, what was Reggie in charge of? Tell me that."

"Our drug supply of course." He gave Pauly a funny look. Why all these questions about the blooming obvious?

"So, guess who's in charge of that now?" and he looked at Mikey with a big grin on his face. "I am. And if you want to be part of it, you can come with me; new horizons, new adventures, more money and more excitement. It can be dangerous; I don't have to tell you that, but then all our jobs can be dangerous. So, whatd'ya say Mikey? You in, eh, Mikey? You want to play with the big boys?"

Was he in? Was he IN? Too right he was going to be IN, and he was going to walk through the door that had just opened before him, right into that golden future that he had been dreaming of.

§§§

There was a lot to learn, and a lot to overcome. Reggie's old team were still together, and it took some time for them to come to terms with Pauly as the new boss. But Boss he was, and rules were rules and so they gave him the respect that his position demanded. However, the 'Rat' was a different proposition; why had he been added to their crew? They knew of his history with Pauly, which gained him some leeway, but he knew nothing of their line of work; he would have to learn the ropes and until he did, he was just another burden for them to carry, a potential liability if the stuff hit the fan, as occasionally it did. The drug world was a tough one; competition from the other families; competition from the Spics and the Negroes. The Police were also a problem; not all of them of course, not the ones on the payroll; but they weren't all on the take and you had to have your wits about you. And the newspapers and the politicians also put their five cents in from time to time, ramping up the pressure. So, no easy life being in the mob, they would say to each other and then laugh, and slap each other on the back, and take another shot of bourbon. OK, so people were 'lost' every now and again, and until you could rely on all your brothers, 100%, life was going to be tougher. Mikey would have to earn his status in the group, and it was going to be tough going for him; they would see to that. There would be tests, and if he didn't come through those, so what. Nothing really lost. They wouldn't cry over that particular carton of spilt milk. There would always be another keen young man waiting to take his place

Mikey's education began. Easy things to begin with; keeping watch as the trucks rolled into their warehouses with the supplies; checking the routes from the docks in New Jersey to those warehouses, looking for anything suspicious, anything new; it had been known for deliveries to be ambushed from behind makeshift hiding places and his task was to check that no such structures had been erected. He got to know his new territory quite quickly, got to recognise the faces that were normally to be seen and spot those that weren't. These he had to follow and check out. Mostly they were ordinary people just going about their business, but maybe, just maybe, somebody couldn't be cleared, and he would look for them the next day and the day after that, until he could be sure they posed no threat. If that wasn't possible, well, then he had to deal with them to make sure they didn't become one.

He'd been doing this for a few weeks when his first real test came. He was told that one of the soldiers who normally rode shotgun on the lorries had been hurt in a brawl in a bar over some damn broad and been given one hell of a beating; a broken leg and arm rendered him incapable of working. So, Mikey got to take his place, riding in the back of one of the waggons for the very first time. With a pump action shotgun cradled in his arms, lethal from short range, he sat in the back as the driver brought his load from the dockside to the dock gate and talked with the guy on that gate about baseball and the weather as the documentation was checked. Mikey wondered if anyone would want to have a look in the back? What would he do if they did? He'd been told not to fire unless he saw a gun, and to keep out of sight behind one of the big boxes, until they were clear of the port. He listened to the conversation, hardly breathing; the baseball and weather had changed to horses when he heard a new voice.

"Let me just take a look in the back pal. Can't be too careful, can we?"

A moment later the tarpaulin at the rear of his ride was untied and he heard someone easing themselves up into the back. Startled, Mikey shrunk back behind the box and prayed that the intruder wouldn't come any further. He heard a box being opened, and then another, and the guy kept on coming back towards him, stopping, opening, muttering.

And then a face appeared around the final crate, its eyes looking right at him; a face surmounted by a police hat; a hand pointing a gun at him; with a jerk he brought the shotgun up and pulled the trigger. Nothing happened. He pulled again, no response. The policeman's gun rose until it was level with his face and at that point Mikey saw his life, short as it was, flash before his eyes and with a moan, he emptied his bowels; the policeman said "Bang, Bang" loudly, and laughed and walked back to the end of the lorry and got out.

"Try not to get too close to your compadre back there when you eventually get where you're going, it's none to savoury," he said, and he and the driver and the driver's mate all laughed, long and loud. Mikey sat in the waggon burning with shame and rage. He checked his shotgun; it was not loaded; it never had been.

Of course, they were all waiting for him in the warehouse when the rig returned; they had nearly all been in on it. There had been no drugs on that run; it had all been set up. Mikey sat where he was for a long time as his supposed colleagues laughed and cheered and taunted until he knew there was no avoiding what was to come; he had better get it over with he thought. A loud roar greeted him as his face appeared through the gap in the tarpaulins.

Somebody shouted out, "Oh my, fellahs, I do believe Little Ratty's crapped himself." And they all broke into a chant of, "he's crapped himself, he's crapped himself, Little Ratty's crapped himself." And when that lost its appeal, "the rat's all covered in crap, the rat's all covered in crap," and laughter echoed off the walls. Pauly came storming out of his office and looked down on them all from a balcony.

"What the hell's going on out here?" he yelled. "What's in hells name is going on? If someone doesn't tell me now, you'll all be in big trouble. So come on, tell me," he shouted, taking in the scene below him and noticing Mikey for the first time, obviously in some form of distress. The noise subsided, and then Joey Spacagna, one of the senior soldiers spoke.

"Aw Boss, we was just havin' a bit of fun here with Mikey." "With Crappy, don'tcha mean," someone else shouted out, and the laughter started again, quickly coming to a stop when the men saw the look on Pauly's face.

"Get over here Mikey," Pauly said, his face showing both surprise and disgust as he took in the state of him, and the smell of him. "Oh for God's sake go and get yourself cleaned up and then come and see me. Now who in hell is going to tell me what's been going on?" he demanded.

As Mikey moved away, Joey started telling Pauly of the events of the trip; "...and it was only a bit of fun, boss; we wanted to see how he'd react and, give him his due he did pull the trigger." "Twice," someone added, and further short-lived laughter broke out.

"Perhaps he'll have learned to check his gun is loaded the next time he goes out, if nothing else," said Joey, and again there was a ripple of laughter.

"Well, children, there's work to be done so get on with it. Joey, my office now."

And so 'Mikey the Rat Gordano' became 'Crappy Gordano'; something he would never forget or forgive. Something for which Joey would pay a high price, a very high price indeed, he vowed to himself.

§§§

The effects of that day's events gradually subsided and the team got on with its work of bringing in the drugs and distributing them to the packing houses for bagging and onwards distribution. Mikey resumed his duties of lookout and scout. In his own time, back in his bedroom, he began to plan in detail exactly how he would extract himself from all of this and with enough money to last him a lifetime. There were several key things that he needed to sort; aliases; passports for those aliases; bank accounts for those aliases; and an escape route known only to him; oh, and the source of his new wealth.

He knew broadly how he was going to get his hands on that, but there was still a stack of detail to sort out. He was certain that one of the other families would be very interested in getting their hands on some of their powder trade. And he was just the boy to help them. Through him, they would get to know who his family's suppliers were, the routes taken, the security regimes and the timetables. They would know the manpower involved, where the storage and packing halls were and who worked them. They would know everything they needed to know to take over, bit by bit. Everything, that is, except who they were getting their information from. Easy peasy, wasn't it? If he was honest with himself, he wasn't too sure about that, but he remembered his humiliation, and his determination to sort out those bastards just grew and grew.

The first part was simple: he selected a few names that he liked by looking through the phonebook of the Manhattan area. He rejected anything too fanciful, or too memorable. He tried them out in his mind over a couple of weeks and at last settled on John Mason, Roger Smith, Kenneth Gordon, Jason Greer and Arthur Thomas. Home alone, he practised speaking in a way that he thought reduced his New York accent; he couldn't do much about his Italian looks, the swarthy skin inherited from the Caesar's, but he didn't want to be obviously from America. There were English actors on some of the TV programmes and he watched and listened, and bit by bit, or phrase by phrase, he thought he began to get the hang of it. His 'whadya's' were replaced by 'what do you'; 'reach out to' became 'ask'; and 'where's it at' by 'where is it.' He rounded his vowels and softened the tone and after a while, he thought that he 'might actually be making a jolly fine job of it, my dear old thing, don't you know'.

The passports were a different problem; he knew he would need help with these; but with help came risk. He had never owned a passport, or even seen one, but he knew they opened all sorts of possibilities for his escape; not being limited to hiding out the rest of his life in the States seemed like a good move. So where to start on this? He couldn't ask anyone in his neighbourhood of course, so he was going to have to go further afield. The question was, how could he get away from the city without arousing suspicion? Not many in the 'family' took holidays so it would have to be something different. A week or so later he saw Pauly and told him that an uncle of his had passed away in a little town south of Washington. With his mom already having passed, he was now the only living relative on his side of the family so felt he needed to go to pay his respects. Pauly readily agreed to Mikey taking a week away.

Mikey didn't go to Washington; instead, he went by Greyhound to Boston. It was a long way from home, and if he went to the right places, asked the right questions then, he thought, he must be able to make a contact there who could help him. Even if there were mob connections there, it was unlikely that anybody would know him or spot him. When he arrived, he focused on the bars down in the Seaport District and on his second night of nursing beers, fell into conversation with a local guy who claimed to be into 'a little piece of this, a little piece of that'. On further pressing, and as the beer flowed, he discovered that Jonnie was tied into one of the local gangs, but not the 'Mob', he was pleased to note.

Gently, almost imperceptibly, he moved the conversation around to the dangers that such affiliation might involve, and the need to lie low from time to time, or even leave the country for a while. Jonnie said, 'if that became necessary, they had a guy who could make it happen'. By all accounts the man was the owner of a reputable bookstore over in Sommerville, near the Universities. Whilst that business gave him a good income, with all the student footfall, he just loved being able to afford the little extras that made his life so much more fulfilling; and it gave him the additional thrill of living on the edge, secretly waving two fingers at the system. Mikey learned further, that he was both good and quick at his job, and eventually, that his first name was Alastair. Talk drifted on into the night, drinks came and went and by the time Mikey left his newfound friend, he was sure that he would have only a vague recollection of his meeting with Herby from Philadelphia who'd been in town on business for his employer, a biscuit manufacturer.

He must be able to find a bookshop owner in Sommerville. How difficult could that be? The phone book came to his rescue again, or more precisely, Yellow Pages. The Boston edition listed fourteen bookshops and five of them were in the broad Sommerville area. Not one of them had an 'A' in their name, so it was going to take a bit of chasing down; but he was used to walking, could read a street map and didn't have anything else to do with his time, did he? He hit paydirt at his third target after only 90 minutes of trying. A bookshop on the corner of Somerville Ave and Park Street, occupying the first two stories of a block built in the 1800's, flanked on one side by a dentist's offices and on the other by a bar. It was called 'The Fountain' and a sign writer had added in smaller case, but also in gold, 'of all knowledge'. Mikey looked carefully at the further information that was provided to the passer-by: 'Est. 1875 Prop A Anstruther'. This had to be his man.

Mikey opened the door and went in. He hadn't been in a book shop before, but it was more or less what he had expected; shelves and shelves of books, new ones on prominent display, older on shelves towards the rear; signs, with arrows, pointing you in various directions, left for the sciences; right for American Literature and American Poets; up for language studies; down, the basement was also in use, for foreign novels. To his left was a long counter, again stacked with books, bearing a cash register and behind it, engaged in a transaction with a young guy, obviously a student, stood a small man, neatly dressed in a tweed brown suit. When the exchange with the student concluded, Mikey made his way over to the counter. "Mr Anstruther? Mr Alastair Anstruther?"

The man looked up sharply from the entry he had been making in his sales ledger.

"And just who would like to know?" he replied, his quick gaze taking in what was before him, obviously leading him to some sort of evaluation.

Mikey had been thinking about this conversation as he had walked the Boston streets. What could he possibly say that would persuade 'Alastair' to hear him out. He was bound to be suspicious, bound to be very wary of any sudden approach coming out of the blue, from someone he didn't know. But he had no time to develop a relationship and so he had concluded that honesty, or something close to it would probably be the best approach.

"My name is Herby. I was talking to a mutual acquaintance the other night and I think you can do something for me for which I'll be willing to pay, as long as the price is reasonable. Is there some place quiet we can talk?"

Another piercing stare and then, "come through to my office. I'll give you five minutes."

Beckoning to an assistant to take his place, he turned and walked off to a room at the back of the store, indicating that 'Herby' should follow him. Once inside he went behind his desk and sat down.

"Sit." He commanded, pointing to a chair immediately opposite.

As he said this, he withdrew a gun from his desk drawer and discretely pointed it at Mikey.

"OK Herby, or whatever your real name is, get to the point, and if you don't pass go,", he paused for a moment to add emphasis, "well, you were trying to rob me, weren't you?"

Mikey told him the tale that he had worked up: he was being pursued by some guys from 'Frisco; a bit of a robbery gone wrong; a body or two where they shouldn't have been; he needed to disappear; needed some new identities; met a guy in a bar; bookshop; a name, Alastair; here I am.

"How do I know you're not a cop? Turn out your pockets. Undo your shirt."

All of which Mikey did. "See, no wire, no gun, no shield. I am what I said, and I really do need to get away, to disappear for good, to be untraceable. So, are you the man I'm looking for? Will you help me? The guy I spoke to said you were very, very good. Oh, and don't worry, he won't remember me. He was quite drunk when I met him and very drunk when I left."

The gentle flattery seemed to ease Anstruther somewhat and he lowered his gun.

"Well, I haven't the time to talk with you now, but depending on what you want, I might be able to help."

"So let me give you a quick idea then," Herby said. "I'm looking for at least three American passports and two British ones and driver's licenses, in the same names, depending on how much they cost of course."

Anstruther looked impressed. He said,

"The passports are $150 each and the licenses are $10, so that would be $800."

Mikey was shocked; he had never dreamed they would cost so much. He didn't have that kind of money. Well, not yet anyway. He had brought $200 with him, all the money he could lay his hands on. Knowing it would not help him if he showed his surprise he said,

"Well Mr Anstruther. He said you were good, but nobody's that good. I think $380 is enough for the lot."

They haggled, and eventually settled on $450 with $200 upfront for three sets of documents; goodbye to Kenny Gordon and Arthur Smith. It was a good job he already had his bus ticket for his journey home he thought. They agreed to meet at the bookshop later that night to arrange things, take pictures and the like, and so they did, Mikey handing over the money. The documents would be ready in three weeks, and he would collect them in person.

On the long trip home, through Providence and New Haven and other little towns that the gleaming bus rattled through, Mikey reflected on his time in Boston: he had accomplished everything he'd set out to do. OK, five identities had been a little ambitious and he still had to find another two hundred and fifty bucks, but he wasn't going to need them for a while yet and he had plans to get his hands on the money. And it was to that that he now turned his attention.

§§§

A week after his return, Mikey accompanied Pauly to a meeting; there had been one or two occasions recently when one family's drug sellers had strayed into another's territory. The 'Commission' was meeting in a New York hotel to ensure that these minor incursions ceased, or at best, stayed at that level. Inside the conference room were assembled the Dons, their consiglieres and their capos; outside, a handful of each family's soldiers milled about, keeping a respectful distance, and a wary eye on each other.

The meeting lasted for three hours. Occasionally the soldiers heard muffled, raised voices but when the meeting ended and the doors opened, the faces of those leaving looked relaxed and content. Mikey looked to Pauly,

"Sorted" was all he said.

"There's something I've got to do Pauly. Alright with you boss? I'll be back in an hour. OK?"

Having received the nod from Pauly, he set off down the carpeted stairway, across the lobby and out onto 5th Avenue, hoping he wasn't too late for what he had planned. As luck would have it, a few of the Gambino family soldiers were ambling down the street, loud, playful, arrogant, forcing pedestrians to move aside as they passed by. Eventually one of them peeled off from the group and turned up 19th Street. Mikey noted the house he went into and ten minutes later, as he walked briskly down the street, he noted the number of the tenement. He entered its lobby and looked over the names on the mailboxes and saw one he recognised. That was enough for him, and he beat a hasty retreat, his heart pounding. Two days later that Gambino soldier received a letter in the mail, addressed to his Don, for 'his eyes only, immediate'.

When it finally reached the Don's office, he and his Consigliere read the note, laboriously cobbled together from words cut out of newspapers, comics and magazines and pasted onto a plain sheet of paper. It said that subject to appropriate terms being agreed, the writer of the note was prepared to provide to them, all the information necessary for their complete takeover of a family's drug business. If they were interested, they should put a personal ad in the New York Times under the heading 'Box $100000'. They were told to just say 'yes or no' and if 'yes' to watch the personal columns for further information.

While he waited for a response. Mikey contacted Alastair. He rang the bookstore from a payphone and when he was through to the owner he said,

"Herby here. I'm going to need some bank accounts to go with those passports and I'm figuring that you might just know someone who could set that up for me. Am I right?"

"For a price, yes," came the reply. "Phone me tomorrow and I'll let you know."

"OK," said Mikey. "But I want one that I can have money deposited in directly and it needs to be done so it can't be traced back to me, or you; and then I want that money to go straight from that account into the other new accounts that go with the new passports. You got that? And you can take your fees for the passports and the bank accounts and stuff out of it until you're paid off. You OK with that?"

There was a loud sigh at the other end of the line and Alastair said,

"Herby. I know what I'm doing. Leave it with me. Call me tomorrow." The line went dead.

When he called the next day, he was told that it was all being set up. The cost was $50 per account.   He took the details of the receiving account he'd asked for and ended the conversation.

§§§

Mikey watched the papers every day for some kind of response to his letter. It was not until five days later that he saw what he was looking for; there, under "Box$100000" was the word "Yes". He was on. Immediately he wrote another entry for the box; 'Contact Telephone number?'.

And in this fashion, Mikey was able to set up a line of communication, always speaking through a scarf and in his new English voice, explaining his needs and how things would go down; he would let them know when shipments were coming into the country; they would pay the agreed fee to the account number he gave them; when that had been received he would tell them the name of the ship, the port of entry and the route the vehicle would take; then it was up to them. His fee for the initial consignment would be $500, an act of good faith; thereafter it would be $30,000 per consignment. After much haggling he agreed to an initial fee of $250 and then $25,000 for each further load. He had banked on having to do only four further deals to get to his $100,000; now it would have to be more, which made him uneasy. Every time he made contact, he upped his risk of exposure, and he knew he couldn't go on forever. But it was what it was, and he would have to cope with that, wouldn't he?

The first consignment was taken two weeks later, the money having been paid into his account. The second was also successfully hi-jacked and his account balances began to grow; he now had just over $25,000. Of course, it didn't go unnoticed that something was wrong. His Family had lost a lot of profit, and face, in a short period of time, not to mention two soldiers; they had a mole somewhere, that was obvious, and they needed to trap it and kill it fast.

Mikey was aware there was a new level of security in operation; information only got passed on at the last minute to those who were going on a run, so there was no time for a leak. He passed this news on to his contact and said he would find a way round it; and since the risk level had just gone up, so would his fee, to $40,000. Everybody would just have to be patient. For the next eight weeks nothing happened and in the way of such things, people began to relax, tongues became a little looser and Mikey picked up the necessary details for the new delivery and passed them on. This time, he was assigned to guard duties on the consignment, something he hadn't banked on, but bodies had been lost and orders were orders.

Everyone was on edge as the truck rolled out of the dock in New Jersey. Joey Spacagna drove, and Mikey sat up front with him. There were two further guards in the back, with the consignment of tinned tomatoes or whatever the heroin was hidden in. There was also a car following with a driver and three armed men. Their route was to take them over the Goethals Bridge, up the New Jersey Turnpike, through the Holland Tunnel and eventually into Brooklyn where their load would be taken into a grocery store on Bond Street. It was here that the processing, cutting and packing, would be undertaken, turning blocks of heroin into the product that would sell for millions of dollars on the street.

They'd been on the Turnpike for about ten minutes when a police car pulled alongside and waved them to take the next exit. It pulled in front of them, put on its lights and started to take the exit. Joey followed, and as he did so he saw that a further police car had dropped in behind them. Of their escort car there was no sign.

"Better get ready for action guys," Joey shouted to the men in the back, "I don't think these cops are cops at all. These are the guys who've been robbing us over the last few weeks."

They were brought to a halt under the turnpike in a deserted, desolate area, the type of place where the homeless came to live in their squalid, rotting tents and boxes. Joey brought up his shotgun.

"You checked yours is loaded Crappy?" Joey asked, turning to look at Mikey. "You're going to need to bring it all this time."

Those were the last words he ever uttered, a bullet entered his forehead through the windshield; Mikey ducked for cover as another bullet flew over his shoulder; then he opened his door and slid out to the ground firing the shotgun in the general direction of the police car. More bullets flew and one hit him in the arm, knocking the gun loose from his grip. He started running towards the place where he thought their support car was, only to be hit in the leg. He fell and lay still.

Back at the wagon, after a short exchange of gunfire, the remaining guards had been silenced. One of the cops pulled Joey out of the cab drove off back up onto the turnpike; too late to be of any help their guard car came down the ramp, only to be raked by a volley of gunfire, the wounded driver losing control, causing it to crash into one of the large cement supports upon which the Turnpike stood. All done and dusted in under two minutes, the two police cars departed the scene leaving four dead and four wounded soldiers behind them.

Mikey's recovery process meant that he did not have to ride shotgun again for a few weeks. The Family's doctor attended to him and, having announced that he was a lucky boy, with no major arteries or bones damaged, extracted a bullet, did some sewing and left.

With time on his hands, Mikey was able to think things through; he had made nearly $65,000 in three months; it was a fortune, but was it enough? OK, one more load would take him over his initial target of $100,000, but a man could live comfortably on what he had already put away, even allowing for his costs; and why take the risk of being exposed? Everyone thought he was one of the good guys, he was in good standing in the group, and as an added bonus, Joey, who had planned and executed his earlier humiliation, had met his own execution. No, it was time to start putting his carefully planned disappearance into motion. And just as he had come to this conclusion, had felt the tension flowing out of his body, he overheard a conversation Pauly was having with Joey's replacement about a shipment coming in, in four days' time.

Four days. Just one more time. He could be well on his way before they even carried out the hit; the south of France sounded great he thought. Once more he passed on the information to his contact, checked that the money had been wired to his account, and having cleared it with Pauly, 'bit of recreation time if that's OK with you boss; down to Florida for a week; let the wounds heal properly etc., etc.', he was on his way to Boston. He had agreed to meet with Anstruther in a café away from the bookstore, and because of what he intended to do after their meeting, he took great care to ensure that he wasn't being followed as he made his way there. You never knew who was watching and you certainly didn't want any surprises later on, did you?

It didn't take the two of them long to complete their business; Mikey checked the documents to see that he had got everything he had asked for. They were perfect, right down to entry and exit stamps they contained showing that variously Mr. John Mason of St Paul Minnesota, Mr Jason Greer of Flagstaff Arizona and Mr Roger Smith of Wokingham in Berkshire, England were all much travelled men. He checked the bank account used to receive his monies had been closed and tried to understand just how untraceable the subsequent transfers were. He felt somewhat reassured on that point, but Anstruther did say nothing was totally untraceable if you put enough time and energy into it. When questioned about the person who had set up the accounts and handled all the transactions he would not be drawn.

"The less you know about that the better. Just know that it was set up by someone who is very skilled and not known to the authorities".

Their business concluded, the two men got up, said their goodbyes and turned to leave. Anstruther paused, placed a hand on Mikey's arm and spoke.

"Oh 'Herby', let me just add that if you are having any thoughts about taking steps to tie up loose ends, me included, then think again. I assure you all the documents, photos and negatives that we created have been destroyed. However, my attorney has a detailed record of all my transactions in his strongroom and instructions that should anything untoward happen to me, then he is free to provide any or all of those records to either the good guys or bad guys, as he thinks fit. You understand me?"

He gave him another of his piercing stares.

"Yes, I see that you do. So, we won't have any problems." He paused again, "will we 'Herby'?"

"No, of course not," said Mikey, realising that he was going to have more time available for himself that evening than he had originally planned. One hour later Mr. John Mason was on his way to O'Hare Airport in Chicago for that Pan-Am flight to Orly, Paris, France.

§§§

Mikey spent a very pleasant three months in Nice. It was so different to anything he had experienced before; the food, the wine, the scenery, the women; the pace of life. Gone was the daily round of the docks, the time wasted in the warehouse doing nothing, trying to ignore it when the others called him 'Crappy'. That was all behind him now. He sat, he sipped his wine, he walked the *Promenade Des Anglais* with a pretty friend on his arm, he ventured to the casinos in Monaco and loved every moment of it.

He would not have been so content if he had known of some of the events back home. There had been no drug shipment on the day that Mikey had heard Pauly mention; it had been a test. Pauly had had various conversations in the hearing of various soldiers to see what happened. Only one truck had been stopped; no shootouts, there was only one old guy driving, and he had stopped immediately on being flagged down and put his hands in the air; no drugs in the back; no guards; no nothing.

Mikey had lived up to his nickname, a rat by name, a rat by nature. It saddened Pauly to think the young boy he had nurtured, the boy he had looked upon as an extra son, could have done this. His dismay turned to anger. Then to fear; would his bosses hold him responsible; would he hear the time-honoured words 'nothing personal Pauly, just business' before the bullet crashed through his brain? He had put a tail on Mikey but that had been lost somewhere in Boston; nothing after that, but they would continue to put the word out to their contacts up there to see if there was anything to be picked up from the gossip and tittle-tattle. There was always talk.

The Gambino family were likewise not best pleased; they were down $40,000 with nothing to show for it; and they had lost a good source of supply. They had little to go on apart from the account details where they had wired the money, and so they started their search from that point. They vowed to themselves they wouldn't rest until they had caught and killed their thief.

Mikey moved on to Johannesburg where he bought a small home in a decent neighbourhood and lived a quiet life for a while. He learned about cricket, a strange game, completely new to him but interesting in its own way. After a year of his leisurely new life, he found himself becoming ever so slightly bored. Selling his house, he moved from the high city to Cape Town. He liked its bustle and vibrant way of life and took up sailing a small dinghy around its harbour waters, a pastime he grew to love. Out one day, using an exhilarating breeze to fly over the blue waves he sailed near an incoming vessel. It seemed familiar to him and as he looked up at it, dwarfing his own craft he felt a shudder as his mind went back to New Jersey and those drug runs. Long, long after the vessel, with its Panamanian flag, all squares and stars, had passed him by, his thoughts continued to linger on his past. The urge to move on again grew strong within him. This time it was to Rio De Janeiro that he went.

Extract Of An Article in The Boston Globe of 15th May 1961

Bookstore Owner Found Murdered in Sommerville

By our Chief Crime Correspondent Nigel Blessed

Police were today saying they were shocked and mystified by the brutal death of Alastair Anstruther a well-known and respected local bookstore owner. Mr Anstruther's father, Bertram Anstruther, had founded the store, known as 'The Fountain' in 1875 and Alastair succeeded him in 1932.

Police were called to the store yesterday morning when Mr. Anstruther's two employees could get no response from him when they turned up for work. 'He's always there to let us in' said Mr Colin Jangle, who has worked in the store for the last three years.

At a press conference yesterday, Chief William Butler told the assembled press there was evidence of a robbery having taken place. Whilst he would not confirm the exact cause of death, my further enquiries have discovered that Mr. Anstruther's body showed signs of having been tortured before he was shot in the back of the head.

Chief Butler asked anyone with any information to contact the police as soon as possible.

Rio proved to be chaotic but good fun. He rented a property close to the beach and resumed his quiet life. His money was lasting well. Indeed, he had made money on his house sales, and he still had over $70,000 in his various accounts. He was a happy man once more. Knowing there would come a time when his funds might come under pressure, he had arranged to meet with the manager of his local bank to discuss investments that might make him money whilst not being high risk. At the appointed hour he walked into the bank and asked to see Senhor Borba; he had an appointment.

He was taken through to the manager's office, where he was offered and accepted coffee. Senhor Borba appeared to be troubled by something, his attention drifting from time to time as they both reviewed the proposed investments, so much so that Mikey halted in mid conversation and addressed the matter directly.

"Senhor, What's the problem? You seem distracted. Is everything okay?"

The bank manager looked at him for a moment and then appeared to have come to a conclusion.

"Senhor, I don't know if this is, how you say, something or nothing. I do not wish to alarm you, but I think you should be aware that we had a gentleman in the bank yesterday asking if we held an account for a Mr. John Mason. He said that he was an old friend of yours and was in Rio and was trying to make contact. He didn't know how to do it but thought asking at banks might be the way. Naturally Senhor Mason we told him nothing. We never pass on any information. I just thought you should know. Oh, and he said that should we see you at any time to let you know that 'Pauly sends his regards'."

Mikey's heart skipped a beat. They knew he was here. Somehow, they knew he was here; they might even be watching the bank now. He had changed his appearance from the old days, no more whiskers, shaved head and some dental work to deal with his 'rodent' fangs, but he didn't know if it would fool a close observer. He looked at Senhor Borba. "I need you to do some things for me Senhor if you will." He went on to discuss arrangements to close his account in Rio, have the money transferred to one of his other accounts and generally remove any traces of his existence. He was assured this would happen immediately. The two men shook hands and Borba showed him out of the bank through a back doorway.

§§§

What now? He had always had escape plans in place for situations just like this, but it felt scary having to actually put one into operation. He returned to his apartment, packed his belongings into one case and headed to the busy central bus station. It would be a long trip to Buenos Aires, over 40 hours; he bought a coche-cama seat to give himself a more comfortable journey and settled back to enjoy it as much as he could, even managing to be astounded by the sight of the falls at Puerto Igauzu. But the thought of Pauly close behind him allowed him little rest.

Through Buenos Aires to Montevideo. It was time to lie low, go deep into the background. He had money, but whilst money could buy you privacy it could also provide a trail that determined hunters could follow. That they were determined was obvious; it was nearly six years since he had left America and yet they were so close to him. He had to disappear for a time, go somewhere where he didn't have to spend, where he didn't have to rub shoulders with all sorts of who-knows-what. He would have to get a job that gave him enough ready money to get by, a job that reduced the number of contacts; the conclusion he came to was a ship.

His time in the New Jersey docks had made him familiar with the ways of ships and shipping lines. Ships had agents who found them cargos and crews, so it was to one of these that he made his way. The offices of Reprimar SA were shadowy, fans blowing humid air and cigarette smoke, full of chatter, phones ringing, papers and files covering desks; it quite reminded him of back home in the Brooklyn office. He approached a desk where a balding guy in an open-neck shirt and braces was checking things off a list on a paper before him.

"Señor, ¿Usted habla inglés?"

A pair of tired brown eyes looked up at him slowly. "Si".

"Great. Sir, I'm looking for a job. What can you do for me?"

"We have nothing in the office at the moment," the man said and looked down to his paperwork again.

"No. No, sorry. Not in the office," Mikey said. "I'm looking for something on a ship."

The man looked up at Mikey, surprised at this turn of events. He had obviously taken in his appearance, the soft hands, the good quality clothes; not what you would expect of a time hardened sailor boy. "A ship? What experience do you have Señor?"

"Not a lot, but I'm a good learner. Something in the galley, or a cleaner, or something similar. Do you have anything like that?" His hand went to his pocket and some banknotes appeared in it. The man's eyes took it all in.

Taking his time, the man looked Mikey up and down, pursed his lips and then reached for a file on his cluttered desk. He opened it and read for a moment or two.

"We have a ship in port looking for a steward; just carries cargo these days. But I'm not sure if you'd be up to it Señor, if you get my meaning?"

Mikey did. His hand returned to his pocket and came back up with a bigger handful of bills. The man smiled.

"Although on second thoughts you might be. Only a small crew to look after you understand."

Mikey's hand made a further trip to his pocket.

"In fact, I'm sure you would be excellent for it," he said, looking up and smiling.

The next few minutes were spent sorting out the paperwork that would introduce Mikey to the captain of his new ship. The man explained to Mikey that he would need a Seaman's Identity card and how to get it. With money having been exchanged and documents in his pocket, he set of for the Panamanian Embassy to get his identity card.

Mikey had a long wait at the embassy. He watched the comings and goings of a wide variety of individuals, passing through its doors, tension rising within him each time they swung open, half expecting Pauly to appear, a smile on his face, a gun in hand. But it didn't happen. Eventually he was shown into a small office, had a stilted conversation with an official, and emerged a few minutes later, less some more bills but bearing the precious card which proclaimed him to be Jan Smith from South Africa. Three hours later, Jan Smith walked up the gangway of his new home and went to look for the captain of the *Western Queen*.

The only stable emotion is hate

Adolf Hitler 1926

I have often wondered if men are born bad or made bad by the things they experience in their lives. Is there a 'bad gene' which once identified could be removed to make people nice? Or, was Vlad the Impaler a lovely little boy whose mother didn't allow him to start a butterfly collection when he was little? I tend to go for the 'experiences' theory, but I'm sure you will have your own view.

The Engineer's Tale

Four middle-aged men were seated around a table in a small private room in a Gasthaus on Meinekestrasse, just off Kurfurstendamm. It was the 30th of April 1960. They had enjoyed a good evening, reminiscing about the old days, as their starter, their main course and their pudding had come and gone, accompanied at various stages by steins of beer and glasses of wine. The fug of cigarette smoke, which had hung heavy all evening, was now fighting a losing battle with a new contender as the diners sat back and lit up large cigars, puffing contentedly. Their waiter came in with a tray holding four small, tulip-shaped glass flutes and a bottle of schnapps, which he placed in the middle of the table.

"Just ring the bell should you wish for anything else Gentlemen," he said as he withdrew, closing the door gently behind him.

One of their number, called Lorentz, took the bottle, and poured four good measures which were passed round the table. As one, they all rose, glasses held high.

"Gentlemen, to our beloved Fuhrer. May he be resting in peace today and for all eternity," said Lorentz.

"Our beloved Fuhrer, God rest his soul," they all said as they clinked their glasses together and drank them empty in one swallow.

"Can you believe it is fifteen years since he died?" Lorentz asked as they settled back into their chairs.

"It still feels like only yesterday to me," said Peter, who sat to his left. "Such a shame. Such a waste. It should never have come to that. We should have done better somehow."

More schnapps was poured and drunk, and then another.

"I blame the British," said Hans. They all laughed together.

"No, no, no," said Hans. "No, they won, we lost; I know that. No, what I mean is that I blame them for not joining us to fight the damn communists like our Fuhrer wanted back in the day. If they'd joined forces with us, we'd be ruling the whole of Europe by now and possibly a bit more besides. No, they were almost with us and then they were gone. Our Fuhrer said, 'the English nation will have to be considered the most valuable ally in the world' didn't he?"

"Well, you can blame Von Ribbentrop for mucking that up," said Gunther. "He upset them all when he was Ambassador, didn't he. Stuck up, pompous fool apparently; got right up everybody's noses. Being allies was not going to happen after that show of his. In fact, you might argue that he lost us the war before we'd even started, looking back on it."

"I met him once," said Lorenz.

They all looked at him.

"Yes, he came to talk to us at Junkerschule one day. And you're right, he was a pompous ass."

"Oh, here we go," said Hans; "'When I was at Junkerschule this, and when I was at Junkerschule that; we all know you went there, we all know you met the Fuhrer there……….."

It was like this every time they met; something they had been doing for the last ten years on the anniversary of their lost leader's death. As the schnapps flowed their conversation became more boisterous, tinged with the tiniest little bit of aggression. They had known each other for years, ever since they had joined the Hitler Youth aged fourteen. From different backgrounds, their parents all shared the same vision of a strong Germany and saw Adolf Hitler as the man to deliver it.

The boys had loved it; what real boy wouldn't? Being trained to fight; the opportunity to fire guns; loads of sports to play; little formal classroom lessons; they thought of themselves as young soldiers, not schoolkids. The chance to go to Nuremburg, to the Nazi Party rally where, as they got older, they were encouraged to 'mingle' with the young ladies of the BDM, was something they remembered as being especially pleasurable. Day after day they received confirmation of their superiority, over the religious twits and the sub-human Slavs and Jews; day after day they were told that they were Herr Hitler's chosen ones who would make Germany great again. And they believed it and longed for the day when they could help him turn that vision into a reality.

§§§

Sitting alone in his apartment later that night, another glass of schnapps in his hand, Lorenz thought back over his life. He had stood out as a strong, capable, and intelligent member of his intake. He had learned quickly and easily, and he had loved what the organisation stood for and his place in it. By the time he was eighteen he had been selected to attend the recently established SS-Junkerschule as a potential SS Officer in the making. For nineteen months he underwent an intense period of training in matters military and matters ideological; military logistics, map reading, weapons handling and physical training were intermingled with sessions on the National Socialist world view and attitude; racial superiority, ruthlessness, toughness; the strength that could be gained from being in the company of similar, like-minded comrades. When he was 21, Lorenz went to his first posting with the *1st SS Panzer Division Liebstandarte SS Adolf Hitler*, the LSSAH, thinking that with people like these at his command, there was not a chance in hell of anyone being able to resist the Fuhrer and the German people in achieving their goals.

He had seen his first real action when his Division took part in the invasion of Poland. All over in little more than a month, he had tasted power and victory and they were both sweet. Sure, he had killed people, soldiers and civilians alike, but these '*Untermensch*' had deserved it. He remembered the terrified looks on the faces of the civilians in Zloczew as they realised what was about to happen. He had thought "this is what my training was preparing me for" as he pulled the trigger and watched their bodies fall to the ground.

From Poland he took part in the capture of Rotterdam; next stop, Dunkirk and the battle with the BEF; his unit, he remembered, had captured soldiers from the Royal Warwickshire Regiment and some French troops; they executed them in a barn.

There was other action, in Greece, a pleasant time, and then his mood darkened as he recalled his service in Russia. The Eastern Front; *Operation Barbarossa*. All had gone well until they attempted to capture KharKov, trying to relieve the 6th Army, which had come under supreme pressure. He saw again the fierce fighting, the sniper fire that was so accurate and so persistent; he felt again, the force of the bullet as it took him in his shoulder and ended his Russian campaign.

He reflected on that for a moment, no bad thing actually. It had led to a period of pleasant recuperation in a small town in Southern France and then in 1943 to a posting as SS Sturmbannfuhrer in the SS Panzer Division. For a time, he had been responsible only for the maintenance and repair of their tanks, a role he had undertaken at other times in his military career owing to his speciality training at the Junkerschule at Bad Tolz; but he found it excessively tedious and longed to be back in a fighting role, which he made known to anyone who would listen.

His face broke into a broad smile, as he recalled that bright, sunny morning when he was summoned to the presence of his commanding officer. After the formalities were over the Standartenfuhrer had said to him,

"Sturmbahnfuhrer Webber, I know you have been telling everyone and anyone who will listen you want a bit more action. Well, I've got something that I think will appeal to you." Lorenz looked slightly sheepish.

"No, don't worry. It is heartening to see your ambition. We have received intelligence that there are three members of the resistance hiding out in Mercy-sur-Cleve. I would like you to take a detachment of men up there and find them. After you have extracted what information you can from them, they do not have to be brought back here, understood? And perhaps the villagers need to be taught a little lesson too. They cannot conceal enemies of ours with impunity."

"Yes, Herr Standartenfuhrer. I will attend to it immediately."

Mercy-sur-Cleve was a very pretty village, typical of villages in Provence; on a hilltop, a church with a spire in a square, surrounded by fields, some carrying the purple hue of lavender; and only four country lanes leading in and out. Easy to close off; easy to contain.

He stirred as he remembered the details, he could almost feel he was back there. He took a sip of his schnapps. He had sent three or four soldiers to each of the roads on the edge of the village, sufficient to isolate it from the world outside, and had then sent others to gather a harvest of farmworkers from the fields and place them in the town's square, under guard. Gradually the village people woke up to the fact that they were being gripped tightly in a German fist; a couple of them attempted to escape but were caught and brought back to their neighbours, in a far worse state than when they had arisen to that beautiful early summer morning. Lorenz had sent soldiers to all the houses of the village and over the next thirty minutes or so they returned with their prizes; women and children were kept on one side of the square, the men and youths on the other.

Having been told that all the houses and barns had been visited, and that all the villagers were now present in the square, Lorenz stood on the steps of the church and asked the Marie to come forward. After a slight pause, a tall man in his fifties, dressed in working clothes, stepped out of the crowd and stared at Lorenz.

"And you are?" Lorenz asked, looking over the man's his head at the assembled crowd.

"Pierre Maison."

"Pierre Maison WHAT?" Lorenz shouted at him.

"Pierre Maison, Sir." The words stumbled out of the man's mouth.

"Right Pierre. We are here for the three resistance members that you have hidden so carefully amongst yourselves; I wish you to point them out to me, now, at once."

"But Sir, we have no resistance people in this town. You have been misinformed sir. We have no such people here. We are all law-abiding citizens, sir, going about our simple lives as we have always done." He hesitated, and then added, "Sir."

The Marie gave Lorenz a beseeching look, hands grasped together.

"Please Sir, we know nothing of the Resistance."

Removing his pistol from its holster, Lorenz pointed to a youth over on the left side of the square.

"Come here boy," he commanded.

The youth moved towards him slowly, his mother calling out to him from the other side. She had to be restrained by her neighbours. The boy turned to look at her, and when he turned back Lorenz shot him between the eyes; he fell in a heap at the side of the Marie, blood beginning to spread out on the yellow sandstone.

Above the cries of shock and horror and wailing of the women and children he said,

"Right M. Le Marie, perhaps that has helped you to remember a little more clearly. Where are they?" He gave the mayor a long, hard cold stare.

"Sir, we do not know," he howled at Lorenz.

He could still see the man's face now, with its look of desperation, deeply lined, tanned by working in the fields under the sun, a grey wispy beard and crooked, yellow-stained teeth. He particularly remembered the teeth; the man was obviously a smoker he had thought.

"No matter, someone will tell me," he said as his pistol fired once more and the mayor joined the boy at his feet.

"Bring me that young woman," he commanded. The same question, no response and the same outcome. And thus it continued for the next ten minutes. Even with twenty of their friends and neighbours lying dead in the square, no one talked. Not even a sign that anyone would. Lorenz was beginning to doubt that their information had been accurate, but he couldn't stop now. If they were here, or even if they weren't, he would sort out this village; he wasn't going to give up, to fail on his first active mission for his commanding officer. He would carry out his orders to the letter; 'nobody has to be brought back'.

"Take the women and children into the Church and line the men up against the church wall."

His troops did as commanded.

When his orders had been carried out, he said, "Oberleutnant, shoot the men if you please."

One by one, the Oberleutnant and his men carried out a series of executions until all 147 men and youths of the village lay dead at the side of the church.

"Now, if you please Herr Oberleutnant, attend to the women and children. I suggest that you lock the church doors and toss in a couple of grenades. That should deal with it."

His junior officer looked startled at the suggestion, but his training overcame any sense of unease at the barbarity of his superior's order, and he went off to do as instructed.

Lorenz sat in his chair in his now cold room, the fire dead, hearing the grenades exploding, the barking of the dogs, the screams of the surviving women and children as the fire took hold; remembering how long it had taken for the crackling of the fire in the church's roof beams and pews to drown them out. He had sat at a table in the square drinking the coffee that one of his men had made for him as another 255 souls sped their way heavenwards.

Back in his room, some sixteen years later, he poured himself another schnapps, raised his glass in the air and said, "and if I had to, I would do it all again. Heil Hitler."

§§§

Two years had passed since his visit to that hilltop town and Lorenz had seen the writing on the wall. He had managed to escape unscathed from the battle at Heilbronn where for nine days his unit had fought long and hard against the Americans, making it so difficult for them to get over the Neckar River. They had made it across once but had been pushed back; and when they had finally got across for good and had wanted to wipe out his Panzer Division in an understandable fit of revenge, they were unable to do so because they had disappeared. When they eventually did make contact with the German column, they found only abandoned vehicles, their occupants gone, dispersed into the countryside beyond. It was the 14th of April 1945.

Lorenz spent the next month making his way to Berlin by foot. He had abandoned his weapons, his papers and his uniform as soon as he could; in an isolated, abandoned house in the little hamlet of Hafenhuas he found some smelly, ragged clothing that just about fitted him; he looked like a down at heel farmworker which suited his purpose just fine. Sleeping by day and travelling by night he managed an average of about ten miles per day. Stealing bits of food here and there, he made his way North East; he faced several steep, exhausting climbs along the way, doubly difficult to do when lit only by the stars or moon. Undetected, he made his way around Würzburg, past Leipzig and eventually ended up in Magdeburg.

He had been stopped at various points by American soldiers as he had come closer to the city, but he explained his appearance and lack of any papers by claiming that they had been lost during the bombing of the city. He was painfully thin by this time; thirty-five days on the road, little food, unwashed; he presented a pretty painful sight, and he was waved on with advice as to where he might get some food and clean clothes.

He took advantage of these offers and a further three weeks passed before he ended up in the west of Berlin, in the sector that would ultimately become British. Again, he was questioned at various points; he explained that he had lived in Magdeburg; that he had been bombed out of his apartment; that he had wandered for days like so many of his displaced countrymen. And the British had bought it. He was directed to a hostel where he could stay and receive a basic diet in exchange for working on the rebuilding of the roads and bridges. He readily accepted and for the next four years he was to be seen working all over the British sector.

§§§

As time passed and the British attitude towards their German charges eased, Lorenz – now calling himself Paul Schmidt – developed a circle of contacts. Through discreet and careful questioning, he identified two or three that he felt he could trust. One of these, Max Fischer, ran a small garage over in Kurfurstendamm. Paul had met him when he'd come one day to recover a broken-down lorry that his gang had been using to carry building materials. Contact made, many evenings spent drinking black-market schnapps together, and Paul became a vehicle mechanic at Autowerkstatt Fischer. Old Comrade groups were hidden away in the shadows, but you could find them if it you knew where to look, and Paul was eventually able to contact a group of his old friends; life settled into a pleasant rhythm. He was a good mechanic, and it was no surprise to anyone that six years after joining up with Max, he was asked to take charge of all garage operations. The firm grew and Paul was able to afford a small, neat and tidy apartment in a pleasant position overlooking Olivaer Platz. Here, he could meet with his friends to drink and reminisce, and he would occasionally entertain some young woman that he had met in a bar.

He was in his office discussing repair costs with a customer one morning, when glancing up into the reception area he saw the face of someone he thought he recognised from years earlier. He couldn't quite place him. Their eyes met briefly, and the man gave him the slightest of nods and sat down to wait. After his customer had left, relieved of a large sum of Deutsch marks, he invited the man in and offered him a seat.

"And what may we do for you Herr…?"

The man cut across him, and without preamble, began to talk

"Well Lorenz, or should I call you Paul now? I see you have got yourself nicely established here; quite a change from your time in France, isn't it? When was that exactly? 1943 I think." He said this without any hint that his statement was a threat. "Yes, I think it was. Well, I'm here because I think you should know there have been several enquiries about your whereabouts. People at the French Embassy have been poking around. They came to our department in Bonn; I met them; they even had a picture of you from somewhere. It seems that someone thinks they saw you here in Berlin recently; they were in a café, you walked by, but by the time they got outside you'd disappeared. Unfortunately, that someone was present on that day in Mercy-sur-Cleve, someone your men didn't find; a Resistance member as it turns out; now a member of the French Government. Well, you can understand how badly they want to find the 'Butcher of Cleve' I think they termed it, even after all this time. Wiesenthal isn't the only one on the lookout for us old boys you know."

Paul's heart skipped a beat, his face drained of colour.

"And you are?" he asked.

"Oh Lorenz. I'm sad that you don't recognise me. I know that I've had a bit of surgery and the passage of sixteen or seventeen years has seen me put on a bit of weight; but not to recognise your old.."

"Commander." Cut in Paul.

"Yes, got it in one. Your old Standartenfuhrer."

Paul looked at him questioningly.

"Oh, I see you're you're wondering how I come to be working for the Government. Quite simple really. I was in the civil service before the war started and I simply applied for a role when they needed people to start putting Germany back together. A few little white lies and a couple of real big black ones on the *Fragebogen*. As if asking you to fill out a questionnaire was going to sort the 'good' Germans from the 'bad' Germans. Quite laughable really, but there's psychiatrists for you, or are they psychologists? Who knows? Anyway, I had to fill it in; as though everyone was ever going to tell the truth, the whole truth and nothing but the truth; they were so desperate to get people who could organise things you see, so they never really checked properly what you said. Anyway, enough of me. It's you we need to concern ourselves with; can't have you falling into French hands, can we? Never know what you might say, do we? Now this is what's going to happen, pay attention." He began to outline the plan for Paul's departure.

Three days later Paul found himself on a ship in Genoa harbour. It had been a hectic time since the visit. He had asked Max for a few days leave; a family matter had arisen that needed his personal attention; see you next week; yes, all's well; no problem.

Max looked at him with a sad smile. "I thought this might happen one day," he said. "I owe you some money I think; take a couple of hundred out of the till. And Paul, good fortune, eh? I shall miss our times together. Now be off with you and take care." The two men embraced; a proper manly hug; a 'goodbye for the last time' sort of hug, and then Paul turned and left with his money.

He had few possessions that he really valued back in his apartment and packing these together with his clothes took little time. That evening, as instructed, he went to Tempelhof airfield and using the ticket provided to him, flew on a British European Airways Viscount aircraft down to Munich-Riem. From there, a shaky old bus carried him to the train station, and he was able to board a train to Bologna; he arrived there at six in the morning. By eleven, he was in Milan; he arrived in Genoa at teatime. He had been travelling for nearly two days and could feel the toll it had taken. He had been given an address for the night, to which he wearily made his way. A women answered his knock, and with the briefest of acknowledgements showed him to a small room with a bed and a jug and bowl on a table.

"Toilet's down the hall," she said, and left him to it.

The next morning, after a brief breakfast of sausage, a roll and coffee, he left and walked to the docks. He'd been told to find the *Eastern Gateway*. After various enquiries, directions and misdirections, he walked up the gangplank of a down-at-heel passenger-carrying ship. He thought the proper term for it was a liner, but its appearance hardly warranted that lofty title in his opinion. Nonetheless it was to be his home, his refuge for the next three weeks or more as it made its way through the Mediterranean via various stops, out into the Atlantic and eventually to its destination, Rio De Janeiro.

§§§

His journey wasn't finished yet. Whilst there was quite a large German community in Rio, those in charge of his disappearance felt Paul shouldn't linger too long in its clutches, it being a well-known hunting ground for those seeking to expose former Nazis. With only one night spent in a downtown hotel he was soon on his way again. The cruise across the Atlantic had been good for him. He was refreshed, relaxed, tanned and raring to go, which was just as well, as he discovered to his horror from the contents of an envelope left in his hotel room, that his guardians had chosen to move him on by bus.

Ten hours after leaving Rio he arrived in Sao Paulo in a dishevelled heap. He had ridden in a bus that seemed to stop every ten minutes to allow people on and off, bulging at the seams with farmers and mothers, old men, old women, shouting children and even dogs. It chugged up hills and seemed to Paul to race down the roads on the other side, at death defying speeds. He could not look out at the sheer drops to potential at the buses side. It was hot, it was cold. Several stops in small villages for toilet breaks and a hasty *Pao De Queijo* or two did little to restore his sense of wellbeing.

And this was just his apprenticeship. He had known hardship in his time in the SS, but that was getting on for what seemed a lifetime ago, and now he had to face a further three days in even more wretched conditions, in an even more decrepit bus as he made his way down to Montevideo. Crossing the border into Uruguay at Chuy, he felt that an overkeen interest was taken in his passport, but nothing seemed to come of it. Even with all the privations of the journey he was still able to take in the beauty of the landscape through which he travelled, and the last part of his route allowed him to watch the Atlantic roll by through his open window; it looked idyllic.

He had been instructed to go to *Bar Facal* at six each evening until contacted. Who his contact would be, he had not been told; and so, he went as directed. His first two nights were uneventful; the bar was full of the usual collection of people you would see in any downtown bar in any port city in the world; businessmen on their way home, working girls, courting couples, old guys drinking coffee together and no doubt reminiscing about better times gone by. But nobody contacted him. On the third evening things changed. He was sitting in a corner, which gave him a great view of the entrance. He had declined several offers of companionship from the girls and sat sipping an espresso. He saw a rather attractive woman enter and watched her with interest as she scanned the room; mid-thirties he thought; nice figure; well-dressed but understated, not showy. She caught his eye and began to walk towards him, pausing a couple of feet away

"I see you are admiring the view Señor," she said in English. "Do you like what you see?" There was a slight smile on her face as she said this.

"I apologise Señorita for my rudeness, but a pretty lady such as yourself cannot be surprised that you draw admiring glances. In my defence I must tell you that I am waiting for someone, and I must admit, that if that someone was to be you, I'd be very happy."

He looked directly into her eyes waiting for her reaction.

"Well Paul, then you better come with me," she said, this time in German. She turned, retraced her steps and Paul got up and followed her out drawing a few looks from the girls; looks that said, 'it wasn't even her turf was it; how dare she?'

She took him on a short walk from the bar, through the narrow streets, to a small flat in a block of grand old apartments, somewhat gone to seed. Once inside, having fetched him a drink, they sat.

"Well Paul. I'm glad to see you made it here in one piece. I didn't know exactly when you'd be arriving, so I left it until tonight to seek you out. Have you been in Montevideo long?"

"Not long," he said, "tonight was my third night."

"Good. My name is Maria; I work with my father on behalf of your benefactors. It is something we have done several times over the last ten years or so and we do know what we are doing. I hope that reassures you." She looked at him and he nodded back.

"What will happen in your case is that I'll take you up to my father's farm where you will wait for the right moment to move on."

He made as if to ask a question, but she motioned him to remain silent whilst she finished what she had to say.

"At this stage we do not know what that will entail, but rest assured, we shall be working on it, and as I say, we have done this before. We need to see how those that seek you are faring; whether they have picked up any trace of your movements over the last few months. We have no wish to bring you all the way here and then rush into doing something that is the source of your eventual undoing. That would be unwise, would it not?"

He nodded again.

"So, we go to your farm and wait. Will you be there too?" he asked in a tone and with a rhythm that made his liking for her quite apparent.

"Well, you'll just have to wait and see won't you," she said and gave him another one of her gentle smiles.

Three days passed before Maria deemed it right to move. He had been left alone in the flat during the days whilst Maria was somewhere in the city. In the evenings they ate and talked.

"Forgive me if I'm being intrusive, but what do you do when you go out and leave me here?" he had asked on their second evening together. "Or is that something I'm not allowed to know?"

"Yes, you can know. We have a small vineyard and winery outside the city, in Canelones; not a big one, but big enough. We also have a wine bar in the city which I help to manage. That is where I go, Mr. Nosey." She laughed at him and then continued, "and I also help to sell our wines into the restaurants and bars, both here and in other towns nearby. It's a competitive business; you must know your stuff and have good products into the bargain. But we do alright."

"Well, if this is an example of your wine, I'd say you must be doing better than alright. It's splendid," Paul said looking at the deep red wine in his glass and taking another sip. "Has this been a family thing for generations? Are you part of a great winemaking dynasty?" he asked playfully.

"My, you do ask a lot of questions," Maria said. "No, Daddy bought it when we moved over here in 1944." She shot him a hard glance, then said, "from Germany."

That really got Paul's attention. "From Germany? In 1944? How was that even possible? There was a war on."

"Yes, there was, but Daddy was rather senior and, well, he thought it was time to leave, and so we did. I was sixteen at the time. Mummy came too, but unfortunately, she passed away three years ago. So, it's just me and Daddy now. But we live well, and whenever it is necessary, we get involved in little projects such as yourself."

"So, I'm a 'project' am I? How do you think it's working out so far?" he asked, laughing.

"You have some potential, I think," she said, then drained her glass and taking him by the hand, led him to her bedroom.

§§§

Driving her jeep out into the country, north of Montevideo, they were soon in a gently rolling landscape. Each hillside seemed to be covered in rows and rows of vines, and here and there people could be seen moving amongst them slowly, bending, snipping, and moving on. A few miles in, Maria swung the noisy little vehicle off the small road onto a lumpy, uneven driveway that eventually ended in front of a collection of buildings; a splendid old farmhouse with a wooden, shaded porch was surrounded on either side by large sheds that Paul assumed to be the winery and storage areas. The sign at the entry had declared this to be *Vinicola Familia Dianne,* and Paul would get to know it and its inhabitants well over the next six months.

The first meeting with 'Daddy' was going to be a rather tense affair, thought Paul. He was nervous. This man, he assumed, had once been very senior in the Fuhrer's regime and as such would require and expect to be treated with great respect and subservience. Paul stood up and came to attention the moment a short, stocky, white-haired man with a neatly trimmed goatee entered the main room of the farmhouse. He was unsure whether a formal salute was necessary, a 'Heil Hitler' perhaps, but chose not to. The man approached him, broke into a broad grin and, very unexpectedly, gave him a big hug.

"Relax young man. Welcome to our humble abode, Paul. How was your trip? You must tell me all about it over dinner tonight. But first let me show you your new home."

Paul was about to move further into the house, but the man caught him by the arm and swung him around and they went outside. They stood on the veranda and looked out across the nearest fields, at the vines hanging with large bunches of grapes that were turning from green to red.

"Splendid isn't it. I loved it when I first saw it all those years ago and I still do; I still work in the fields you know, as will you whilst you are here; and I believe you are a handy mechanic too, so you won't be idle I can assure you."

He patted him on the back once more.

"Sir, I don't know how to thank you for all your help, but if I can repay you through work then so I shall."

"No need for the 'Sir' young man; my name is Lucas." He paused, "well, out here it is; you may call me that. And as to our help, well we owe it to those of the old country who committed themselves to the cause, as I believe you did. My boss did go a little wild towards the end, but don't mistake me, he had a great vision for our country's future, and it was so sad to see that being lost. We're on the way back now though, aren't we? Soon be in charge of them all once again I'll wager. Who would have thought that back in '45, but here we are; you can't keep a good country down. Never forget that young man. A shame that so many had to be lost, but that's the way of war as you know."

Paul happily settled into the work of the estate, out around the vines, repairing machinery, or helping with the general chores to make the prosperous little business run smoothly. His relationship with Maria blossomed. Paul was concerned that her father might disapprove, but there was no hint of that. The harvest came and went, with all the ritual and partying associated with it; Paul learned how the Tannat grapes were processed and transformed into that beautiful, punchy red wine they drank round the barbecue. Paul loved his life at *Familia Dianne*; he wished it could last forever, but that was not to be.

The blow came early one morning. He had heard the phone ringing and had thought nothing of it; they were running a business from here after all, so phone calls were not unusual. But when he saw the look on

Lucas' face as he entered the room, he knew there was a problem; not necessarily for him, but something was obviously up.

"What's wrong Lucas?" he asked. "You're as white as a sheet."

"I'm afraid your time here with us is coming to an end Paul. I've just had a call from Maria; she's in Montevideo and was talking with a contact of hers. It seems your journey to Uruguay has been traced. The French Embassy has been talking with the Uruguayan Government about you. The Uruguayans never were very well disposed towards us; look what they allowed with the *Graf Spee*. Anyway, it seems they have offered to help, and have set up an investigative team. It's a long shot, but they may just find some traces and I cannot afford for them to find you here or discover links between you and my Maria. You do understand that, don't you Paul?"

Paul nodded. "Yes Lucas, of course I do. What's to happen now then? Is there nothing that can be done to keep me here? I love it; I love Maria as I think you know, and she loves me. Can't I hide somewhere till this all blows over?" he pleaded.

"Well yes; that's our intention. But no, that can't be here. We think it would be better if you were out of the way for a short time. No, don't look so worried," he said quickly as he read Paul's face and saw what might be going through his mind. "No, we are arranging for you to take passage on a ship, a working passage that is. There is a ship, cargo mainly, sometimes a few passengers, that goes up and down the coast here and they need an engineer. It's docking in Montevideo tonight and we have arranged for you to be on it. I know it's sudden, and difficult to take in, but we will know where you are, and when things quieten down, then you may return here."

At ten that night, after a last meeting with Maria, Paul walked up the gangplank of an old rust bucket, called the *Western Queen*.

Cut your losses with evil people. For everyone else, the merely flawed, find a way to forgive them

Unknown

Another of life's little mysteries for me: who is most guilty; the one who gives in to temptation or the one who creates it?

The Boatswain's Tale

Barry and Jan were both off duty. The ship was in port in Hong Kong, and they were enjoying a little bit of shore leave. Purely by chance, they both happened to end up in the same, dimly lit bar and once they had caught each other's eye, they made their way over to a table in the corner of the saloon, sat down and started to drink. They knew each other a little of course, but not much more beyond what you might call a nodding acquaintance. The bosun didn't have too much call to see the captain, or his steward, reporting as he did to the First Mate, and so their contact was mainly composed of crossing in the ship's passageways, or in the mess when meals were being served. Their conversation was therefore a bit hesitant at first, on matters that weren't particularly personal; things like the state of the ship, a rotting old heap of junk, was their shared opinion; about Hong Kong and how humid it was; and about their captain; an 'old soak', was Barry's take. Jan surprised himself by feeling the need to offer some sort of defence of Captain Olaf.

"He's not that bad a guy really. I don't know what happened to him in the past but he's a sad old so and so. I think he wants to do the right thing by everyone, but there's something just gets in the way and cuts him down…"

Barry made to speak but Jan carried on over him, "…yes, I know, the bottle you'll say, but really, I think there's something more behind it than that. It's as if he's carrying some deep, awful secret and he's drinking to forget. I really don't know what it is."

"Just like the rest of us, eh?" joked Barry, "secrets, that is," he added, fixing Jan with a meaningful stare.

"Anyway, why should you worry," said Jan. "Your boss Tony sails the ship, doesn't he? And he's very good at his job isn't he," more of a statement than a question.

Barry agreed. "Yes, Tony's good to work for. Doesn't bother me too much as long as I do my job and make sure the others do the same. He's a really nice guy actually, helpful to a fault; I've had to stop people going to him all the time, asking for this and for that and every other blooming thing under the sun. I think that if you asked him for an ostrich, he'd have one on board, all tied up in a big bow by the end of the watch. He makes it hard for himself sometimes, he really does."

"He's from Malta, isn't he," said Jan.

"Yes, Valetta. He can remember the war and what it was like there. Hunger, bombings and the like. That's why he doesn't have a lot of time for Paul, you know. Bad blood there I'm thinking."

They talked on like this for a while and the drinks kept on coming, bourbon on the rocks for Jan, rice wine for Barry.

"Bourbon eh?" said Barry. "I thought I could hear a bit of a Yank in there somewhere, although you've gone to some lengths to cover it up, I'd say." He looked sharply at Jan, who said nothing.

"Anyway, as I was saying, I thought I heard the Yank in you, probably New York, am I right?" again he gave Jan a long hard stare. "I've worked with a lot of your fellow countrymen over the years; some good, some bad. Take as I find."

"Where I'm from is my business if you don't mind," said Jan, a little touchily.

"OK, OK. Keep your hair on. I'm sure we all have our little secrets. I know I do. It's why I'm on this flipping boat to tell the truth; a little something best avoided if you know what I mean." He winked at Jan.

Suddenly interested, Jan said, "OK, spit it out then, Mr Bosun. What are you running from?

"Have to kill you if I tell ya," Barry said and laughed. Then they both laughed together and ordered another round of drinks.

"Well, heck yes, you got me. I was in the Big Apple for a while, working with some guys, doing this and that, but it wasn't my kind of thing, so I left," said Jan, casting a little bit of bait on the water in front of Barry. The wine having relaxed him, Barry rose to the surface like a hungry fish and swallowed. Three hours later, they both staggered back on board the *Western Queen,* arms around each other's shoulders. Jan now knew an awful lot more about his newest best friend Barry Briggs.

§§§

He had known he was British, that was obvious from the way he talked, but he didn't know the accent. He thought all the world knew a New York accent when they heard it, part of his reason for working so hard to erase it, but this accent was a teaser. It wasn't like the ones he had heard on the movies. No, this wasn't one of those posh southern things, so up north then maybe. Barry had put him out of his misery.

"I'm from Newcastle on Tyne up in the North East; Geordie born and bred. Me dad came home on leave after the Battle of the Somme, and nine months later I appeared. Silly fool got himself killed before that, at the Battle of Arras would you believe, so I never knew him. Me mam looked after us but before I was ten, she upped and died, silly woman. I was put in a children's home; terrible place it was; poor food, beatings from the staff for the slightest thing, and the older kids used to bully us something rotten. But I got through it. By the time I left I was this thin, wiry, kid who'd learned to take care of himself in a fight. I was a lot stronger than I looked, still am. Nobody got the better of me after I was fourteen, I can tell you. Well anyway, I was working in the Rope Mill over the river in Gateshead when I saw a recruiting poster for the Royal Marines; I was seventeen so I was old enough and before you could say Jack Robinson I was in, a Royal Marine. Best thing I ever did; made a proper man of me and that's a fact."

He had paused for a moment, taken another mouthful of his drink and Jan had asked, "So what happened then? Did you have to fight in the war?"

"Yes," he had said. "I saw plenty of action in that war, and then it was Korea, and after that, Vietnam."

"Vietnam?" Jan had a look of surprise on his face. "I thought we were the only ones that fought over there, not you Brits."

"Oh. You'd be amazed sonny boy, about who got involved in what, and where," he laughed, "really amazed."

Out of the blue Jan had asked, "did you ever kill anyone, you know, up front and personal. I did." He stopped, astonished by what he'd just revealed.

"Well yes, of course, that was my bleeding job, wasn't it?' Barry had continued, as if he hadn't heard Jan's confession. "Yes, we killed plenty. Took out quite a few of Paul's fellow countrymen as it happens, but we won't tell him that will we? I'd become a commando in '42 when they was first set up, and we was used in places all over; I was in Tunisia, Sicily, D-Day, …" here he had paused and given Jan a knowing look.

"You know Sicily do you Jan? Ever been there? Well, I have. Lovely country but some rum blokes." He gave Jan another old-fashioned look. "Well, 'appen you do, 'appen you don't."

"So where was I? Oh yes, we were also in Normandy and eventually in Germany. And then we were disbanded. I went back to the marines and then along came Korea, and we were all put back together again, unlike Humpty Dumpty."

Jan had had no idea what he was talking about; Humpty who? He let it pass.

"So, there we were, 41 Commando again if you please; I sometimes wondered if the Brass knew what they were doing with all the changes we went through; or maybe they used to spend their Friday afternoons in Whitehall playing 'who can we bugger up next'. You know the sort of thing," here he assumed a very posh English voice and continued, 'OK Archibald, let's toss the dice old boy and see who we send where and when and for how long. What? No support available? Well, they'll just have to fight a bit harder then will they not? Send the order Carruthers'. Anyway, Churchill had said we had to go set Europe ablaze when we were first formed and that was pretty much what we were told to do when we went to Korea. First time I really got to know your lot up close and personal, so to speak. They fitted us out when we got there, and we did a lot of work together. I even won a medal."

Jan's mind had started to wander as Barry had been droning on about the commandos, but his ears had pricked up at the mention of a medal. "You did? What for?" There was a note of awe in his voice.

"Not a lot really," said Barry. "We'd already made a few raids from the sea, blown up some tunnels, you know, general sort of disruption, nothing major. Then a month or so after that, we went in with some of your US marine boys; place called Hoisin Reservoir." He paused for a moment and then said, "I wonder if that is where the sauce comes from?" A further pause, then, "no, that's Chinese, isn't it? Well, no matter, we had quite a bit it of fighting on that jolly. Some of our guys got pinned down and me and a marine went in and cleared out the nest of commies that was causing us a problem. Our guys got home safe."

Jan had looked at him with a new level of respect. He'd been in some tight corners himself, but nothing that came close to this, unless, he mused, unless the fact that one bullet was all it would have taken, be it in Korea or the Bronx; sort of levelled things up when you looked at it that way. Still this guy was a hero; he had just been a thug.

"Sounds like you were a lucky guy. Did you ever get wounded? I did." He froze. The booze was certainly loosening tongues, but again Barry had seemed unconcerned.

"No, luckily, I didn't. I got transferred out to Malaya for a while and then returned to the UK. That didn't last too long though. Little thing called the Vietnam War came along, didn't it?"

Jan had cut in. "But what were you Brits doing out there? I never heard that before."

Barry moved closer to Jan, heads nearly touching, and in a low, conspiratorial tone said,

"Well, our government didn't want it to become generally known, but yes, we were there, a few of us, offering advice and training to the South Vietnamese, and doing a little bit of this and that; some fighting, but not a lot. We managed supplies and logistics and the like. I had a good time out there. Cushy posting, for most of the time. And the women were nice too. Anyway, in the end I actually married a Vietnamese girl, lovely woman she is. She's back home with the kids in..." he paused, "well, you don't need to know that do you Jan? No, you don't. Anyhow she's back there in our lovely apartment and I can't wait to get back home to them all I can tell you. Shall we have another drink?"

§§§

The waitress had brought them their refills and after she had left them to it, Jan had said,

"Well, if you can't wait to get back to wherever it is, what are you doing on the old *Queen*? Sounds like the last thing you'd want. Surely with your background there are plenty of jobs you could do, you know, security and protection and the like, aren't there?"

Barry had looked slowly and carefully round the bar, slightly one eyed as the drink increased its hold over him, and then motioned to Jan to come even closer. His voice dropped to a loud whisper.

"There are a few people I'd like to avoid if you know what I mean, and something tells me you do; similar bedfellows you and me, I'm thinking. No, so, when I was in 'Nam, I got involved with one or two things that perhaps I shouldn't have. I said I was dealing with the supply side didn't I. Well, we handled all sorts of bits and pieces. You can imagine what a mighty great number of items an army needs if it's to keep going can't you?"

Jan had nodded.

"Well occasionally, some of those supplies found their way to places they weren't supposed to be, if you get my meaning. And cash flowed back the other way, lots of it; I'd never seen so much money. Well, I suppose it went to our heads and we did what every idiot criminal does; we got greedy. A big shipment of medical supplies was coming in and we arranged a buyer. What we didn't know was that it was the other side."

"What? The commies?" Jan had said.

Barry had given a sad little laugh at this point, spilling some of his drink as he set the glass heavily down on the table. "Yes, the blooming Cong. God, what fools we were. And people had been watching us, which we didn't know, didn't even think about it. As I said, we were blooming fools. Thought we were untouchables. Like your Elliot Ness"

Jan had not pointed out that Elliot Ness had been on the side of the good guys. Barry carried on.

"We were lifted and shuffled back offshore to one of the US ships. Well, long story short, they didn't want a big fuss, it going public and all. In a way that would have made them look incompetent wouldn't it, us getting away with it for so long. No, it was all hushed up, dishonourable discharge for me and some of the others involved, and not even a lift home. I was dumped back into Saigon."

He had finished his drink and waived to a waitress for another.

"But that was another bit of luck for me. The Yanks, your lot, were known to feed their troops on all sorts of substances to get'em going at the enemy, you know, like Dexedrine and hash and the like."

"I didn't know that," Jan had said, a hint of surprise in his voice.

"Yeah, they did. They were stoned a lot of the time on those things, but it left some of them looking for something stronger, and that's where we came in. My contacts were still there; I knew a lot of people and it wasn't hard to set up a supply chain. Most of it came from Cambodia; we took our cut, and I sent my money back home and was able to buy some nice property. Again. It was all going so well but remembering what had happened last time I decided to get out, and as you might just know yourself, getting out ain't that easy. People don't trust you to keep your mouth shut I suppose."

Jan had given him a sharp look at that point; he'd been a little bit too close for comfort there. Looking back on his own experience, he silently agreed that getting out from under was not easy. He longed to get back to his previous lifestyle; he still had money hidden away, enough of it for a very comfortable life for the rest of his life. But each time he had contacted his banker he had been told to continue to keep in the shadows; people were still around, still asking questions. It was so frustrating. But it would pass he kept on telling himself. It would pass.

§§§

Barry was still talking, and Jan had tuned back in "...I remember my last few days in 'Nam. I had this mate, American helicopter pilot – it's how we moved stuff around – and he comes and gets me one evening.

"Wanna go to Saigon, sir? Your carriage awaits." So I hopped into his jeep and we go out to the Huey .."

"Yeah. I heard of those," Jan had said.

"Yeah? OK, good. Well, we get in the Huey and take off for Saigon. We normally flew high, to keep away from those nasty people on the ground with their vicious shooty things, but this night Big Joe he says,

"We gotta to stay low tonight because of the cloud cover, so it's over the treetops we shall go."

And so we went. It wasn't a long trip up to town, about an hour or so, and we'd been going for nearly half an hour when an alarm goes off in the cockpit. Jeez it was loud; scared me half to death; I hadn't heard one before had I, so I asks 'is that important?' And he says, 'why hell yes bro! It means we've been lit up by anti-aircraft radar. There aint supposed to be any near here. Must be the Cong. We need to move about a bit. Hold on to your hat.' And with that he's swooping and turning and whizzing all over the sky, nearly touching the treetops. We thought we'd made it, but then we see it."

"What?" Jan had gasped, riveted by what he was hearing.

"Well, a bloody rocket of course. Whooshing up out of the trees and heading right for us. It hit us just behind the rotor. And then there's Big Joe wrestling at the controls, but we both knew it was futile, we were going down. 'Good luck brother' was the last thing he said to me; ground fire got him just before we came into the trees. Somehow, don't ask me how, I got thrown out of the chopper into the trees and I remember how I bumped and scrapped and tumbled through that canopy thinking any second now! But I'm a lucky beast me. I hit the ground in a tangle of vines and creepers and was OK. It took me a few minutes to get my breath back, so I just lay where I was."

Barry had looked into the far distance, reliving it all. "And then what?" Jan had asked, eager to hear the next part of this action hero's story.

"Then what? Well, after a few minutes, I hear talking nearby. The Cong, obviously looking over the Huey which had crashed a little way away from me. It was on fire, but I knew that they'd soon work out that there had probably been more than one bloke in there and come looking. So I backed off, crawling on my belly through the vines and grasses, and after half an hour or so I couldn't hear them anymore. It was dark by then, and I just decided to stay put for an hour or two. Then I'm on the move again and as the dawn comes up, and I'm creeping along, I see the gates of an army post, one of ours, looming up out of the dawn. So, I step out on the path, put my hands in the air and walk up to the sentry and ask to be taken to the duty officer. He looks at me strangely, well you would have too wouldn't you, me, in civvies, all ripped and torn, blood, scratches, coming out of the jungle at dawn, you would, wouldn't you?"

Jan had admitted that he would.

"And then I'm cuffed and marched across a compound to an office and shoved through the door."

Barry's face had broken into a big grin,

"And whose face am I looking into? I couldn't believe it. It was only the face of my brother-in-law wasn't it. He couldn't believe it neither. He said 'Right Corporal, you may leave this ugly specimen with me. I'll deal with him.' And when the guy had gone, he smiles at me and gets the cuffs off and gives me a big hug. 'Barry, what are you doing here, looking like that?' he asks and so I tell him. And then we go and have some breakfast."

Barry had paused and waived the waitress over for some more drinks.

"So, there we were having breakfast, as though nothing was wrong in the world, and me thinking I was nearly dead six hours ago and Big Joe is, when Nguyen says, 'I hope you're looking after my sister properly. I know what you western men are like', and we laugh. And then he gets all serious like, and he says, 'we're going to have to slow down our operation for a while brother -in-law, and..'"

Barry had seen the look of puzzlement on Jan's face.

"Oh, didn't I say? I was working with Nguyen. He was in the supply chain. We were all making a packet. Anyway, he says, 'we're going to have to slow it down for a month or so. I keep hearing that investigations are on the go; signs are, that they're getting uncomfortably close, so, time to lie low. And I hear your name has been mentioned in despatches more than once, so perhaps you might want to get out of Vietnam for a while. Then you come back.' He had paused and then said, 'even without all the heat, it might not be too long before bloody Cong are all over the place; that the most powerful army in the world can't defeat peasants on bicycles is beyond belief, but there it is.'"

"So, here I am. I got a lift into Saigon, made sure I wasn't being followed and made it home. I told my wife what was happening and that we needed to move. We'd got this place in, well, as I said, you don't need to know where, but we'd got this place abroad and she should go to it with the kids. The money was all set up for her, so she'd be ok. And I would go off the scene for a while, lie low for a bit, and then come and join her. And that, my friend, is how I come to be on this old heap along with you and the rest of our motley crew. Not for long, I hope. Just until it all dies down."

He had paused, and then had said,

"Next time we're in port Jan, you'll have to tell me your story. Let's have another drink shall we?"

Seize the day: trust not to the morrow

Horace

I once heard a father talking to his son as they walked my deck. "So, you're in love with her you say." The boy replied, "yes Dad. Every time I see her my stomach does a somersault, and I can't breathe. I love her, I really do." There was a pause and then the father had said, "You do know it's all chemicals, son, don't you? A chemical imbalance in your brain. You get the red mist, the 'rose-coloured glasses' my dad used to call them; it clouds your judgement. And then, when you get over it, as you surely will, you suddenly look and think to yourself, 'what did I ever see in her?' Give it time; sleep with her if necessary, but don't, for goodness sake do anything like getting engaged, or worse still, married"

I thought that harsh. Where would we be in this world without love?

The Marconi Man's Tale

They were sitting in a quiet corner of the saloon bar in the Marquis of Granby, down by the Cemetery Junction. A bombshell had just landed.

"You're what?"

Bryan looked at her sharply, the colour draining from his face.

"You're WHAT?" he asked again, this time his voice had a low, sharp edge to it and an incredulous tone.

"I'm pregnant" Dorothy said again.

"How can you be pregnant?" he said.

She gave him a look that said, 'don't be silly'.

"OK. But how do you know? I mean, we've taken precautions, haven't we? You can't be. How do you know?"

"A girl knows," Dorothy said. "I haven't had my monthly for a couple of months now have I, so I do know. Anyway, aren't you pleased? I thought you'd be pleased. I know it's not what we'd planned, but we do love each other don't we?"

There was a tiny hint of desperation in her voice as she said those last words. She carried on,

"We can get married. It'll be alright. My dad will stump up for the wedding and we can stay with them or your mum and dad 'till we can get our own place, can't we?'

There was even more of a note of desperation as she tumbled out her last sentence. She had been watching his face and what she saw had not been encouraging.

There was silence, a silence that grew and grew until Bryan whispered back at her

"What about an abortion? There are people aren't there? We could ask about. I could pay for it."

"An abortion?"

She was astonished. The words jumped out of Dorothy's mouth as the tears fell from her eyes. She looked at him as if seeing him for the first time, seeing what he was really like, who he really was.

"Keep your voice down, or everyone will know," he said, looking nervously around the bar.

"You can't mean that Bryan, surely you can't. This is our **child** we're talking about here and there is no way on God's earth that I would kill it. You can't mean that, can you?"

Looking slightly abashed, he said,

"Look, I'm sorry for upsetting you Dotty, I really am. But it's such a shock, you know. Coming at me out of the blue like that, I don't know what to think. We've got our whole lives ahead of us, don't we? We've got to think this through, don't we? "

"There's no 'thinking' to be done," Dorothy said. "A child's a child and that's all there is to it. I can't believe you're not happy that we're going to be blessed like this."

She looked at him again, the tears flowing once more.

"OK, alright," he said in a more soothing tone, pulling her into him and cradling her in his arms. "We'll think it through and see what's best to be done. It's just the shock, you know. One minute you think your life's all on track and going along nicely and then, well, wham! And you have to think it through. That's all I'm saying, you have to think it through. You've known for some time, haven't you, and I bet you had some mixed feelings when it dawned on you what was going on, didn't you?

"Well, yes, it was a bit frightening at first, but I've always wanted children and so it's God's will I thought. So be it. Aren't you a little bit pleased Bryan? Aren't you a little bit excited by it all. A new life, our baby. Aren't you?"

He wasn't, but instead of answering her question he said,

"Do your mum and dad know yet?"

"No," Dorothy said. "I wanted to tell you first. And then I thought that we could go together and tell them, and your mum and dad too. Shall we do that Bryan? Can we go and do that now, please?"

"When do you think it will start to show?" he asked.

'What?" Again, she was hurt and dismayed by his response. "Oh, I don't know. In a couple of months maybe. What's that got to do with it? Why do you want to know?"

"And isn't there still a danger that you might lose it? I remember my Auntie Eileen saying she hadn't told us all until she was 'more than three months gone' as she put it, since there was a high chance of losing it before then. That's right isn't it?"

"Yes, I suppose that's true," Dorothy said hesitantly, losing hope. This wasn't going how she had expected, nothing like. She had thought Bryan would be happy, over the moon. Yes, it would be a bit difficult at first, with the money and a place to live and such, but he was coming to the end of his apprenticeship, and he would start to earn good money then as an electrician, and both sets of parents would see them alright until that time. But here he was talking about abortions and possible miscarriages and the like as if he didn't want their child, her child. Summoning up as much dignity and composure as she could, she tried one more time,

"Bryan. Face it. I'm pregnant with our child. There's no history of miscarriage in my family that I know of and I'm not going to have an abortion. I love you. I'm pleased you're the father of my child. I want us to share it with those we love and love us. What's the problem with that? I can't see one."

Again, he became uncomfortable. "Like I said, it's a shock. I need a bit of time to get used to it, to think through the best way for us to deal with it. I'll get used to it, I know I will, but just give me a little time to think before we tell anybody else. Please?"

"OK," she said reluctantly. "We'll tell my mum and dad next week. That should be long enough for you to think it through, shouldn't it?" a hint of bitterness in her voice.

They had parted an hour later with no further resolution, and each had gone home, deeply perplexed, and unhappy.

Bryan had never faced such a big dilemma. So far in his short life, the biggest decisions he'd had to take had been about what subjects to study for 'A' Levels and whether to go to university or not; he had chosen an apprenticeship since he wanted to start earning there and then. And now, here he was staring at a marriage, and a child, and a life of boredom and monotony and... he knew not what else. What he did know was that it wasn't an attractive picture he was looking at. Dorothy was a nice girl, he liked her, he really did. They'd been going out together for two years, but he didn't know if he really loved her. How did you know that? He didn't know, but he was sure he wouldn't be feeling like he did now if he did truly love her. So then what? Was it a simple choice between 'do the right thing' by her and suffer the potential consequences for the rest of his life, or don't do it, and suffer the potential consequences. Which of those two 'potential consequences' was the worst of the two evils, he asked himself?

On the one hand, staying, getting married, having a child, eventually a house and a decent job wasn't a truly bad option was it? Their parents would be shocked at first but would rally round. There would be a bit of gossip, a nod here, and a wink there, jokes about shotguns and the like, but that wouldn't be too bad now, would it? And there were plenty around them in their part of town who had gone through it already; he'd heard his mum talking to his dad about this one or that one who'd got a girl 'into trouble', and they seemed to be doing OK, didn't they? And he'd have a job and earn money and, and what; live the rest of his life in this town and never experience anything out of the ordinary? He had plans and hopes for his future didn't he? Of course he did. He would qualify, get some experience, and then make his way out of this Godforsaken place. Travel, maybe join the navy as a ship's electrician or some such. See a bit of the world. Experience life. Meet other women. Become something, not squander his talents in this nondescript, middle-class, southern town.

He knew if he did that, if he left, he would become the pariah; the one who 'did the dirty on that lovely girl Dorothy, poor soul', who he'd left to fend all by herself with a child. It would wreck the standing of his mum and dad in the community. How could they have brought up a son who didn't know about honour and doing the right thing. Such a scumbag, to be loathed and vilified by all right-thinking people. Perhaps his mum and dad would even have to sell up and move to a different town. It would be hard on them, but they could do it if they really felt they must. Dad had a good job in the bank; a good transferable skill and they had inherited their house from his grandma. So, they could do it if they really needed to. It wouldn't be easy for them, but they could get over it, would get over it given time. All these thoughts and more raced through his head throughout the night. When he woke in the morning, his mind was made up.

Dorothy had also had a bad night. She couldn't get rid of her feelings of surprise, disappointment and anger at the way Bryan had reacted. Sure, it was a shock for him, and yes, she might have found a better way to let him know, to prepare him for the news. But it had just seemed opportune, sitting there in the quiet corner of the bar. But it was what it was. She couldn't change things and she really, really did want this baby, her baby, his baby. Would he stand by her she had asked herself? She realised for the first time, that she wasn't sure of that anymore. She suddenly decided she wasn't sure of his love; nobody who loved her would have reacted so coolly, even coldly, to that news would they? What was she going to do if he didn't do the right thing? Girls had been tossed out of their family homes for bringing the shame of an unmarried pregnancy to their parents' door. Her family wouldn't do that to her would they? They loved her, she loved them. But one never really knew, and the weight of public opinion might leave them little choice but to comply with the received wisdom that that's what you did under these circumstances. And then what would she do? She eventually cried herself into a disturbed, troubled sleep.

She didn't leave her bedroom until she heard her dad go off to work. She didn't want to face him just yet. Her mother turned as Dorothy entered the kitchen,

"Morning love, how did you slee………?"

Her voice trailed off as she saw her daughter's face; it's usually clear complexion replaced by great red blotches, her eyes puffy. She looked like she hadn't slept all night.

"Oh love, whatever is the matter? Come here," and she opened her arms to give her daughter the cuddle that she so obviously needed. She made soothing noises as she held her close and rubbed and patted her back, just as she had done when Dorothy had been a baby and needed comforting.

"Have you had a row with Bryan, is that what this is? What have you two argued over?"

Mrs Lowood liked Bryan; he was polite, bright, and quite handsome. He was going to have a good trade and income and would be well able to look after her little girl. He would make a good son-in-law she thought.

"Don't take it too seriously my pet. There're always a few bumps along the road, you'll get over it, whatever it is, I know you will."

She gently pushed her daughter away, so she could look into her face.

"Is that what it is dear?"

"Oh Mum," wailed Dorothy, and then it all came tumbling out.

A stern, ashen faced Mrs Lowood sat opposite her daughter at the kitchen table.

"You silly, silly girl. How could you have been so stupid? How many times have I warned you about that sort of thing. Men are all the same these days, after one thing and one thing only." Her opinion of Bryan had gone rapidly downhill.

"Your Dad wasn't like that; he knew how to behave, how to treat a girl properly. It's all this modern thing, all this Elvis blooming Presley and his shaking hips. It's disgusting is what it is. And how could you have fallen for it? How could have been so foolish eh, what did he promise you?"

She stopped. She could see she was only making things worse.

When her dad came home that evening, Dorothy and her mum sat him down and gave him the news. He was a nice man. He'd taken care of his wife and his daughter as best he could, given them love and warmth and support. There wasn't an aggressive bone in his body. But as he listened, he could feel the anger rising inside him. Bryan bloody Willowtree was not going to treat his daughter like this. He was going to have to do the right thing by her or there would be consequences that he would not like, of that he could be sure.

"Right Mother, get your hat and coat. We're going to go and see Bryan and his parents and get this whole thing sorted out. Dorothy, you will wait here."

It was a chastened couple that returned an hour later.

"He's gone" was all Dorothy's dad could say.

§§§

Bryan had risen at six that morning and had got ready for work in his usual way. Unusually he had come down the stairs with a small suitcase in his hand.

"Oh, are you going somewhere son?" his mum had asked.

"Yes Mum. Mr Davidson has got a job in London that's going to take a few days and he wants me to work on it with Jim. I'll be away all week.

I'll see you on Friday." With that, he had given her a peck on the cheek and gone out the door. Later, with Dorothy's parents camped in their sitting room, Mr Willowtree had found out from Mr Davidson that no such job existed. He said that Bryan had called in that morning, said he had to go to see a dying aunt in Minehead and asked if he could have the wages he was due to see him over the time away. Mr Davidson had duly obliged and wished his aunt well. He had added he was somewhat surprised to see Bryan take his tools with him but had thought no more of it.

Bryan had arrived in London by lunchtime. He needed to get a job, quickly, his small amount of wages and an even smaller amount of savings would not keep him going for long. One of the decisions that he had taken the night before was that getting away for a bit, where nobody might find him, would be a good idea which led him on to revisiting his daydream of life at sea. Given his current position, it had a certain attraction. Just how did you go about it though?

First things first; he looked for some digs; there were a few cards in a newsagent's window, and he found a place at his second knocking. A small room, bathroom down the hall, and breakfast, all for 17/6d a week. He paid up front out of his small cache of money. Now for that job. He walked into the Labour Exchange on Conroy Street, passing through its swing doors, to be met by the sight of a large room, full of people, some seated, some standing, some walking aimlessly around. He'd never been in one of these places before and was at a loss as to how to go about it. He looked round for some sort of guidance. Not finding anything that was helpful, he attached himself to the back of a queue that seemed to be making slow progress to a counter, sectioned off into windows, staffed by a handful of officials. It took him about forty minutes, but eventually he was standing in front of a tired looking man in his fifties wearing a brown suit, balding, a thin moustache and heavy rimmed glasses.

The man was writing something on a card. When he had finished, he proceeded to put the card into a long thin tray, searching for the right place in the alphabet Bryan thought, and without looking up he said,

"Yes. And what can I do for you?"

"I want to know how to get a job on a ship, Sir."

"A ship is it? Well, we don't do ships in here son," the man said, looking up at Bryan for the first time.

"You'd need to go to one of the shipping companies in the docks out at Tilbury. Or you could try their London offices I suppose or, there's a thing called the Shipping Federation, or pool. That's probably out near Tilbury too.

He looked past Bryan and said, "Next."

A whole hour and not really any further on. But, OK, he would have to try one of the companies themselves. Bryan moved out of the way of the next customer and left the building.

Not as easy as he had hoped then. Sitting in his small room, he took some time in the evening to think things through again. He was in London, with very little money and no job. His first try at finding a job on a ship had been a failure. He had parents back home who would by now know everything that had gone on and would be worrying about him; about where he was and whether they would ever see him again, about whether he was going to do the right thing by Dotty. He had to deal with that. He knew he had to, but how? He'd burned his boats, hadn't he? "Burned my boats," he said out loud and gave a sarcastic laugh; "I can't even find one, let alone burn one," and he laughed, a sad, despairing laugh, again.

"What am I going to do?" By the morning he had a fresh plan.

He returned to the labour exchange that he had visited the previous day and got into the line that would take him back to the man he had spoken to before. When he arrived in front of him, he waited for the bald head to lift and the heavy rimmed glasses to point in his direction. Light bounced off the lenses and he couldn't see the eyes behind them.

"Oh, it's you again," the official said, his voice carrying a disappointed tone. "What can I do for you now? Haven't found a ship yet? I suppose you've come to sign on have you." He muttered under his breath, but loud enough for Bryan to hear, "Think the world owes them all a living these blooming kids."

"No Sir, I haven't. But I wonder if you could help me please. I'm new into London; I've just completed my apprenticeship as an electrician and I'm wondering if you know of any jobs going in that line?" He hesitated, then added, "Please Sir?"

The man, whose nameplate on the desk advised all and sundry that this was 'Mr. A Brent' looked at Bryan for a moment and then after a slight hesitation, got up and went to a filing cabinet and began flipping through some papers. Over the general hubbub, Bryan could hear the occasional word passing Mr Brent's lips; 'no'….. 'that one's gone',… 'oh, what's this still doing in here?', ….'a joiner, no he said electrician didn't he',…. 'ah, here were are', and he removed a sheet of paper and returned to his place on the counter.

"Right Mr," he hesitated. "What's your name son? I shall need that for my records." Bryan told him. "Well Bryan, it looks like you might be in luck. We do have a job for a job come in for a junior electrician at McKirgan's. It's just down the road from here. They do general contracting, work in homes and factories and the like. Let's fill in some paperwork and then you can go down to see Mr Mckirgan. Nice man he is. Yes, a nice man."

Mr Brent's tone had changed; perhaps having a trade had risen Bryan up in his esteem. He and Bryan spent the next ten minutes filling in a couple of forms for his records. "Off you go son, and good luck."

Ten minutes later, Bryan was standing in the reception area of *McKirgan's Electrical Contracting*, along with two other young men. His heart fell. He hadn't thought that there would be other people interested. 'What a fool', he chastised himself as he handed the card Mr Brent had given him to the pretty girl sitting behind a desk.

"Take a seat. Mr McKirgan will see you presently."

At that moment, a tall, thin man with curly black hair, dressed in smart overalls and with a pleasant smile on his face, came through a door behind the reception desk and walked over to it.

"OK Sylvia love, who have we got waiting to see us?"

She handed three cards over to the man.

"That's the order that these gentlemen came in Mr McKirgan," she said.

"OK. Mr Johns, it seems that you were first, so please follow me," and he turned and went back through the door, taking one of the young men with him.

Thirty minutes later, the next candidate was called through, leaving just Bryan, sitting, thinking things through as to how to deal with an interview. He'd only had one before in his life, when he applied for the apprenticeship with Mr Davidson, and his dad had been with him then. There was no one with him now, he would just have to cope by himself and that was that he thought. Part of his 'learning curve'.

"Would you like a cup of tea, Mr Willowtree?" It was Sylvia asking. He said 'yes', and noticed that she had nice ankles as she went out through the door to make it for him.

Bryan had liked Mr McKirgan immediately and the interview had gone well. It focused on his experience, and he thought he'd managed to answer all the technical and practical questions that were asked of him well. The work he would be required to do was pretty much the same as he had been doing for Mr Davidson. The questions surrounding his circumstances were slightly more problematic.

"So, you've just come up to town have you Bryan?'

"Yes Mr McKirgan. I've lived in Reading until now."

"Oh, so not too far then?"

"No sir."

"And why did you make the move? Seems like you were quite well set up, just come to the end of your apprenticeship with," he looked at his notes. "Mr Davidson was it? Ready to move on to proper wages. Did he not have room for you in his business then?"

Bryan was basically an honest young man. He'd been brought up to tell the truth; he knew that sometimes got you into bother. Would Mr McKirgan follow up with Mr Davidson? If he did, then he would be told everything, and probably in a way which would sound awful. So, get his story out there first? Tell it his way? He came to a decision.

"Well sir. I want to be honest with you and you should know before I start that it doesn't reflect too well on me as a person. But I'm a good electrician. Mr Davidson will vouch for that, I know he will."

And so, Bryan told the tale of the last 48 hours; he was amazed, only 48 hours and his life, his world had been turned on its head. He told it as simply as he could. He finished by saying that if he was successful in his application he would contact his parents, send money to Dorothy to help with the child, their child, but he would not tie himself down so young, when the world and all it had to offer was still out there. He finished, surprised by how open he had been, and looked into the face of the man opposite him. He'd blown it he thought. McKirgan looked back at him, the silence grew longer, and then he said,

"Well young man, that's quite a tale, but I thank you for your honesty. You're in a difficult situation but then most of us have been at some time or another. You've interviewed well and I'm going to take a chance on you; don't let me down. The job's yours if you want it."

When they had finished talking through the terms and conditions, Mr McKirgan stared steadily into Bryan's eyes; "One more thing Bryan that I want you to take note of. Don't fool around with Sylvia, she's my daughter. God help you if you do."

After his interview, Bryan went into the Post Office he had found down the road. He wanted to send his mum and dad a telegram. He took a form from the rack and thought long and hard. You paid by the word, three shillings for the first twelve words and then a thruppenny bit for each extra one. He made several attempts but eventually settled on:

SORRY STOP AM FINE STOP GOT JOB STOP MORE LATER STOP WILL SEND MONEY FOR DOTTY STOP LOVE BRYAN STOP

Five shillings, but he felt better for it.

§§§

Bryan settled quickly into life in London. With the money he was being paid he was able to move into better lodgings, with a pleasant couple in their fifties. In exchange for the odd bit of electrical work, some rewiring and repairs to an old lamp that they were particularly fond of, Mrs Marshall did his laundry and cooked him his tea, Monday to Friday. He started to send a money order to Dotty every week for £2 and felt a little better about himself.

Three months after he started at McKirgan's, he came out of the door from the workshop they used, to find his mother waiting for him. He stopped dead in his tracks. His heart raced and he swallowed hard.

"Oh, Mum. You gave me such a shock," he managed to stammer out. "What are you doing here? How did you find me? How are you and dad?" He stopped, feeling like a fool, like he had felt when, as a small boy, having done something wrong, he had stood and waited for his punishment. His mother rushed up to him and folded her arms around him and gave him such a hug. She clung on to him for what seemed like an age, but eventually she let go and stepped back to look at him. She looked tired he thought; tired and worried and sad. He blushed. For a moment he turned his gaze away from her; he felt so ashamed.

"Oh Mum. I'm so sorry. I really am."

"I know son" she said simply. "Let's go and have a cup of tea, shall we?"

Seated at a table by the window of a local café, steaming cups of tea in front of them, his mother started their conversation. "We got your telegram Bryan, thank you for that at least." Bryan winced. He deserved that he thought. "You look like you're doing okay up here. Do you like it?"

He was about to say that it was fine, that he was fine, it was just the start, there were better things ahead, when he thought better of it and said "you do understand why I did it Mum, don't you? You and Dad do understand?"

"Well, apart from the blooming obvious, that you didn't want to get married to Dotty, no. She's such a lovely girl. I can't see what you had against it. Your dad and I haven't always seen eye to eye, but we've rubbed along together fine, haven't we? So it can't have been us that put you off, was it?"

"No Mum, of course not. Yes, Dotty is a lovely girl, but I'm only twenty. There's loads I want to do, places I want to go, and I couldn't give up on those dreams. By the way, how is Dotty?"

His mum said, "She's gone to stay with one of her aunts up near Blackpool I heard. You know, until it's all over. Her mum and dad are still in shock you know. People were just starting to notice her bump, so they sent her off. She'll no doubt be back some time with the little'un, but it's hit them all hard, really hard. And of course, no one's talking to us now word has got out. You know the kind of thing, 'how could we have brought up our son like that? Didn't we teach you right and wrong? How did we fail to teach you a proper sense of your responsibilities?' And worse. But, there you are, what's done is done and it'll all wash out in time I suppose."

Once more Bryan said how sorry he was. His mother waived it away.

"So how are you doing then Bryan, on this 'life of adventure' that you're so keen on?" There were notes of sarcasm, of bitterness, in her voice. "Seems to me that you've gone thirty-five miles east from one electrician job to another. Not exactly the earth-shattering change you were seeking, is it? Or am I missing something?" this time, more sadness than anger in her tone.

"No Mum, it's not. But it will be, I promise. I'm not putting everyone through this just to stay a simple electrician. I just needed a job while I sort myself out, and so I could send Dotty some money, for the kid, you know. I thought I had to do that at least, but I really want to go to sea and I'm going to when I get enough things in place."

"The sea is it?" Bryan's mum did not look too impressed. "Mrs Hobson, down the road, her husband was a sailor, not that it did her much good. He left her for another woman. And the money you're sending. Don't bother. Mr Lowood came round our house two weeks back and virtually flung your postal orders in my face. 'We don't need money from your cowardly brat to look after our daughter. If he can't do the right thing by her then he can stay the hell away from us, and good riddance'. So, I've got them here if you want them back," and she went to get them out of her handbag.

"What? Oh I'm so sorry I've brought this on you and Dad, I really am. But no Mum, you keep them. Will you put them in a bank account in your name and I'll keep sending you some money and then when she needs it later on, we can give it to her, for the kid. It'll no doubt need stuff, won't it?"

They talked on for a while. At one point Bryan asked, "how did you find out where I was working, how did you know to come here today?"

"Simple," his mum replied. "Your Mr McKirgan got in touch with Mr Davidson, to check you out I suppose, and he mentioned the name of his firm and Mr Davidson told me and, well here I am. Took me a while to convince myself I was doing the right thing, but your dad and I talked it over. We can understand how you feel, and in a funny way I suppose, it shows a strength of character, not that we're condoning what you've done to that poor girl mind. But, what's done is done and I thought I should have one last go at seeing if you would change your mind. Which its clear you won't, and anyway Dotty would probably never have you back now, and…..oh my goodness, listen to me rambling on like an old fool. But I just wanted to see you and check you were OK and," at this point the tears flowed and Bryan went round the table and gave her a big cuddle.

"It'll be alright Mum, you'll see. I won't be a stranger. We can meet up here every month if you like; I don't think I should come back to Reading for a while, do you?"

She dried her eyes and smiled up at him. "No Bryan, I don't think that would be a very good idea at all."

He had stayed at Mckirgan's for another eighteen months. He met his mother regularly, and his father occasionally. He learned that Dotty had produced a daughter, who was doing well, and was going to stay up in Blackpool for a while more. One morning, as he was getting ready for work, his attention was caught by the radio; he always had it on in the morning to listen to *Today*. He heard Jack De Manio say,

"…it was fifty years ago to this very day that the unsinkable *Titanic* did just that, and sank on its maiden voyage, the victim of a collision with an iceberg. Over 1500 lives were lost, lives which might have been saved if the radio communications between ships, which were not well managed and controlled in those days, had been up to modern standards. Such a tragedy. But that tragedy led to significant changes in the way these matters were handled, across the world. I'm pleased now, to be able to talk with Captain James Anderson, who heads up the training college for Merchant Navy radio officers at Wray Castle in the Lake District. Good morning, Captain Anderson. It was a sad day fifty years ago was it not, but things move on I'm happy to say. Would you be kind enough to take our listeners through the changes that have taken place in the intervening years please?"

Bryan listened with increasing interest as the Captain outlined those changes.

"Thank you, Captain Anderson, I'm afraid were going to have to finish there. It's been most interesting and wonderful to see just how much things have moved on from that dreadful day. Just before I let you go, if there are any people out there who are interested in joining your college, how might they go about it?"

A pencil and some paper were grabbed and Bryan wrote down the gist of what he had heard; two year course for an OND or three if you wanted an HND; need maths and an "A" level and have a technical mind. He had carried on doing his 'A' levels at evening classes during his apprenticeship and he had passes in two subjects, so no problem there. Wasn't this just what he had been waiting for? Travel, use his skills, see the world, do an important job, become an officer. That might go some way to restoring his parents' pride in him. He decided to apply.

§§§

He started in September that year. He was a personable, bright lad and had flown through the interviews and tests which had been part of the admissions process. He had obtained a local authority grant to help fund the course and had started reading books in the library which might help him get ahead of things. On the 4th of September he formally entered Wray Castle as a student and his journey to become 'Radio Officer Willowtree' began. The instructors were nearly all time-served on ships, and between them had sailed to most of the ports on the globe. As well as knowing their stuff, they often held their students spellbound with tales of their experiences. Bryan studied the law governing safety at sea and the radio procedures and regulations associated with that. He learned Morse and how to operate a radio correctly; how to diagnose faults on the communications equipment and put them right and how to operate, maintain and repair radar installations. They learned on old equipment; they learned on the latest technology since there was no telling what vintage of kit they would find in any vessel they were on. Wray Castle itself wasn't in the best shape, and it was often damp and draughty when he went to his bed. But, he survived that, taking part in lots of the outdoor activities that the school offered. He received one or two knocks from his teachers, but he could be a cheeky young man and they were well deserved. He had a good time overall.

His parents were present to see him receive his diploma when he graduated with an HND in June 1965. They were pleased and proud of what he had achieved, but their happiness was, as ever, tinged with regret. Regret that he could not be home with them, that they could not spend time like normal grandparents, fussing over their granddaughter, spoiling her, watching her develop as they had watched him, although this time, with less responsibility and more enjoyment.

After the ceremony, they went into Bowness for a celebratory tea. The subject of Dotty came up, as it usually did. He'd been kept in touch with developments in Dotty's life; their daughter Caroline was nearly five years old now and by all accounts was progressing as five-year-old girls should. Dotty was married. She had met a nice young man through her aunt's church, fallen in love and had wed when Caroline was two years old. David, her husband, worked in his father's bakers shop in a suburb of Blackpool and his family were very happy with their son's union.

"Do you think Dotty will let you see Caroline in the future, you being the grandparents and all?"

"Not a chance Bryan. I don't think they want anything to do with us. You must be able to see why, can't you?" His mother looked sharply at him and then carried on, "surely you can understand why? They're married, their daughter will never have known anyone other than David as her father. They will not want to mess that up will they? I wouldn't, I know."

"No, I suppose you're right Mum. I'm sorry I screwed it up for you, I really am. But it just wasn't for me. Maybe one day they'll come round, eh, maybe one day."

There was a silence as their thoughts turned inward. After a while, Bryan's dad asked, "So what now Bryan, now that you've passed out or whatever it is? What do you do now?"

Grateful for the change in tack, Bryan said, "I have to get experience on a ship before I can work alone as a ship's radio officer. It's a requirement. No new graduate can go straight into that role. So, I'm on the hunt for a ship. I'd like one of the big cruise ships if possible, one of the major lines, like P&O. I've been talking with one of the senior lecturers at the Castle and he's fixing it up for me to have an interview with them, possibly for the *Canberra*." His voice filled with excitement. "It's one of the biggest ships they have and it's only four years old; it's massive and it's beautiful, and I might get a job on it as a junior wireless officer. What do you think of that? Once I've done that, and met all the requirements, then I'll get a certificate that will allow me to operate by myself. Until I have that, I have to work under supervision. I can't wait."

In truth, it did sound good to his parents too, but nothing would totally overcome his mother's worry about him becoming a sailor and going to sea.

Bryan loved his job on the big cruise liner. He worked under Radio Officer Shay McConnan, a quietly spoken Irishman; a man with a wicked sense of humour, who had been at sea for twenty years or more. Two hours on, two hours off from 0800 to 2200hrs was the daily routine, operating Morse code with a Marconi transmitter and receiver, listening for distress signals during the allotted 'silence periods' of 15-18 and 45-48 minutes each hour, recording and filing all the radio traffic that they received. The radar was a bit unpredictable, going off-tune, and Bryan would be required to go out in all weathers to the equipment box on the deck to fix it, but he didn't mind that at all. He enjoyed putting his training to practical use and it turned out that he was good at his job; at the end of his six months, he was awarded his Radio Officers Certificate.

The Canberra carried over two thousand passengers, with nearly a quarter of them in first class cabins. In their relationships with them, the crew were expected to be polite, speak if spoken to and generally be of assistance with information, guidance and support, as and when required. Bryan was a good-looking man of 25, the white uniform suit and his tropical tan enhanced his appearance further and drew admiring glances from both the young, and the more mature ladies on the ship.

He had never been short of female company since his relationship with Dotty had finished. The dalliances had typically been short-lived, just a bit of fun; once bitten, twice shy as the saying goes. He liked women and they seemed to like him. When off duty and out of uniform he would walk around the decks, not officially countenanced, but doable if you knew how. His eyes would run over the passengers by the swimming pool as he passed. They were on a long cruise, down to the far east and Australia, via the Panama Canal, and ever so slowly, over the days, his eye contact became longer and more pronounced with one passenger in particular, and she seemed to respond. He would slow down, looking to see if she was there, in her usual spot, and their eyes would meet and hold each other's gaze for a moment or two, and then he would move on, with thoughts in his head that he knew could not become reality.

On one such walk, he saw that his 'friend' as he had come to think of her, was missing from her usual spot. He felt a small surge of disappointment but shrugged it off. Turning a corner, there she was. She had obviously been lying in wait for him. His pulse jumped, but he made to walk by, not engaging in any eye contact. She moved into his path, and he stopped.

"Well Mr Radio Officer, how are you today?"

In her forties, tall, tanned, expensive jewellery, American, pretty, a hint of a sophisticated perfume that he didn't recognise.

"I'm very well thank you Madam, and you?"

Twenty minutes later they were in her cabin. They were rushed, pulling at each other's clothing, open-mouthed, lips brushing, hearts pumping, the excitement building to fever pitch. They fell onto the bed. Then the cabin door opened. A man walked in. They froze.

"Just what the hell do you think you're doing with my wife Sir?"

Bryan started to get up but didn't see the punch coming; he was unconscious by the time his head hit the cabin floor.

§§§

Bryan walked slowly into the Staff Captain's office. It was a day after the event. He had a large purple bruise on the side of his face where Mr Gruman had hit him. Following his punch, Mr Gruman had summoned a steward and asked him to bring him one of the ship's officers immediately. The Staff Captain had appeared five minutes later and took in the scene; Bryan groggily rising to his feet, a lady in the background, one of the ship's luxurious dressing gowns wrapped round her, a rumpled bed and an angry man ready to confront him.

"Just what sort of penny-ante outfit do you think you're running here?" he had shouted at Officer Ranworth. "I come back to my cabin after my bridge game ended, to find this, this, this," he had searched for the right word and one not being immediately forthcoming, said "officer of yours, assaulting my wife. What have you got to say about that Sir? What are you going to do about it? This is the last time that I ever use your company, of that I can assure you. Well my good man, what are you going to do about it?"

Officer Ranworth had done his best to calm Mr Gruman down, which had taken some time, had assured him that the matter would be dealt with, with urgency, that a full and proper investigation would be undertaken, starting immediately. He asked another officer to take Bryan back to his quarters.

And now they were all assembled for the hearing: Bryan, Bryan's 'friend', his senior officer Shay McConnon, the master at arms, a writer to take notes of the proceedings and the staff captain, Graham Ranworth.

"So let's make a start shall we," said Ranworth. He looked down at a sheet of paper in front of him and read aloud from it,

"Junior Wireless Officer Willowtree, you are here before this disciplinary hearing to answer the following charges:

One. That you did force yourself into the cabin of Mrs Sandra Gruman, a passenger of this ship, without invitation to do so.

Two. That you did attempt to have sexual relations with her, against her will.

Both offences are contrary to the code of conduct applicable to all employees on this ship and you have appended your signature to this document, acknowledging your understanding of it and your agreement to abide by its terms.

If found guilty of these offences, especially of the alleged sexual attack on Mrs Gruman, you are liable to be handed over to the appropriate authority in this ship's home port for appropriate criminal action to be considered."

He stopped at that point and looked at Bryan.

'Well Willowtree, what do you have to say to these charges?"

Bryan had been in despair since the events of the previous day. He had asked 'Bugsy' Tanner to be his 'friend' for the hearing, as Bugsy had experience of such things. He wasn't quite sure if that was a good thing or a bad thing, but on balance, having some experience in his corner might come in useful.

In the time they had together, Bugsy had said,

"Just deny it Bryan. It's your word against hers, isn't it?"

A moment of hope flickered in his chest. That was one way of dealing with it. But it was extinguished just as quickly as it had come.

"But I was in her cabin Bugsy, and her damned husband found us there together."

He thought for a moment or two and then continued,

"He couldn't have seen anything much, because we didn't have the time, to, you know, do anything. But I was there, and we were on the bed together. How can I explain that away?"

"As I said, just deny it." He paused, then continued,

"OK. OK. How's this work? So, you were there; but she had asked you to come there to look at the way the air conditioning was working; and, being a good company man, you went down there simply to see if you could help one of its paying customers." Bugsy was warming to his task, "and when you went in, she jumped on you, to your surprise obviously, and you were simply trying to ward her off when the husband came in; he got the wrong end of the stick and smacked you one; he's the one that should be on a charge, not you; a case of grievous bodily harm if I ever saw one."

Bugsy had stopped at that point, a look of triumph on his face. "See, that's all you have to say. It's her word against yours, isn't it? They won't be able to touch you for it."

He had thought long and hard about Bugsy's suggested approach. It had much to recommend it, not least that it might save his job. Now he opened his mouth to speak,

"Captain Ranworth, Sir. I cannot dispute that I was present in Mr and Mrs Gruman's cabin yesterday afternoon. But things did not happen as they have described to you. Mrs Gruman stopped me on deck. We talked about the ship and its operations for a short while and then, Sir, she invited me to go to her cabin. I knew it to be against the rules, but she insisted that I accompany her. In order to avoid a scene in front of other passengers, I assented. I know that I shouldn't have done so, but I was trying to avoid trouble, not cause it. This you have to believe Sir. I did not force my way into her cabin, as claimed. I did not force myself onto her, as claimed. Indeed, she took the lead in everything that happened. Now I suspect she is lying to avoid trouble with her husband."

Bryan had once again gone for honesty as the best policy. He would have to see if his luck held this time, as it had with Mr McKirgan.

"Well thank you for your honesty Willowtree," said Captain Ranworth. "Have you anything to say Radio Officer McConnan, before I consider my decision?"

"Sir, Junior Radio Officer Willowtree has performed all his duties in an exemplary fashion whilst he has been on this ship working for me. I think that he has further shown his admirable character today, by not seeking to deny that he was in the Gruman's cabin. He has explained the circumstances leading up to the husband's arrival and I, for one believe him. He's a good-looking lad Captain. We have all know situations arise in the past where one of the ladies has taken a shine to one of our own, and, speaking from experience, it can be hard to resist as you know. Sir, I would ask you to take those points into consideration when you are deliberating upon the outcome of today's proceedings."

"Has anyone else anything to add? Captain Ranworth looked at everyone in the room. "Very well. We will adjourn whilst I consider what should be done."

Two hours later they reconvened. Bryan stood in front of the Captain. Captain Ranworth said,

"Junior Radio Officer Willowtree. This is a very serious case and a very difficult one, I can assure you. Whilst the facts of the case have been disputed, and it is in a sense, one person's word against another, the one fact that has not been disputed is your presence in the cabin of a passenger for no official reason or purpose. This is expressly forbidden by the contract that you signed, testifying to your understanding and acceptance of that and other requirements.

Bryan nodded his agreement.

"Now, I have listened to your senior officer speak glowingly of your conduct and of your honesty. I have taken further soundings from others that you have had contact with on this ship and they all speak well of you."

"Coming to the charges; on charge one, by your own admission you were present in the Gruman's cabin, although the reason for that is disputed.; on charge two, again whether you forced yourself upon Mrs Gruman or were invited, as you claim, I find there to be insufficient evidence to prove it either way; regarding prosecution, again I find there to be insufficient evidence to justify the taking of such action. Of course.

Mr Gruman may pursue the matter in another place, if he so choses. I will do my best to ensure he will now let the matter drop."

Bryan's spirits lifted a little; perhaps he would survive, receiving a reprimand only, or the loss of pay and privileges. His hopes were soon dashed.

Captain Ranworth said, "However, I have no alternative but to dismiss you from the service on this ship. I cannot allow any member of our team to brazenly disregard the code by which we all operate, a code which enables the passengers we carry and care for, to have confidence in us. Put simply, to trust us. You were in her cabin, which is expressly forbidden. You will continue to carry out your duties until such time as a replacement is obtained. When you are not working, you will be confined to your quarters. You will have No, I repeat, No contact with any passenger on this ship again."

Although this outcome, had been half expected, he was shocked by it, nonetheless. He felt tears gather in his eyes and he fought strongly against them. The Staff Captain looked at him. "Junior Radio Officer Willowtree, please let this be a lesson as regards to your future conduct. When you leave us, your discharge book will carry the usual stamps of VG relating to you ability and conduct but I will be informing the Marconi Company of the events and I do not believe that they will be hastening to find you another position anytime soon. I would urge you to think about your future conduct. You are a young man, good at your job, personable and bright. You will find another job; of that I have no doubt. But please, do not mess up again. This hearing is closed."

Rangoon was their next landfall. The company was duty bound to return him to his port of embarkation, Southampton, but a new junior wireless officer having been provided, Bryan felt no qualms as he toured the dockside offices seeking some form of employment. Eventually he heard of a ship that needed a 'Marconi man'. Bit of an old wreck apparently, on its way out to Montevideo when it could find someone to handle the radio traffic. It wasn't a hard sell. It obviously wasn't going to be a step up the career ladder. How did he feel about it? He hesitated for only a moment; beggars can't be choosers he thought, and besides his whole future still lay ahead of him didn't it. That evening he found the right dock and walked up the gangway of the *MV Western Queen* to begin a new chapter in his life of adventure.

We are our choices

Jean-Paul Sartre

We all have dreams when we are young. I know that. I've heard many of them being shared as the miles have passed under my keel. To be famous, to be rich, to be a doctor, to be a mum, to be a dad, to be…. who knows what? Yes, we all have them, but over time the realities we deal with can cause those dreams to change, to be lost. Some hold on, manage to live their dream, but at what cost? There is always a cost.

Captain Olaf's Tale

Jan was staring into space. On the galley worktop sat a simple silver tray with a glass of rum and a little jug of water. It was 9.00am, or 'two bells in the Fore-Noon Watch' as he had come to learn; time for his Captain's first formal drink of the day. The captain was the reason for Jan's reverie; in his three years on the ship, he had had more contact with him than with any other person on board and he still couldn't make up his mind about him. He knew that others in the crew thought their captain to be a complete waste of space, especially the First Mate, Tony. Tony was a nice guy, friendly with nearly everyone, but he had no respect for Captain Olaf Peterson, either as a sailor or a person. It was all he could do to keep a civil tongue in his head when dealing with him. Jan had once overheard one of the watchkeepers ask Tony

"What's wrong with the captain today, Mate?"

And Tony had replied,

"Don't you know?"

"No."

"He's sober."

Peterson was always polite in his dealings with Jan, as he was with most of the others who reported to him, but whilst Jan couldn't put his finger on the reason for it, he got the sense that inside his captain there was a deep, deep pit of sadness. He thought back to his old bosses, back in the day; they all commanded respect; they were involved, busy, took decisions and made sure those decisions were acted upon; and if they weren't, then you better have had a very good reason as to why. He saw none of these things in Captain Olaf. There was just some sort of void where the man should be; and he saw Olaf try to fill that void every day, with alcohol.

He came out of his trance, picked up the tray and walked the few steps to the door of the captain's cabin, knocked and stepped over the threshold. Petersen was asleep in his chair, a glass with some amber liquid already in front of him. An empty rum bottle lay on its side, rolling gently across the desktop with the motion of the ship. Jan put down his tray, picked up the bottle and glass and left quietly, not wishing to disturb his captain's slumbers.

When Olaf had fallen into to his bunk the night before, befuddled by drink, his usual deep sense of self-loathing and guilt hanging over him, his last waking thoughts were of the past. He hadn't always been like this he thought. Once upon a time he had been a bright, eager young officer with lively career ahead of him...

§§§

He had always wanted to go to sea, ever since he could remember. The tales of the Viking adventurers' explorations and conquests that had been read to him by his father, and subsequently read and re-read by himself when able, had lit a fire deep within him that would never be extinguished. He was a bright boy and performed well at school, he was a good athlete and, much to the envy of his friends, grew into a tall, handsome young man, able to charm any girl in his neighbourhood that he happened to choose. When the time came for him to leave school, there was only one possible route for him; with the support of his parents, he sought an apprenticeship with one of the many shipping companies in Oslo. Even then, he pictured the time when he would stand on the bridge of one of those beautiful, magical liners that he saw in the harbour every day, as its Captain.

With his school record, it wasn't long before he was in the employment of *Den Norske Amerikalinje*, one of Norway's largest shipping lines with nineteen ships. The Company had plans to expand; Norwegian tonnage was growing and there was always going to be a demand for good, well-trained officers. Olaf found himself as an apprentice deck officer at the age of sixteen. Initially, his training was mainly shore based, or on ships in port but after nine months he began to spend more time at sea and eighteen months into his service he was full-time on the voyages across the Atlantic via Stavanger and Bergen, to New York.

There was much for him to learn; cargo operations, maintenance, passage planning, navigation, loading and discharge; the list just seemed endless. But he kept at it and was appointed Fourth Officer soon after he turned twenty. The cruises across the Atlantic were non-stop, unlike those of other lines. The officer contingent, when not formally on duty, were encouraged to mingle with the passengers, especially those from First and Second Class, to explain the ways of the ship and of sailing. It was their role to entertain, and keep spirits up, especially on those days of the voyage when nothing, other than the sea, could be seen whatever direction you turned your eyes. With his polite manners and good looks, Olaf became adept at charming the older ladies with his tales of the sea; he reminded them of their sons; he also had a very winning way with the younger members of the fairer sex who found him quite a dashing and romantic character; it was not unknown for him to end up in their cabins when unchaperoned.

He impressed his superiors and by the time he was 28 he was Second Officer of the SS *Oslofjord*. Only two steps to go and a captain I will be, he thought, maybe by 1945 if I keep my nose clean and the passengers happy. But the best laid plans can be thwarted; on the 9th of April 1940 Norway was invaded by Germany and his life, together with so many others of his countrymen and countrywomen changed. After hasty discussions on the bridge, their captain decided to ignore the German instruction for them to put into a German controlled port and they continued to New York. Here they idled away their time whilst Norwegian and British bigwigs sorted out insurances and the like and in quite a short space of time, considering bureaucrats were involved, they were advised that they were now under the control of a newly formed body, Nortraship, which now had responsibility for all Norwegian shipping. From New York they went to Halifax, Nova Scotia where work began fitting out the *Oslofjord* as a troopship, work which continued in Liverpool. Olaf was kept very busy during this period; he loved the hustle and bustle of the fitting out process, getting involved in any and every aspect that his first officer would allow; secretly he was exhilarated by the prospect of the danger that would now accompany their future voyages. He was convinced that they would win the war and then they would need even more captains and ships; his future would be assured.

Over the next four years his ship carried more than one hundred and fifty thousand troops to destinations all over the world, sailed three hundred thousand miles and was at sea for over nine hundred days. It had transported prisoners of war to safe havens. It had been part of big battles like Operation Torch and Operation Husky and he, and it, had survived. Of course, it hadn't all been sunshine and roses; aircraft tried to sink them with their bombs, they were shot at from land, sea and air; torpedoes and mines had been miraculously avoided. They saw sister ships sunk with many lives lost, and death, sorrow, and destruction on a scale they had not dreamed of, but the *Oslofjord* remained largely unscathed. Whilst it brought home to him the precarious nature of his existence it confirmed in him a sense of invincibility that would contribute to his downfall a few short years later. But he had loved it, and he had prospered, being promoted to First Officer in 1945, when his boss had been killed in a freak deck accident.

When the ship returned to its former owners, they decided it would make sense to sell it, which they did, to a Panamanian company. Nils Bergenson, the head of the *Den Norske Amerikalinge*, had decided that the time was ripe for growth, and he and his Board had announced that they were to build a further five liners over the next five years, all to be state of the art, the best technology, the best performance, the best cost profiles in the industry. Most of the officers from the *Oslofjord* were put on shore leave to await further engagements but some, including Olaf, were brought into Head Office. Bergensen had asked that the design team be augmented by a few of their brightest officers to ensure the designs would meet all the stated goals in practice as well as in theory; Olaf's captain had recommended him.

§§§

Once again, Olaf found the work to be of great interest, and he became absorbed into its rhythms, often working long into the night on some knotty problem with the siting of the loading equipment, or the right type of radar, or the automatic pilot system. Automatic Pilots were hated by the watch officers; they didn't trust the things, sometimes with good cause. Even when they were installed, they weren't used at night. Olaf sought out the best equipment of the time and developed a training programme to ensure it would deliver the right results in the hands of the Watch on the Bridge; autopilots often saved fuel on a voyage and therefore costs.

As he was going back to the design office one morning, a sandwich of cheese and juniper berries in his hand, he noticed a woman sitting at a desk outside the office of one of the Directors. He was sure he hadn't seen her before; but how could he have not noticed her he asked himself? She was, by far, the most beautiful woman he had ever seen, and he had seen a few in his time. He stopped in his tracks, thought for a moment, and then walked over to her, adopting what he thought to be his most appealing look.

"Good morning Miss…..er. I don't think we've met before, have we? I'm sure I'd have remembered if we had. Are you new? Yes, you must be new." He was gabbling on, he knew that. He felt so clumsy; he was making a complete fool of himself he thought. He blushed.

The woman noticed this and smiled a little smile to herself.

"Well sir, yes, I am new here, I started yesterday. As you can see, I'm working for the Finance Director." She indicated the nameplate on the door over her shoulder. "And it's Fru, Fru Bakke. And you are?"

Olaf told her his name, and then quickly told her what he was doing there in the offices and what he had been doing at sea. It all came out in a rush again, and he felt mortified once more; where was his poise, his legendary charm? He couldn't remember being so thrown. But she was so lovely; up close, even more lovely than he had at first thought; but she was married, the 'Fru' told him that. Well, that hadn't necessarily proved an insurmountable obstacle in the past had it. But he would have to go very carefully here if he was to stand any chance with this auburn haired, blue-eyed wonder who sat before him. He cleared his throat and bidding her adieu walked back to his office. She watched him go, that little smile twitching her lips once again.

He looked out for her every day after that, several times a day in fact. From various observations he had noted how tall she was, how elegantly she comported herself, her lovely hair, her measured tones, soft and lyrical, in short, just how classy she was. He knew he was head over heels besotted with her. But what could he do about it? He wracked his brain; he couldn't just ask her out could he, she was married after all. He couldn't hang around her desk all day, she'd think that creepy, wouldn't she? So, what to do?

One evening he waited for her to leave the building and, keeping out of sight, he began to follow her. Not a long walk as it turned out, just five minutes before she turned into the entrance of a block of flats and disappeared. He looked for her name on the row of bells beside the entry door and there she was, "F. Bakke" apartment 12. The next morning, he was outside the apartment block nice and early and he waited for her to leave for work; he noted the time, 8.15am. The following morning, he just happened to be walking past her apartment building when she came out. Feigning surprise at this chance meeting, he quickly fell in beside her and they walked to the office together.

This happened nearly every working morning for the next two weeks. By the end of this time, he had learnt: that her name was Frida; that, to his joy, she was in fact single, her husband had been killed by the Germans, fighting in the north of Norway; that she had survived the war by going to Sweden, like many other Norwegians; that she loved Oslo more than any other place in the world; that she did not have any children; and she did not have a current boyfriend, nor was she looking for one. That last piece of information cast a temporary shadow, but nothing ventured, nothing gained. He told her things about himself and his life at sea and his daring-do during the war years, and by the end of the first month of their walks together she agreed to meet him for a coffee on the next Saturday afternoon.

He had never, ever felt what he felt for her about anyone else; of that he was certain. And slowly he saw that she was beginning to feel the same way about him. He held the taste of their first kiss together in his memory for a long time. After six months they made love and after ten months he proposed to her, and she said "Yes."

It was still a time when a young man felt the need to meet the conventions associated with getting married. Olaf talked with Frida about asking permission from her guardian for her hand in marriage. He knew both her parents were dead, and that her grandfather had acted as her guardian until she was old enough to take formal responsibility for herself. He pressed her to set up a meeting with him. She was reluctant to do so, which puzzled him.

"What? Do you think he won't see me as good enough for you? I'm a senior officer in a large company, one who is going places. He'll surely see that I'll be able to keep you in the style to which you are accustomed, even better if things work out like I think they will. What's the problem? I really don't understand."

This conversation went on for nearly a week. They were rehashing it all once again when she turned to him and said,

"Look, there's something that you should know; when I've told you, you can make your decision as to whether you want to carry on down this route."

His face drained of colour. Was she about to tell him that she didn't love him, that she had found someone else? Surely not. He couldn't bear for that to happen. He loved her more than life itself.

"My Grandfather is Nils Bergensen."

"What?" he said in astonishment, "*the* Nils Bergensen? The Chairman of my Company, Nils Bergensen? How come you never told me this before? How come I never knew before? I mean, how come no one else ever told me?"

After he had calmed down, he said, "but what difference does that make? Why have you been so mysterious about it? Surely, he would be pleased for you, my working for him and all; you know, keep it in the family."

His face brightened as his thoughts raced ahead; this lovely girl his wife; his rapid rise through the company; Commodore of the Fleet perhaps; Chairman eventually. And then he saw her face, and stopped.

"He once told me his opinion of sailors," she said. "He said that whilst he worked with them every day, and they were often very professional and good at their jobs, he did not want me ever to marry one; never there when you need them; woman in every port; a lonely, solitary life for me; not what I want for you, etcetera, etcetera. So, I know it's not going to be as easy as you appear to think it will be. I don't think he'll give us his blessing."

"So, if he doesn't, what can he do to us?" Olaf said defiantly, his picture of that bright future momentarily fading. "We'll get married even if he says 'no', but I'm sure he won't, will he darling? He looked at her imploringly, seeking some sign from her that it wasn't as bad as she had implied. "I'm only asking him because I think it's the right thing to do. And besides, I'd like to meet him. I've heard a lot about him."

They talked on and on about it and Frida eventually agreed to seek a meeting with her grandfather for them both.

§§§

At the appointed time, they walked up a long drive to a beautiful house in a very select part of Oslo. They had passed other grand houses set discretely along the road here in Bygdoy and he had marvelled at each one as they passed by. Olaf had only been in this part of town once before, when visiting the Viking Ship Museum. He was about eleven years old he remembered; he recalled the smooth flowing lines of the beautiful *Oseberg* ship and had felt for a moment the wonder and the pride that had swelled within him; he was descended from the navigators and the explorers that had built that ship. It had fuelled further his desire to be part of ships and the sea. What greeted him now, as they walked up the drive was one of the most gorgeous houses he had ever seen; turrets, tall chimneys, balconies, picture windows, beautiful gardens, massive front door made of polished oak. It even had its own little jetty stretching out into the fjord and a lovely yacht was moored at its side. He was overawed.

They were admitted by a maid and asked to wait in a small room off the grand entrance hall. They were both very nervous and talked in whispers to each other. Olaf felt like he had, when waiting for his first job interview. But that hadn't turned out badly, he thought. And neither would this, would it? Eventually the door opened, and the maid reappeared and beckoned to Frida to follow her, indicating that Olaf should remain where he was. A bad sign if ever there was one, he thought. He waited for her return, and waited and waited; five minutes became ten, ten became twenty, twenty became thirty and he was becoming very edgy and restless when the door opened once more, and the maid escorted him across the hallway to what was obviously the grandfather's study.

Frida was nowhere to be seen. Bergenson sat in a chair, behind an exquisite oak desk, his face devoid of any expression. He did not ask Olaf to sit but instead indicated that he should stand in front of him; just like the headmaster's study Olaf thought. He made to speak. But Bergesen raised his hand and spoke.

"Be quiet young man. You will speak when and if, I say that you may." He gave Olaf a long cold, hard stare, apparently not liking what he was seeing. "I have just told my granddaughter that she cannot, must not, marry you under any circumstances; she does not have my blessing for your proposed union. I have further told her that should she be mad enough to go against my wishes, then I will withdraw all support from her in any and every way possible; her job in my company, her pleasant flat, any possibility of inheritance, and all the other little benefits and treats that she currently enjoys, and which make her life pleasant; all will cease forthwith." His tone softened a little. "Now, I am sure if you love her as much as she tells me you do, you will not wish for any of this to happen. I therefore expect you to cease your relationship immediately. I have arranged for you to be posted to a ship of ours that is sailing for the Far East tonight. My secretary will give you its details as you leave. After today, you will never see my granddaughter again. I hope that is clear. Now you may go."

Olaf was stunned. He had never expected anything like this to happen. He turned to go but anger took hold of him. It was going to be his only chance to stop this madness; he halted and turned back to face the man.

"I…"

Bergensen looked up at him. "Did you not understand me young man? I told you leave my office. Now get out before I have you thrown out."

"No Sir. I will not. But before I do leave you, I want to know why it is you hate your granddaughter so much. Why would you even think about taking such harsh and cruel decisions where she is concerned? I had been led to believe that you loved her; she believes you love her. But these are the actions of a…" he hesitated, searching for the right word, "…a tyrant and an evil-hearted bully. We love each other for God's sake.

Please, please think again. Tell me, please tell me what can I do to show you that I'm worthy of her? Just tell me and I'll do it. I will, I promise. Do you really wish to destroy her chance of happiness? What have we ever done to you to cause this. You don't even know me," he shouted, "so why this awful, dreadful, cruel decision?"

Bergensen stood up, his body bent forward over the desk in front of him, his knuckles clenched and white, forcing hard down onto the beautiful gold tooled leather of its top. His voice was cold, harsh, his words were spat out like bullets. "Hate my Granddaughter Sir? I assure you I do no such thing. I love her and I am doing this to save her. And 'I don't know you' you say. Well Sir, I know your kind and I do know you to be one of the worst of them. Sailors like you give a bad reputation to the profession. You don't think that I haven't enquired about you? You have been under my eye ever since I was told that you were seeing Frida. I've talked with all your previous captains and shipmates. And what have I learned you ask? Self-obsessed; thinking only of your own career; a girl in every port; a girl, or two or three or as many as you can get on every ship you've ever served on. You're a disgrace. How could I approve of your marriage when I know that should it ever happen, Frida would be here weeping on my shoulder within six months, telling me of your other women, saying how you have left her to rot in misery, fending for herself. Well, I won't allow that to happen. She's already lost one husband, a good man incidentally, who fought and died for his country. I'll never let you inflict more sorrow and pain on her. This is your only deal; much against my better judgement I will allow you to remain in my company's employment and you will be on that ship leaving Oslo tonight. Should you persist in your gold-digging adventure, for that is what we both know this to be, then, I will ensure that you never sail on another Norwegian, European or American ship again. You know I have many connections in this industry. People listen when I speak. Word will go out to all our agents all over the world and people will be warned against letting you on board a ship ever again. Do you understand me? Now, for the final time, get out of my office," he shouted as he pointed towards the study door. "I never want to see you again."

§§§

Frida was in tears when they met again outside, and continued to cry as they walked, drawing curious looks from those they passed. Now, back in her flat, they sat opposite each other, dazed by what had just taken place.

"I just don't understand it. How can he hate the people that work for him so much? How can he hate me so much?"

"I don't think it's you he hates Olaf; if it had been any other sailor, it would have been the same. When I was with him, he told me something he had never spoken of before, about my mother, his daughter. He said he had never wanted me to hear what he was about to tell me, but the time had come to tell me the truth, to stop me from ruining my life. My mother died when I was five, I can hardly remember her. Anyway, he said she was happily married to my father, and they had me and that made them very happy; then she met someone. Well, you can guess can't you? A sailor of course. And the rest is history, as they say.

My parents separated, she went to live with her fancy man; he left her after a year or so; grandad wouldn't take her back; she lived in squalor, and then she died in the Spanish Flu outbreak and so did my father. Grandad thought, and still thinks, that if she had been living her old life none of it would have happened, he wouldn't have lost his daughter. So, he blames that sailor, all sailors if you will. It's not just you darling. As I said, any sailor; same result."

"Right. But that doesn't solve anything, does it? I'm supposed to be on a ship tonight, never darkening your door again; or I don't work again. And you lose your flat he said. Is that true by the way?"

"Yes, he can throw me out if he wishes. Don't worry Olaf, we'll be fine."

They talked on into the evening. The time for the departure of his ship came and went and still they talked. Two weeks later, they were married in a little church just around the corner from her flat surrounded by a small group of their friends.

Three years passed and things were decidedly not fine. As promised, Grandad had moved quickly to evict Frida from her flat, and though Olaf had enquired of captains of ships from freighters to fishing boats he could not get a job at sea. They were living in a very small flat in one of the less salubrious areas of the city. Frida's work in an office paid for most of the rent and the odd jobs that Olaf found in shops and warehouses covered the rest and provided their food. They were still in love with each other, but Olaf was becoming increasingly frustrated. How could he be kept from his other true love? How could a man of his talent, a man of his potential, a man with the capability to be a captain of a big ship, be unable to fulfil his destiny simply because of the word of one old fool? It niggled at him. It kept him awake at night; it woke him early in the morning; it plagued him; and on a growing number of occasions, it caused him to take one drink too many.

He continued to keep his ears open for any possibility of a return to the sea, but it was obvious it wouldn't happen any time soon. Unless, he thought, unless he went beyond the reach of Bergenson. The old boy didn't control all the shipping of the world, did he? There must be something for him in the Middle East, or Far east, or South America or somewhere.

He still talked with sailors in bars. He listened carefully to those returning from the other side of the world, asked questions and eventually had a few contacts he could use to seek a role outside Bergenson's parish. The trouble was it would mean his leaving Oslo and he knew just how difficult that would be for Frida. Ever so gradually, he introduced the notion of him working abroad; he would get contracts for six months; he would send money home; Frida would be able to get out of this 'rat hole' and find a better apartment for them. And he might get a permanent job, like he had had before and then she could join him, and they could live a life of luxury in Malaysia, or Hong Kong or Rangoon, or wherever. And didn't she know how frustrated he was living this shore life, working menial jobs, watching every penny, when he was capable of so much more? She must know that surely? These conversations took place over several months, gaining in intensity, often ending in a bitter argument, and with Frida in tears.

One evening he came home, again a little the worse for drink with a sheepish look about him. After they had eaten their simple meal together Olaf cleared his throat and said,

"I know you're not going to like what I'm about to tell you, but please listen. I've signed on a ship as Second Officer. It sails for Rangoon tomorrow. I've found someone at last who isn't afraid of your grandad."

He saw the sudden, startled look on the face he loved, the tears beginning to fall slowly from those beautiful eyes.

"No, hear me out," he said quickly. "If all goes well, I shall be out there for a year or so. They say there's the possibility of my own command in a couple of years and we could live so well there. We could darling. Just think of it; a house with servants, golden sandy beaches, great food, and no scrimping and saving and worrying where our next meal is to come from. We'd be free from your grandfather. I'd be happy. You'd be happy. I know it. I do"

He grasped her hands across the table "Oh please say I can do it, please say you'll come when I call. Please, please, please."

She looked at him. "Olaf, I think I'm pregnant."

He snapped upright, a big grin spreading across his face. "You're pregnant? That's such wonderful news my darling" he said as he came to her side and embraced her and kissed her. "That's such wonderful news. You say you 'think' you're pregnant. Are you sure?"

"Well, yes. I'm sure. A woman knows about these things.

"Right. Yes, I get the picture. It's wonderful news." He paused for a moment and then continued, "but don't you see? That makes it even more important for me to get a proper job. You won't be able to carry on in your job; we shall need me to be earning a proper wage, especially now there are going to be three of us."

"I don't want you to go. I need you here with me. I'm frightened. I'm not that young anymore and it might be a very difficult time for me. I really don't think I can do it without you."

She gave him a pleading look. "If you love me like you say you do, you'll stay. Perhaps you could go after our child is born, it does sound like a good life. But not now Olaf. Not when I am going to need you so much. I beg you, please don't go."

He heard himself say, "Frida, you'll be fine, I know you will. But we need the money now, surely you can see that? I have to go darling, for all our sakes. I can't pass up this opportunity, it will be the making of us. I'll send money, you'll be fine and in no time at all I'll be back to take the three of us off to our new, better life. Plenty of sailors' wives have babies whilst their husbands are away at sea. You'll be fine."

Frida knew she had lost. She simply turned and walked away to their tiny bedroom and closed the door.

§§§

He had looked back at that moment many, many times in the years that followed. How could he have been so callous, so heartless, so self-centred? And he could never come up with an answer to those questions that didn't lead him to the conclusion that he was a selfish, arrogant, unworthy human being who didn't deserve to be alive.

Olaf left the next morning without saying goodbye; he couldn't face another scene. He left her with all the spare cash that he had, and a note that said he would think about them both every day, that he would send her money as soon as he got it, that he would look for a place for them to live, and that he loved her, loved her with all his heart.

And he was true to his word; he had sent letters and money. His ship docked back in Oslo eleven months later. He was so looking forward to seeing Frida and their new baby, his baby, and he was singing a little lullaby as he rushed up the narrow alley to their flat, turned the handle on the door, finding to his surprise that it was locked. Odd that, he thought. It was always open when Frida was home. He put his key in the lock; it didn't turn. After scratching his head and trying the key several more times he gave up, perplexed. He turned and went to their next-door neighbour's flat and knocked. After a wait that seemed to him to last for minutes, but was only a few seconds, the door opened and Olaf's smile of greeting disappeared as he noticed the woman's face turn dark when she saw who was on her step.

"I don't know how you have the bloody bare-faced cheek to turn up here" she shot at him.

"What?" he said, taken aback by her aggression. "I've just come to ask you if you know where Frida is, that's all. I can't get in."

"Where Frida is you ask, you heartless sod? I'll tell you where she is. She's in heaven you bastard, with her little one, that's where she is. They wouldn't be there if you'd have done your duty and stayed with her. But, oh no, you had to go off on your fancy boat. She told me all about it after you'd gone. I hated you for it, but she didn't; said you needed to sail, that you were off to get them a better life, I'd see. Well, I'll tell you what I saw. I saw a poor woman, frightened for her life and her baby's life, getting by on scraps, not looking after herself properly, getting sicker by the day and not able to pay for medical care. We all did what we could, but it wasn't enough. She died here in my arms four months ago. She's buried in a pauper's grave. You can go find it for yourself." And with that, she turned back indoors and slammed the door shut in his face.

Olaf found the grave later that day; a wooden cross marked the spot. On it was nailed a piece of wood with the simple inscription 'Here lie Frida and Kari Peterson'; nothing further, no dates, nothing.

"I had a daughter," he said to himself. "Our Kari. Frida and Kari. Christ! What have I done?" and he crumpled down onto the grave and wept and wept and wept. Later that night, it was all he could to drag his drunken body up the gangplank of his ship. He was leaving Oslo for good.

Eaten by grief and guilt, he turned to the bottle for refuge. He was thrown off the Panamanian ship when it reached Rangoon. He picked up little jobs here and there, but they never lasted. He even gained the captaincy of a small tramp steamer for a short while, hauling cargoes to Israel and Hong Kong. But the bottle always reared its head, and everyone in those ports knew of the alcoholic captain, who given half the chance would recount the tail of his shattered marriage to anyone who would listen, like some modern-day Ancient Mariner. A brief spell in the drug trade, an even shorter one in people smuggling, yes you still needed to be reliable in those businesses, and he found himself all washed-up on the shore, a drunken, laughingstock.

He had endured two years of this, when to his amazement, and to the amazement of all who knew him, he was appointed captain of an old ship called *The Western Queen*. She had been bought for a song. Her new owner was aware that she only had a few working years left, but he planned to run her into the ground, making all the money he could out of her, and then pick up a final payment when she was scrapped. He had heard of Olaf and knowing that he would be hard pressed to find a skipper of quality for his new venture, he installed him as captain, for a paltry fee. A good deal all round he thought.

If you knew how your day would end, would you still begin it?

N' Zuri Za Aust

The Epilogue

The MV *Western Queen* was showing her thirty plus years of sailing. Trails of rust streaked her sides and things that had once shone brightly in the sunshine of many oceans and sparkled from the care and attention lavished on them by her crew, were all things of the past. She was sailing to Montevideo with a cargo of scrap iron and had crossed the Bay of Bengal, skirted Ceylon, passed the Cape of Good Hope and was approximately ten days out from her destination. All had gone smoothly on their twenty days or so at sea. The weather had been especially good for their trip and the crew were looking forward to some time ashore. Spirits were high. Captain Olaf had not shown himself too often and Tony had been left to his own devices, just the way he liked it.

Tony had just advised the helmsman of a new course to steer, when Bryan, their Marconi man came onto the bridge.

"Hey Mate, I've just had a bit of news over the radio. Apparently, they're experiencing a bit of bother further west. Seems like there's a big old storm growing; the lads are saying its one to avoid if at all possible. It's coming up from the south and currently is around 39.9 degrees South and 10.00 degrees West. They say it's moving up quite fast and veering to the west."

He and Tony and the second mate went over to the chart table and huddled over it. Dividers were opened and adjusted and applied to the chart in front of them.

"Well, if we slow down to about ten knots, we might avoid it I suppose, but you'll have to keep us advised Bryan. Any information you get, on the double, OK?"

Bryan nodded agreement and went off to his shack.

Keith, the second mate said,

"Do you think we should let the captain know?"

It was the obvious question to ask. The captain, be he a drunk or not, was still in charge of the ship and carried the ultimate responsibility for its safety and that of the crew.

"Yes, I think we should, though what good that'll do us I don't know, but you're right as usual Keith."

Tony left the bridge, went down the companionway and popped into Jan's galley.

"Hi Jan."

Jan stopped what he was doing and looked over to Tony.

"Hello Mr Mate, what might I do for you? Bacon roll, cup of tea, glass of …."

Tony cut across him.

"No thanks Jan. Not just at the moment thanks. How's the skipper today? Is he able to have a visitor?"

He gave Jan a knowing look.

"Yes, he's not too bad today actually. I've managed to get some food into him, and he's only partway down his first bottle of rum. So yeah, you might have a good chance."

Tony thanked him for the information and went along to his captain's cabin. He knocked and heard a quiet 'come in' and in he went.

Olaf was at his desk, uniform trousers and shirt on. He was looking at a book of pictures. Tony caught a glimpse of the title as Olaf fumbled it out of sight; some words in a language he didn't know but the word 'Oslo' stood out clearly. He was obviously looking back into his past Tony thought.

"Mr Mate, what can I do for you?"

Words not slurred, thought Tony, eyeing the large glass of amber liquid that sat on the desk near his captain's right hand. I might be in luck for once. He straightened himself up and said,

"Captain, I've had information from the Marconi guy that there's a storm brewing down south, ahead of us. It seems like it might be a big beast, and I thought I should let you know, so that we," he hesitated a moment and then corrected himself, "so that you can decide on what to do. I've already had a quick look and we might be able to avoid it if we slow down a few knots, or we could alter course to go down south of it and then follow it back up the coast. But I thought you should know so you can decide sir."

His captain sat still for a moment, looking deep in thought. Then he said,

"I'll come up to the bridge. Just give me a moment."

Tony turned and went back to his station on the bridge, by the chart.

A few minutes later Captain Olaf appeared at his shoulder, dressed in his full uniform, even though it was a warm day.

"Doesn't look as if it could hurt a fly," he said, as he looked out for'ard through a salt-streaked bridge window at a calm blue sea, "but we all know how deceiving that can be don't we? Come now Tony, show me where this thing is."

The pair huddled over the chart, Tony pointing and tracing the possible path of the storm.

"I mean, we don't know exactly what it'll do, so I've got Bryan primed to bring us any and every bit of news he gets. But, for now, that seems its most likely course, Captain. So, if we were to drop say, to nine knots, it would move us to about here in five days' time," and he pointed at a spot on the chart, "and it could have passed us by; or we swing down towards South Georgia, or the Falklands. That could add another seven or eight days to the trip, but we'd be in one piece."

He looked at his captain once more.

After a while, Olaf said,

"The thing of it is Tony, our owners were very clear with me, to the point of insistence, that this cargo had to get to Montevideo by the scheduled date. Don't ask me why, it's only a load of scrap metal as far as I'm aware, but they were very clear. So, for now, we need to keep going as planned. Obviously, you need to keep your eye on the situation and let me know what's going on with the damn thing. If we must, we can change our minds later."

And with that, he said, "thank you gentlemen," and left the bridge.

§§§

For the next thirty-six hours Tony and the rest of his team, charted the progress of the storm very carefully. Bryan brought them every piece of information he could get from his colleagues on the ships in the storm area. It was moving as they had expected. Tony knew that if they maintained their present course and speed they would come into its clutches in less than two days' time and it scared him. He'd been in storms on many occasions, of course he had, he was a sailor wasn't he; but there were some things he was hearing about the exceptional ferocity of this storm that really worried him. Contact had already been lost with one of the ships that Bryan had been in touch with, and the general word was that the storm was still growing in intensity. If it changed course, and they did nothing, it could be on them in less than a day; or it might pass on by leaving them unscathed. Tony had been at sea long enough to know that discretion might prove to be the better course of action and he went to see Captain Olaf once again.

This time, he was a little the worse for wear. His rum bottle was nearly empty. Tony hoped it was the first bottle of that day.

"I'm afraid that I'm thinking we should change our plan Sir," he said.

A bleary eye was turned on him. "An' just why do you think we should do that Mr Mate? Sea seems just fine to me."

Tony knew what he wanted to say but he bit his tongue.

"Well, Sir, the reports we're getting indicate that this one is a real brute, force 10 at present and strengthening. It only needs to change course by a few degrees and it would be on us in less than twenty-four hours and quite honestly Captain, I don't like our chances in this old girl if it really came at us. I've also talked with the Chief Engineer and he's also concerned that we wouldn't be able to hold our way properly in anything that serious. So, my recommendation," he really wanted to add 'you drunken old sot', "Sir, is that we cut our speed to six knots and turn down south for the next twelve hours. Then we shall have a better fix on it, and we can act according to what we see, Sir."

He waited. For a moment he thought the old fool had dropped off to sleep, but Olaf stirred.

"You heard what I told you the other day didn't you Mr Mate. We have to get to Montivideo as scheduled. You may come back to nine knots, and we hold our course. Is that clear Mr Mate?" and he gave Tony a long, hard look.

"But Captain, better to get there a little late than not at all. Surely our owner will understand. He must be aware of what's going on out there. Shall I ask Bryan to send them a message, seeking permission for our plan?"

"Mr Mate, you've heard my order. Now go and carry it out, at once. Oh, and no messages to anyone out there either. I'm in command of this ship; it's what they pay me for. I'm not going to go running to the owner like some little kid to his dad when he's a bit scared. Do you understand me? Remember Mr Mate, ships aren't democracies."

Tony had never seen him like this before. All he could say was "Aye, aye Captain." He hastened away out of the cabin and back up to the bridge.

When he got there, an angry and worried Tony gave the order to drop the speed to 'slow ahead'. The captain wouldn't know. The light was fading from the sky and the sea had started to become more active, he noted. He needed some sleep. Now was the time to get it, and he asked to be roused should anything of significance occur. He went below to his cabin.

It must have been about two in the morning when he was shaken awake by the second mate.

"Mate, I think you better come up top, things are starting to change, and quickly. I don't like it, and I don't think you will."

He was correct in his assumption. What Tony saw when he got back up to the bridge was a massive transformation from the choppy sea that had surrounded them as he had gone to his bunk. Now the waves were rising up to near the height of their hull and the air was thick with spray. The old ship was listing one way and then another, as she rose up, crested a wave, and lurched down its other side.

"I've already altered our course onto a more southerly heading, but I think we need to turn a bit more so that we can face into the sea and stop this twisting. It's not doing the old girl any good. I just didn't want to go too much against the captain's orders, but I had to do something."

Tony could see his second mate needed some re-assurance. "You've done the right thing Second, and I agree we need to bring her further round, so if you will," and he allowed his subordinate to issue the order. At the same time he was thinking, 'and bugger the captain'. He said, "Can you get Jan to come and see me?"

When Jan appeared, Tony took him to one side of the bridge. He noted some signs of fear in Jan's eyes as he looked at the spray battering onto the bridge window and out into the gloom.

"Yes Mate, what can I do for you? And don't tell me you want me to take a cup of tea out to the man on the bow." It was his attempt at a little bit of humour.

Tony smiled. "No nothing like that Jan. Do you know how the captain is?"

"Oh. The captain is it? Well, yes, I looked in on him when I was coming up to see you. He's asleep. Curled up on his bunk. He's finished his second bottle and that usually means he'll be out of it for another four or five hours I think."

"Thanks Jan. Let's try and keep it like that if we can. I think we're in for a bit of a bumpy ride, not too bad I hope," he added, seeing the fear reappear on Jan's face. "Be better if he was out of the way while we deal with it."

"OK Mate, I'll do my best. Good luck, eh, for all our sakes eh?"

Tony clapped him on the back and Jan went back down below.

The change of course had smoothed their ride a bit and Tony sent for the Marconi man.

"Well, what news do you have for us Bryan?"

A very dishevelled looking Bryan said, "Well, I've been by that radio all night. There's hardly been any radio traffic at all, and there's been absolutely zero for three hours now. The last thing I did pick up was that it was getting worse out there, but no real detail beyond that. I'm sorry Mate. I can't tell you what I don't know, but I'm thinking one thing's for certain; radio silence like this usually means that weather conditions are making it impossible for the radio signals to get through, and that means very bad weather indeed. I'll go back and listen and if I get anything else I'll let you know at once."

The wind had strengthened further in the short time that Tony had been on the bridge and once more the ship was labouring through the waves. He had a message sent to the Chief Engineer and in a couple of minutes Paul appeared.

"Well Chief, you can see what it's like, and I think there's every chance that it's going to get worse. How's she holding up down your end?"

"She's quite steady at the moment Mate."

Tony waited for more, but nothing more being forthcoming, he said, "it's about gale force now, but some of the last reports we got were saying that it was at storm force ten over to the west, and possibly swinging our way. If that's the case, how do you think she'll cope?"

"Well Mr Mate, she's an old ship, with a full cargo of scrap iron so your guess is probably as good as mine. You're the sailor after all. I'll provide the power; you do the sailing. You and your team should be capable of that, should you not?" He stared at Tony.

Typical arrogant, German sod thought Tony. He had never liked this man. Possibly something to do with their backgrounds; but no, there was more to it than just that. There was something hard, something chilling about the way Paul behaved. He had joined the ship as a engineer a couple of years back. When his boss failed to return from an evening ashore, he was promoted. Tony had thought at the time it was very convenient for the German. The Chief had never shown any inclination to jump ship before, so why now? Tony came back to the present to hear Paul saying, "Yes, Mr Mate, all you and your team have to do is keep her pointed in the right direction. Think you can manage that do you?" He gave Tony a long, hard stare.

"You just leave the ship to me Chief and give me the power when I need it. Thank you. You may go." Tony turned his attention to the bridge windows and what lay beyond. Paul looked at his back for a moment or two, then turned and went back to his engine room.

§§§

The black, black sky began to lighten and what the enfeebled light started to reveal to them caused all on the bridge to begin to be really concerned. The seas were massive now, between force 10 and 11 Tony thought. He had, of course, been at sea in all kinds of weather; he knew storms had to be respected. Mother Nature's powers were immense, frightening to behold, way beyond the comprehension of landlubbers, but sailors the world over had to deal with them. That's what they were paid for. So, something had to be done and he was the one who had to do it. To his dismay though, he knew he didn't actually have many options.

"Second, I think we should keep her at slow-ahead. Hold the wind just on our port bow if you please." And we'd all better hope and pray that this old ship keeps afloat and in one piece he thought to himself.

For a few hours this ploy worked. The *Western Queen* did what was asked of her and lumbered through the ever-increasing waves and wind, still maintaining a course of sorts, and keeping the worst of the sea's efforts to damage her, sink her, at bay. Then the feel of the ship changed; her stability seemed to waver, the helmsman and his partner suddenly had more trouble holding her line and this issue became ever more obvious over the next ten minutes.

"I think the cargo's shifted. We need more speed Mate, to stop her paying off," said the Second Mate.

Tony was about to agree and ask for half-ahead, when the ship's bow smashed into a wall of water, ripped a hole in it and lifted to the crest, only then to plunge down into what seemed to be a bottomless trough. The whole vessel juddered and strained; its plates came under immense strain as the mighty forces of the sea began to twist and contort the fabric of the ship.

Above the din, Tony heard the whistle of the bridge's voice-pipe; he lurched across to it and when he bent to listen, Paul was in his ear, full blast,

"What in the name of all that's holy are you useless lot doing up there?"

Tony's blood boiled. Just who did this man think he was? He was about to tell him leave the sailing to him and focus on his job of keeping the engines running, when Paul continued,

"The way you're letting us be tossed about is putting far too much strain on the engines down here. If you don't get a grip soon, then something is going to blow, and I will not be able to do anything about it. Understand? Now get a grip will you?"

Tony put the stopper back into the pipe without a word.

"What on earth does he think we're trying to do?" He muttered under his breath and turned his attention back to the increasingly chaotic scene before him.

There was worse to come; the biggest wave yet came upon them. The *Western Queen* started to rise but couldn't make it to the crest. Water thundered down onto the length of the ship, ripping at the deck equipment, at the derricks, the lifeboats, the capstans, tearing things free wherever it could, smashing a couple of the bridge windows and causing the cargo to shift further in the holds below. Tony knew defeat when he saw it, but called for an assessment of the damage, a futile gesture he knew. Another two or three blows like that and the ship would be gone. It was most likely already on its way out he thought. They could either all die on the ship as it went down, or they could take their very slim and final chance of abandoning the ship and getting into the lifeboats, if they had any left, and trusting to their luck.

"Pass the word Second, abandon ship. Sound the general alarm, ship's company to muster stations." As the klaxon sounded out its alarm and the tannoy issued the order, Tony thought about the drills they had all carried out every week, typically on a nice sunny day on a flat calm sea. They'd all gone like clockwork of course; everyone had known their role; where to go, what to do, which station they were on, which lifeboat was theirs. Now it was bedlam. The spray felt like bullets, the seas continued to pound the *Western Queen*, not as big as the one that had knocked her into near submission; every seventh one was a biggie was the received wisdom, so maybe they had two minutes to get off.

People began to emerge from below, staggering onto the deck looking for a lifeboat, a lifeline. Three deckhands were making their way unsteadily towards safety when a further large wave crashed across the decks, washing them into the sea, drowning both them and their hopes. Others clung on frantically to any piece of railing or rope that they could find, waiting for their opportunity to dash across the slippery deck to safety. The ship was starting to list now, and members of the crew were making frantic efforts to free the lifeboats from their davits before the *Western Queen* took them all with it on its journey to the bottom of the sea. In the event, they found only three of their boats were serviceable and men were in the process of getting them into the bubbling, foaming water. Tony looked round to see Jan appear at the side of the ship, supporting Captain Olaf. Tony, half in, half out of the lifeboat was about to go to help his captain when Olaf held up his palm indicating that he should stay where he was. Surprised, Tony did as bid, and Jan followed him into the boat. There were a dozen men in it. They were expecting their captain to join them, and Jan shifted along to make space, but instead, Olaf clawed his way to the edge of the ship and with much effort, freed the lifeboat from its last rope; he gave it a push away from the edge, saluted them and turned away. The last sight they had of him was as he inched his way back towards the ladder to the bridge. He had chosen to be free of his daily torment, the time had come for him to go to be with his beloved Frida. He just hoped she would accept him back with good grace.

§§§

The storm pressed on, stinging spray, howling winds, great, rolling, crashing waves that showed no mercy for anything caught in their path. *The Western Queen* had been sailing with its cargo-carrying crew of forty-five men, so there was ample room in the three lifeboats for those that remained. One of the boats, which had pushed off from the ship's side, slid down a wave and emerging from the little protection its hull afforded, was flipped over by a mighty gust of wind. There it sat, keel upright, water crashing around it. A couple of the twenty heads it had been carrying appeared beside it, arms flailed against the water as the two surviving occupants made towards Tony's boat. One disappeared under the waves, never to be seen again, but the other sailor managed to get alongside, and he thrust his arm up, waiting to be pulled into their sanctuary. Paul reached over and hit his head with one of the axes that the lifeboat carried. It was a glancing blow, but sufficient to loosen the man's grasp on their boat. He started to cry out in surprise and Paul hit him again; he disappeared under the water for good. Everyone on the lifeboat stared at Paul in horror and sheer surprise at what they had just witnessed.

"The fewer we have on this boat the better our chances of survival," was all he said, securing the axe on his belt.

Tony couldn't believe his eyes. He was just about to launch himself on Paul, when Jan pointed back towards the ship. She was just visible through the soaking air, a great, looming dark shape, now listing well over, water pouring into her holds where her hatch covers had been ripped off. The twelve people in the boat looked out sadly at what had been their home, their place of practical jokes, of hard work, of joy, of arguments, and in some cases, of love; their place of safety. The *Western Queen* settled lower and lower into the raging sea. Five minutes later, she was gone. Now they were on their own.

Tony looked at the shocked faces in the boat. Shocked by the loss of their ship, shocked by the actions of Paul. What had he been thinking of; how could he have done that to one of their own? He gave up his idea of taking Paul to task; right now he had bigger things to think about he decided; their immediate survival. Here they were, who knew how many miles from who knew where, in the middle of the most horrendous storm that he had ever encountered, with a bloody murderer in their midst, unimaginable seas raging about them, and in a howling, screaming wind. They must survive the next few hours he thought, then perhaps he could worry about Paul. Survival first, no time for inquests or recriminations.

"Bosun," he shouted, struggling to make himself heard over the roaring wind and seas, "if you please, can you and some of the others get the sea anchor over our bow. It will give us a bit more stability," and God, don't we need that, he thought.

There was a rummaging around the lockers of the lifeboat as they sought out the sea anchor. It would bring them round to face more into the sea and calm some of the bucking bronco effect they were experiencing. It was duly found and let out, and within a minute, the ride of their boat became a trifle easier.

"Okay, let's see what items we have on board," Tony shouted, "call them out to me please."

The message was relayed from one to the other and answers came back by the same process. A list was gradually developed. Tony had expected to hear most of it, he was, after all, responsible for things like provisioning the lifeboats. That they were carrying flares, matches, lamp oil and lamps, buckets, barley sugar, high-protein biscuits, coconut oil, condensed milk, a rudimentary first-aid kit, waterproof cannisters and some drinking water came as no real surprise. What he hadn't heard anyone say worried him. Where were the charts and the compass that they would need to navigate their way to safety if the ever got out of this damn storm. So, he asked them to search again. To everyone's relief, they were eventually discovered in the locker that he was sitting on, along with some rope and oilcloth.

"Did you manage to get the emergency radio off her Bryan?"

Bryan looked shocked. "Sorry Mate, in all the panic I'm afraid that I didn't."

"Well, did you manage to get a mayday call out before we got off?"

"Sorry Mate, it was all a bit rushed. I did try but with the weather like it was, all that spray and the height of those waves, I don't think it would have got out to the rest of the world. I think we're on our own I'm afraid."

They sat back, clinging on to the hope that they were going to survive this. The lifeboat, kept on track by its sea anchor, provided a reasonably stable ride and they had been its passengers for a couple of hours or more when Jan said,

"Is it my imagination Mate, or are things calming down a bit?'

"Yes, I was thinking the same thing," said Bryan.

They weren't having to shout quite so loud in order to be heard, and the sky definitely seemed to be brightening.

"Don't get too excited," said Tony, "we might just have managed to get ourselves to the centre of this damn thing, and if we have..." his voice trailed off, and they all knew what he meant; there would be more of this life-threatening horror to come. Two more hours passed, and they were certain they were clear of the storm. The seas were still big, but the wind had abated, and the clouds were definitely thinning.

Tony knew they were approximately fifteen hundred miles from the coasts of South America and Africa, give or take. If they were lucky, and if the storm had truly passed them by, then once they could get a sighting of the sun, they could begin to plot a course that might take them to safety. Their best hope was that they would be carried on the south Atlantic gyre towards the west coast of Africa. He estimated that it might possibly carry them at two miles per hour, so maybe fifty, or so, miles in a day, maybe a bit more if they could rig up some kind of sail. That meant maybe thirty days to reach land, if they were lucky. They might be picked up by a passing vessel of course, in which case, problem over, but, he thought, their tiny boat, sat on the sea in all those thousands of square miles of ocean, their chances of seeing another boat were minimal; needle in a haystack minimal.

The weather continued to improve; 'so we are over the worst of it,' thought Tony. Time to plan. The lifeboat held Tony, Jan, Bryan, Barry, Paul, two of the ship's engineers and five other seamen. Twelve mouths to feed, on their minimal rations, over thirty days; not impossible, Tony thought, with careful rationing. But the big issue would be the drinking water. Men can survive for a surprisingly long time on only a little food, but the lack of water could kill in three or four days, depending on age, general health and the like. It was fairly cool at the moment, but if it began to warm up, then the process of dehydration would speed up, and without water the body would slow down and eventually stop.

Tony called for, and got, the attention of them all. He gave them an outline of his thinking, telling them of his calculations of possible days at sea, and where they might end up; all in stark detail, holding nothing back. They had to understand their position in order to accept the rules and restrictions that he was going to impose on them.

"So, everyone, the biggest threat to us making our way out of this is water. Or the lack of it. Without it we will die, you all know that. We have roughly sixty gallons on board right now. We must therefore do several things; firstly, water is on immediate ration. No person will be allowed to have more than one and a half pints per day; Barry, will you please organise and administer this for us?"

"Yes Mate," the boatswain said.

"Secondly, we need to find some way of getting more water, and for those amongst us who think that we're surrounded by it, so what's the problem, well, drink sea water and you will die more quickly than you would otherwise do. That's a no-no, understood?" He looked round and saw them all nod their agreement. "So, any ideas on getting more drinking water?"

"We have tarpaulin do we not?" said Paul. "We could rig that up to catch any rainwater that comes our way, and condensation at night. And we have some buckets we could catch it in."

"OK Paul, will you get that set up for us please?" said Tony.

Paul nodded his assent and spoke briefly to his engineers.

"Right, next. Food. We have some, but not a lot and it's not the sort of thing that's going to help with our hydration. High protein biscuits and barley sugar might just give us some energy, but we aren't going to need a lot of that for now. It's going to be about conserving our energy, keeping as still as possible and keeping as cool as possible. All of those things will help us out. We might try to supplement our stock of food by fishing. We have a handline." He saw the look of disapproval on some of their faces. "Hold on men. You might not like fish under normal circumstances, but these aren't 'normal circumstances'. If sucking on a piece of cod or some such, keeps you going, then all well and good. Anyone here think of themselves as a fisherman?" He looked round; one of the seamen put up his hand. "Good lad. Well, you're in charge of that, Tim, and you might as well start now. Jan will no doubt create a wonderful dish for us all to share." There was a slight smile on some of their lips.

Tony carried on, asking Jan to take charge of all the rations and devise a programme of sharing them out over something like twenty-five days. Eventually he had given everyone something to be responsible for and then he reminded them all of his advice to remain as still as possible and settled down for the ride.

§§§

The first week passed uneventfully. The weather calmed, the sun appeared, and the winds were gentle. By their observation of the sun, they gathered that they were indeed heading in a north-westerly direction, but where that would take them, they knew not. They ate little, drank even less and pretty much stayed put. Paul's rain catcher had provided them with a few drops of condensation and a little shade. Tim had caught a couple of fish, some of which had been shared out, raw, amongst a generally unenthusiastic crew; Jan said he was short of the necessary rice and seaweed, or he might have prepared a sushi feast for them. At night they lit a lantern in the hope that a passing vessel might spot them and come to their aid and there was always someone on watch, but nothing came to pass; they couldn't give their light much elevation so most of them thought it a waste of time.

On the tenth day, their privations were beginning to tell; the older and heavier crew members were beginning to show clear signs of dehydration. They had stopped urinating and were asking for more food, more water. They even accepted some of the raw fish Tim was becoming proficient at providing for them. They were moody and snappy with their colleagues, said they had headaches, and started to get cramp in various parts of their bodies. By day fourteen, they were slack skinned, blistered, virtually comatose and incapable of talking, drinking or eating. On the fifteenth morning they found three of the crew dead. They were tossed over the side, Tony saying a few words of a poorly remembered burial service, as the people they had worked with slipped down into the ocean never to be seen again.

And that left nine. Tony decided, and they all agreed, that they should stay with the present restrictions on their water and food. They knew not where they were, or how long things would have to last. There had been no rain and the water supply was becoming a real issue in Tony's mind and in everyone else's; mild signs of dehydration were to be seen in all of them.

Three weeks of this torment had passed. A further crew member was found dead, one of the engineers. They were preparing to put him over the side when Paul spoke up in a raspy, croaking voice,

"Just before we get rid of Milo, I want you all to listen to what I have to say. We still don't know where we are, or for how much longer this will be going on. It seems foolish to me to simply put him over the side. I think that we should, how do you say this," he hesitated, then carried on, "I think we should make use of him." He looked round at the seven faces that were staring at him.

"What do you mean 'make use of him'?" asked Tony, a look of repulsion spreading over his face. "You mean eat him don't you, you German bastard. How could you even think about it; he's one of your own men for goodness sake. You've worked with him, drunk with him. How can you even think of it?" For all his lack of strength he was nearly shouting, but it came out as a hoarse whisper.

"Well, has anyone else got a better idea about how we survive this for long enough to get to land?" Paul looked at each one of them in turn, a long hard stare. One by one they looked away. Even Tony had nothing further to say.

"You have, what do you call it, Jerky isn't it Yank?" He looked to Jan as he said this, who lay quite still, eyes glazing over. "Yes, well, they do. And they have Biltong in South Africa. So, we could lay in a little store, dry out the meat. There'd be enough to last us for some time I'm thinking."

In a last effort to stave of the unthinkable Tony said, "water's our real problem. How much we got left Barry?"

"Unless we get some rain, two or three days. We're down to a pint each as it is. We could go a bit lower to give us an extra day or so, but that's about it." His voice tailed off. Everyone looked to the horizon, to the heavens; nothing but clear, blue empty sky and sea.

"Well, I'm not just going to sit and wait to die," Paul said, as he crawled over to the body of Milo, a knife in his hand. It took some time, but by the end of that day every single one of them, even Tony, had eaten a piece of Milo, their former colleague and friend.

In the small hours of the morning Tony was woken by something pulling at him. It was Jan. He was in a bad way. "Tony, you just gotta listen to me man. I'm going, I know it. Just toss me over when the time comes, don't let that bloody German carve me up. You gotta promise me that." His voice was barely above a whisper and his New York twang was back.

"You've got my promise Jan," said Tony.

"I got some money Tony, in a bank." He fumbled a piece of paper into Tony's hand. "Them's all the details you'll need. It's yours if you get out of this alive and I really hope you do." He gave a rasping cough and fell silent for a minute. "I had such plans, you know, such plans." They were the last words he ever spoke. When the dawn light came up, it fell on the dead body of Jan. In accordance with his wishes, whilst they struggled with his body, they were eventually able to get it over the side where it slipped into the deep blue water.

They passed another twenty-four hours of torment. Not a cloud in the sky. Fisher, one of the deck hands went around mid-day; his colleague, O'Flynn, followed him five hours later. Both were put over the side, Paul's eyes looking hungrily at them as they went.

"All the more water for us," he croaked out and started to laugh, a strange, strangled, cackling thing that ended in a fit of coughing that took the breath out of his body.

Bryan woke up in the middle of the night. The sky was clear, beautiful with its sparkling carpet of stars. Had he had tears, he would have cried at its beauty and at the contrasting awfulness of his position. He tried to lick his cracked and blistered lips with his rough, cracked, dry tongue. 'How has it come to this? What's the blooming point of it all,' he thought. 'I knew the sea could be a dangerous place, but I never thought this could, would, happen to me. I might understand it if I was on some little boat, but I was on a liner for God's sake. I was going places. I was going to get onto one of them big liners like the Queen Elizabeth 2 and then who knows, I could have met some rich young woman crossing the Atlantic, and fallen in love and…' He sighed and looked at the huddled figures dotted around the bottom of their boat. 'The 'what ifs eh' Then anger surged inside. 'Why me?' he wailed inwardly. 'Why me?'

He was left exhausted and started to doze but something caught his attention, something moving at the corner of his eye. What? Was it a light out there on the water, was it? Yes, he was sure of it. A light, a long way off, but it was a light. It was a vessel of some sort he was sure of that. He looked up to their lamp, eager to see it sending out their ray of hope. If he could see theirs then they might see his. To his dismay, they had no lamp shining out. It had not been lit. He tried to get to his feet, a great struggle, but he made it, and he started calling out and flapping his arms. The others were roused by his movements and slowly took in the fact that Bryan had, apparently, gone mad.

"What's going on with you Bryan? Sit down for God's sake. You'll have us over if you're not careful," said Barry.

"No, no, I've seen a light, out there, look. Look for goodness's sake," and he pointed out across the water.

"Seen the light, have you,' said Barry, "well you'll be alright when you get to heaven," and he croaked out a short laugh.

"No, damn you, I HAVE seen a light. Out there," and he pointed once again.

All the others had heard the conversation and in their various states had struggled as best they could to look out in the direction that Bryan had indicated. At first, they could see nothing and then they noticed the occasional flicker of a far-off light. Tony looked towards their lamp and groaned.

"God's teeth, the lamp's not lit."

Then it dawned on him; that had been Jan's job and Jan was no longer with them God rest his soul. He had forgotten to appoint someone else to do it.

And slowly, oh so slowly they watched their chance of survival move off until it's light could be seen no more.

Attention was dragged back to their boat by a loud splash. Bryan had fallen overboard. They reached out to him, almost grasped a hand; his weak, fitful calling ceased within a minute. It didn't register with any of them that Paul had been by his side a moment before he went over.

It had always been unlikely that they would make it out of their situation. They had all known that, but Pope's line, 'hope springs eternal in the human breast' had been as true for them as it had been when it was penned two centuries before. But no longer. Their chance, their needle being so nearly found in their haystack, their ride back to civilisation and life and fun had been so close, but not close enough. This had robbed them of that hope. They were doomed and they knew it. They were angry, they were depressed, they were close to dying and they had had the one thing that might have sustained them ripped out of their souls.

"You stupid moron," growled Paul, "you stupid, stupid man. How could you not have had the sense to have lit the lamp."

Tony did not respond.

"All it would have taken was a single match and we would have been out of this hellhole. But no. Your dear friend Jan" he said this in a sneering tone, "had gone and you didn't think to do it yourself. You idiot, you stupid, stupid man."

"Shut up," came Tony's strangled response. "We've seen what sort of a man you are," he choked out. "You have nothing to be proud of and a lot to answer for. And did you think to sort out the lamp? No, you did not, so if there is any stupidity, then you share it. So shut up and save your strength."

Their hope, their exertions to attract the attention of the passing vessel and their emotions had taken a lot out of them and they spent the rest of the day in fitful, agitated sleep and in despair. Hubert, the engineer was gone the next morning. They didn't have the strength to move him. The sun still shone, the water was calm and blue, and they were all but dead themselves.

§§§

Tony was awakened by raindrops hitting his face. It was dark and the lifeboat was moving to a choppy motion, but rain, beautiful, wet, cool rain was falling onto his face. He opened his mouth and let the big drops fall in. They gathered at the back of his throat, and he coughed and spluttered and slowly heaved his way up into a sitting position. He turned to look at Barry. He was still, lying on his back. In the dim light he could see that his chest was rising and falling very slowly. He shook him but he did not respond. So not dead then; maybe in a coma. He shifted his gaze across to Paul. The man was sitting up, his eyes wide open, staring down the length of the boat to a horizon he could no longer see. The rain, the lifesaving rain, fell onto his bare head, gluing his thinning hair to his scalp, it ran down his face, slipped into his open, blackened mouth, but brought him no relief; it had come too late for him, he was dead.

Tony sighed with a sense of relief; rain and no Paul to worry about anymore. He turned his attention to the device they had set up to capture the rain. It seemed to be working. He could see a steady stream running into the cannister they had attached to the tarpaulin. He would have to see to that he thought. He would fill up the large container with it, and if the rain lasted long enough, they might gather sufficient to see them through a few more days. He knew recovery would not be quick; you don't get over severe dehydration simply by taking a glass of water; it would take days for him to begin to feel anything like normal and he didn't know if he had that time. He would try his best, try to keep Barry alive and just trust that somehow, someone would find them and end this nightmare.

The rain continued well into the day and then gradually came to a stop. Tony calculated that they probably had enough water to see them through the next six days if they were sensible, even if Barry managed to drink, which, at the moment didn't seem likely. And then hope started to fade once more. Barry departed this world two days after the rains came, never having regained consciousness. Tony was alone; feeling a little better it was true, but not a lot. The smell in the boat was beginning to irritate him, but he didn't have the strength to do anything about it.

Three days later a small fishing vessel moved alongside the lifeboat and three bearded faces stared down into it. The smell was overpowering and one they knew, rotting flesh. They saw four bodies sprawled out. Having secured the lifeboat to their craft they jumped down into it and checked out its occupants. Three were obviously dead, but the fourth man showed signs of life, they saw his chest was moving ever so slowly. On checking they found he had a feeble pulse, and his lips were moving, though they could hear no sound coming from them. They quickly searched the other bodies, taking anything they thought might be of value and then picked them up, and gently, and with respect, lowered them over the side and into the water and watched as they settled, one by one, into its embrace.

They lifted Tony up onto the deck of their ship. It wasn't large, about fifty feet in length, with a single wheelhouse, an engine set below its deck and winching gear for the nets, which were currently floating out behind it. They made sure he was in shade and then discussed what they should do. The man was obviously very close to death, probably would die unless they could get him into port and to a doctor. That would cut their trip short, and that would cost them money which they could ill-afford. Tony coughed and stirred and moved his arms. Then his eyes opened. It took him a moment or two, but he slowly registered that he was looking up at three men. They were dark-skinned, bearded, bare to the waste and they were all looking down at him. He managed to rasp out the word "water." The men didn't respond immediately. They looked at each other and he heard them talking in a language he didn't understand. Then one disappeared out of view, reappearing seconds later with a cup in his hand. He bent down and put it to Tony's lips, supporting his head, and letting him take in the liquid at his own pace.

"Thanks" Tony croaked.

The man nodded and looked up at his colleagues. There was more conversation and eventually they seemed to have come to a decision. A pillow was produced and put under his head; the winch was started up and the nets brought in and the ship turned to the east and headed back to its home port.

Ten days later Tony was sitting up in a hospital bed in Port Elizabeth, reading a book. A drip was attached to his arm, and he was regaining the look of a man who wanted to get up and move about. His rescuers had brought him to their village near Cape Recife and he had found his way, in a ramshackle old van, across the peninsula to the city in which he now found himself. He had been questioned about his experiences but feigned memory loss, and after a while the questioning had stopped; he had been left to make his recovery.

Sixty days after his ordeal had started, Tony walked out of the hospital. He had a broad smile on his face and nestling in his pocket was the piece of paper that Jan had given him the night he had died.

The End

Printed in Great Britain
by Amazon